I0539290

SALVATION

HUGH A. FLOWERS

Copyright © 2004 - 2014 Hugh A. Flowers

All rights reserved.

No part of this book may be reproduced or transmitted or transferred in any form or by any means, graphic, electronic, mechanical, including photocopying, recording, taping or by any information storage retrieval system or device, without the permission in writing by the author

Any resemblance to actual people and events is purely coincidental.

This is a work of fiction.

Paperback-Press
an imprint of A & S Publishing
A & S Holmes, Inc.

ISBN: 09911805-5-0
ISBN-13: 978-0-9911805-5-4

TABLE OF CONTENTS

CHAPTER ONE

I first met Olivia when I was just ten. I awoke in a hospital bed to the unfamiliar smell of antiseptics and later awareness that my right leg and arm were in casts. This was my first time in a hospital and I panicked as I yelled for my mother until a nurse hurried into the room.

"Now, now let's quiet down in here. What's your problem young man?" She said as she checked the monitors and then placed a cool hand on my forehead.

"What happened to me and where is my mother?"

"You were in an accident. Don't you remember anything about it?"

Immediately memories returned. I was in the front passenger seat next to my mom and a truck turned into our lane, but before mom could do anything it hit our car almost head on. I must have hit my head as I was flung from the car because I seemed to be caught by a very large white bird that surrounded my body with its wings. I'll never forget that its scent was that of fresh baked cookies.

The bird opened its wings from around me and I gaped in surprise at a winged woman, who looked at me solemnly.

"Jack, I am Olivia and we will meet again." She said before I blacked out.

I was brought back to the present by the scent of cookies again and wasn't surprised when I saw Olivia standing in the doorway. It took me by surprise when a doctor walked through Olivia as if she wasn't there and made his way toward my bed. Olivia gave me a sad smile before disappearing.

The doctor asked me my full name and I replied, "Jackson Pearson. Where's my mom?"

"Your mother is not able to talk right now. Who is your next of kin?"

"Grandma Pearson. Dad was killed six months ago in Afghanistan."

The doctor wrote down where Grandma lived and after checking my vitals, left me with the nurse. When I woke the next morning, Grandma was sitting next to my bed. She hugged me the best she could with casts on my arm and leg. She then stared into my eyes.

"Jack… Your mother died in that accident and you and I are the only ones left in our family. As soon as they release you from here you'll come and live with me."

"Mom died too? Grandma what are we going to do?" I sobbed as tears rolled down my face.

Three weeks later I was living with Grandma, my home now that everything I owned had been moved there. The house was part of 160 acres which Grandpa and Grandma used to farm until Grandpa died fifteen years ago. Most of the acreage is now leased and Grandma keeps a small garden and a few chickens that roam free.

Grandma fixed a room downstairs where it was easier for me to get around in my wheelchair. We soon established a routine which included home schooling for me. Grandma used to teach at the middle school in nearby Baxter Springs, Kansas.

I was in the fifth grade when my studies were interrupted by the accident. I was a good student, at least until we received word of Dad's death. Grandma got me the school books I needed for my grade level at the local school and proceeded to take my mind off my losses. Two months later we had finished those books and started on the sixth grade level.

My casts had been removed, but I was as weak as a barn kitten. Grandma started me on light chores around the farm until my strength returned. I was clearing out junk in the barn when I found my dad's old weight equipment. After getting Grandma's permission, I set them up and started building up the muscles on my right arm and leg that had weakened from disuse. After three weeks I started jogging down the long half-mile driveway to the county road and back until I reached three miles, then I increased my pace until I could do it in five minutes.

In the fall of my eleventh birthday I started sixth grade in the Baxter Springs school system. I had a huge advantage over my classmates as I had been studying their subjects for over six weeks. A month later I was jumped to seventh grade in middle school. Not only was everyone else older than me, they were also bigger - even the girls. However, the boys seemed determined to make my life a living hell.

My first time returning home with a black eye and a cut lip, Grandma asked, "Were you the winner or the loser because it's hard to tell from your appearance."

I winced when I tried to smile. "He was almost twice my size, so it took a little time to beat him down to my size."

I handed her a slip of paper. "Principal Blake told me to give this to you when I got home."

Grandma snorted back a laugh when she read the note. "He told me to tell you to not beat up on his football prospects unless they come back for seconds. Did the boy look like he wanted more?"

"No Grandma. He said uncle where everyone could hear. Maybe they'll leave me alone now."

* * *

Six years later Grandmother was fussing over my first new suit. She had insisted that we travel to nearby Joplin to shop for clothing and when we arrived at the Mall she herded me into several men's clothing stores until she found what she wanted for me.

"You're not going to that fancy school with only your Baxter clothes to wear. They'll think you're a hick from the sticks."

"I do need a nice suit, but when I visited Lawrence I noticed they wore jeans just like here."

"Well, maybe so, but I want you to wear new clothes. I had you save your insurance money so you wouldn't have any money worries for college. Why, your dorm and food is even paid for. That VW bug you bought should be easy on gas, so be sure to come home and visit your old Grandma."

I arrived in Lawrence three days early so I could get settled and find my way around campus. I found my way to the gym and checked it out; however, when I arrived at the check-in counter I met a young woman who looked familiar. She smiled at me and spoke, "Jack, it's nice to see you again. What can I do for you?"

I smiled at her and asked, "Do I know you?"

"Why Jack, I'm Olivia. Don't you remember me?"

My memory of her came crashing forward as I gripped the counter trying to center myself. "You're Olivia? You looked familiar, but now I see a resemblance. It's been a long time ago and you're missing your wings. What's going on?"

"I've been assigned to watch over you."

"You mean like a fairy godmother?"

"No. More like a guardian angel."

"Why would I need a guardian angel? I haven't needed saving since the night my mother died."

"You have the potential of becoming a man of substantial influence in the future if dark forces are kept at bay. My goal is to help guide you through the choices you make and protect you from mortal threats you will encounter. I want you to enroll in a Judo class. It begins tonight at six."

I looked at Olivia doubtfully, but then remembered she was an angel and had saved me once already. "Where do I sign up?"

I returned to the gym a little early to change into the new uniform all class members were required to wear. It felt strange walking into the class barefoot as I joined three others in the middle of the room. I was the largest of our group of two men and two women. Before we had a chance to exchange greetings our instructor arrived.

Somehow, I was not surprised to see the instructor was Olivia. She introduced us to each other and I learned my classmates were Jason Campbell, Barbara Powers, and Ann Drake. We were instructed in the proper etiquette of greeting and told this was a self-defense class where we would be taught moves to disable an attacker. She explained that the white uniform we wore was called a gi, and the white belt or obi, designated us as a novice. Since I was the largest class member, Olivia named me as the designated foe. She started throwing me around the mat demonstrating the various defensive moves and that a smaller person can defeat a larger, stronger foe by using his own movements against him.

I was soon given the opportunity to try one of the moves against our instructor. Somehow she had failed to mention that for every move there are counter moves, and I found myself in the air again. However, I then got to watch Olivia throw the other students across the mat at will. Jason and I were tasked as foes of Barbara and Ann and to our dismay found that the girls had paid attention to our instructor, as we both found ourselves flat on our backs.

The remainder of the class period were matches between the students which left everyone sore by the time the class came to an end. Olivia told me to stay as she dismissed the others, telling them to meet here each Monday at six.

She then proceeded to give me advanced lessons in counter moves for each defensive move. An hour later I was trying to remove my body aches under the hot shower. I couldn't remember ever being so sore. When I left the gym I was surprised to find my classmates waiting for me. Barbara spoke up as I approached them. "After our showers we watched Olivia beat up on you. Did you do something to her that pissed her off?"

"No, I paid extra for that. Do you all want to go get a soda?"

Later, after arriving in the rec center and finding a empty table with our drinks we started getting acquainted with each other's backgrounds. Jason was also a freshman, whose interests were in computers, and he came from Topeka. Ann was a second year student studying under an Honors Scholarship from Ft. Scott, with an interest in medicine. Barbara was a freshman with an interest in teaching and art, and came from Coffeyville. Since they were all from Kansas, three from cities near each other, we shared many common experiences.

Barbara said, "I've been through Baxter Springs several times with my family on shopping trips to Joplin. It's really a small town, even smaller than Coffeyville."

I laughed. "Yeah, and you went through its only traffic light. Not much goes on after dark except for a few restaurants and a Wal-Mart."

Everyone smiled and Barbara asked about our girlfriends. Jason and I smiled at each other. I answered, "I didn't have any serious girl friends and you two are the only girls I've met since getting here. How about you two? Did you break any hearts when you left home for college?"

Jason chimed in. "Yeah, what's your story."

Ann gave the boys a coy smile. "I guess we are all unattached. Do we have any classes together this semester?"

The next few months progressed with the four of us becoming close friends, with Barbara and I, and Jason and Ann pairing up. Ann, the smartest in our group, volunteered her help to the rest of us when we were stuck in our studies. Olivia's extra time with me working on Judo moves made me the most proficient in our group and I ended up helping the others perfect their moves. Jason helped all of us when we had computer problems or questions. We were a perfect team.

Christmas break arrived and I volunteered to drive Barbara to her home, as Coffeyville was on my way and only about 50 miles from Baxter Springs. I planned to drop her off and continue on to Grandmother's. As I pulled into the long drive leading up to a huge house with a separate six car garage, I realized Barbara's parents were wealthy.

Barbara indicated a spot next to the garage where I parked.

"Leave my luggage," she said. "I want you to meet my family."

I knew Barbara had a younger brother and sister, so I wasn't surprised when we entered the large country kitchen and found a ten year old boy and a fifteen year old girl helping an older woman prepare a meal. Barbara was in the lead and when she yelled, "I'm home!" They jumped in surprise and hurried to welcome her home for the holiday.

"This is Jack, the one I've told you about."

Her mother grabbed me and gave me a hug. "I'm Alice. I want to thank you for bringing Barbara home."

I smiled at her, "I see where Barbara gets her looks. She looks like a younger version of you."

Barbara and her mother blushed. I heard her sister mutter, "Better watch out sis, this guy has a silver tongue."

I laughed. "You must be Jennifer, or do you go by Jenn? Barbara didn't tell me her younger sister was so pretty, just that you were smart and had a sharp tongue. Ben, I was your age when I started living with my Grandmother. Are you interested in any sports?"

Ben grimaced. "Mom and Dad won't let me play football, but I like baseball. Maybe we can throw a ball around later." He said hopefully.

"Maybe another time. I should get home before Grandmother begins to worry where I am."

"Mom, it's lunch time and I think we owe Jack at least a meal before he heads home." Barbara said, giving her mother a meaningful look.

"I thought it was understood that Jack was going to eat with us. It's ready and I want the time to get to know him. Jenn, go get your father out of his office and we'll eat."

Jenn soon returned with Jamison Powers, who shook Jack's hand and said, "let's eat." Barbara and her mother had a salad, while everyone else ate cold cut sandwiches and potato salad. Jack was kept busy answering questions from the two parents about his family history and his goals in life. Barbara told me her father was the manager of a local oil refinery. When the meal came to a close, Jamison asked, "Jack, we want to invite you and your Grandmother back here for a Christmas meal and celebration and spend the day so we can get to know you better."

Out of the corner of my eye I saw Barbara soundlessly mouth, please. "I would like that very much, but I need to check with Grandmother first to make sure that she hasn't already made plans. I'll give you a call either way. Ben, I think I have a little time before I leave if you still want to play catch."

Ben was out of the room in a rush saying, "I'll get the ball and gloves." Barbara and Jack went to his car to unload her luggage, with the others offering their help. Jamison looked over the VW before commenting. "It's got a lot more room inside than I thought. How's its power and gas mileage?"

"Oh, it's not as quick as a V-6, but it gets about 40 mpg on the highway and rides nice. Barbara even likes to drive it."

Ben returned with the ball and gloves and the others moved out of our way as we begin playing catch. The glove Ben gave me was a little small for my hand, but I made do. Ben was quite good, so I had him move a little further away as we continued. He had a good arm and had no problem getting the ball to me. After twenty minutes I called an end to the play and asked Jamison if he wanted to continue throwing with Ben. He nodded and took the glove from me.

Barbara followed me to the car and gave me a quick kiss. "Talk your Grandmother into coming if you can."

CHAPTER TWO

I called Grandmother to let her know when to expect me and was home in less than an hour. She walked out the front door and waved as I pulled up. I gave her a big hug and kiss on the cheek before unloading. Once inside and settled I told her about the Christmas invitation.

"Is your relationship with Barbara serious?"

"We spend most of our free time together, so I guess we are getting serious and from the invitation from her parents, Barbara must think so too."

Christmas day we arrived at the Power's home at 9:30 a.m. Barbara met us at the car and gave me a kiss before hugging Grandmother. She was surprised at the variety of food we brought with us and helped us bring it into the kitchen where Barbara's mother showed us where to set everything. Alice smiled at Grandmother.

"My, I'm glad Jack warned me not to fix any salads or deserts because you planned on bringing enough to feed an army."

"Oh poo! I love to cook and I like to show off some of my favorite dishes to new friends." Looking over at Jack and Barbara leaving the kitchen holding hands, she added. "It looks like we may be seeing more of each other in the future."

Alice smiled at her. "Jack always referred to you as Grandmother.

What's your first name?"

"Elizabeth, but my friends call me Lizzie. Jack is the second son I've raised and they both had the same name. My first was killed in the war and his wife April, died only a few months later leaving their son for me to finish raising. Jack has been a blessing for me after losing my first boy."

"What have you brought for us to eat?" Alice said as she put her arm around Elizabeth.

Barbara was leading me to her favorite place. I soon found myself in a large room over the garage that appeared to be an artist's studio. She squeezed my arm asking, "What do you think of my inner sanctum?"

"You paint! Let me look at what you've done." I said looking around at several stacks of paintings leaning against the wall. Each stack appeared to represent a different subject starting with still life with the oldest at the bottom of each stack. I started pulling out several pieces as I worked through the paintings, placing them side by side as I admired her work.

"Babe, you do good work. I'm no art expert but these speak to me. The style, subject matter, and colors grab my attention and emotion." I then noticed another picture on a covered easel. "Can I look at that one?"

Barbara came over to me, putting her arm around my waist. "That's my Christmas present to you. I finished it after you brought me home for Christmas break. I've never tried a portrait before, so I hope you like it."

Seeing her concerned and vulnerable expression, I had to smile. It seemed so natural to bring her into my arms and kiss her. "That's for the thought, even if its hideous." I said with a crooked smile.

"You better not laugh or you'll get a punch you won't forget." She said as she moved to uncover the painting.

When she slid the cover off, I beheld the most beautiful woman I had ever seen. I stood, my mouth open, not making a sound until Barbara asked. "Well, do you like it?" There was a nervous quiver to her voice.

I turned to her, tears in my eyes. "Babe, that is the most beautiful picture I've ever seen, and it's of you. How did you do it? I've never seen the background or that dress you're wearing. This is the best of your work that I've seen."

Barbara hugged me with happiness. "I'm so glad you like it, but I want you to pose for me so that I can do one of you for myself. The one of me, I had Jenn take a photo of me that I enlarged and placed beside the easel. The background I took from places I've taken photos of, and the dress came from a magazine picture."

"Well, I'm not taking this back to the dorm because something might happen to it. Can I take this to show to Grandmother or would you prefer your parents not know about it?"

"Oh, I'm sure that they know I'm crazy about you, so this picture will not be a surprise." Barbara said with wistful smile.

She fit into my arms perfectly. I kissed her again, feeling her soft lips open to mine. Afterwards, she rested her head on my chest and sighed in contentment.

Barbara and I took the painting with its easel and returned to the main house looking for the remainder of their family. I found everyone except Jamison in the kitchen and asked them to meet Barbara and me in the living room, while Barbara sought her father. It wasn't long before everyone was gathered and I pointed to the covered picture on a easel. Barbara and I moved to the easel where I removed the covering. Alice and Grandmother uttered a soft gasp of surprise and admiration. While the other family members sat in stunned surprise.

"This is Barbara's Christmas gift to me, her first portrait. I wanted you all to share this unveiling and witness our declaration of love for each other." Jack took her hands in his while she appeared to be about to faint. "Barbara, would you consent to be my wife?"

Barbara rushed into my arms with happy tears in her eyes, and pulled my head down for a passionate kiss. "I guess that's a yes." Jenn said, smiling.

The family members gathered around us, with words of congratulations. Looking up, I caught sight of Grandmother, smiling then winking at me. I felt like I was in an surreal fog as the remainder of the day progressed with Barbara close by my side.

Before Grandmother and I left for home that evening, Barbara and I promised to discuss our future plans before we returned to school for the next semester. Once back home I walked around the house trying to decide where to hang Barbara's painting. I took down some old landscape pictures in the living room that had been hanging for over forty years and replaced them with my most prized possession. Grandmother and I gazed at the picture, she with her arm around my waist.

"Jack, I'm so happy you have found someone to love. Barbara is a very beautiful in appearance and spirit, and I mean that truly."

"I know. I count myself very lucky to have found her. Now I have to plan for our future together. I've been thinking what career I should pursue, one that interests me and will provide sufficient income to raise a family."

Jack, remember that this farm will be yours when I'm gone and the lease payments pay its taxes and provides some extra income, no matter what you decide to do."

Hugging her, I said, "I'm not in any hurry to see you gone, so don't talk about leaving me anytime soon."

CHAPTER THREE

The next day after breakfast and completing some farm chores, I was cleaning up before calling Barbara. When the telephone rang, I smiled, thinking Barbara beat me in calling first. However, it was Jamison who called. "Jack...Barbara's been in a car wreck and has been taken to the hospital. Don't kill yourself getting here, but you need to hurry."

I yelled, "Grandma! Barbara's been hurt and we need to get to the hospital right away."

I don't remember much of the drive to the Coffeyville hospital, but when we arrived I knew from the expressions on the faces of Barbara's family that I was too late. Jamison's face was a mirror of his extreme emotional suffering as he took me aside and said, "Jack, she died shortly after she arrived at the hospital. There was nothing they could do for her."

"I don't understand. What happened to her?"

"Her car was struck on the driver's side by another that ran a stop sign. Ben was in the car with her and didn't get a scratch, may the Lord be praised, but her neck was broken by the crash, which caused her death."

I went to a chair where I held my head in my hands and wept. Grandmother came and sat beside me and placed her hand on my shoulder weeping herself. Barbara's family watched us grieve along with them.

Alice came over and requested that we stop by their house for a time until we could compose ourselves before returning home. We agreed and several hours later we left for the farm.

I sat before Barbara's picture for three days until the day of the funeral, taking little of the food and drink that Grandmother set out for me. When it came time to leave for the funeral she dressed me and drove me to the church in Coffeyville.

The funeral was a black hole of misery for everyone, especially for me as I grieved about losing Barbara after just finding my true love. When I returned home I sat in front of the picture of Barbara and grieved for hours until I collapsed in my bed and didn't wake until late the next day.

I found Grandmother in the kitchen. She looked up as I entered the room and I was shocked at her appearance. She had grieved almost as much as me, but she managed to smile and asked. "Are you ready for some food now?"

I nodded and then gave her a hug and a kiss on the forehead. "I guess this has hit both of us hard. I've got to pick myself up and continue because Barbara would want that."

I smelled baking cookies and looked up expecting to find Olivia. She was standing next to Grandmother, who was looking at her with surprise and uncertainty. Olivia had arrived without her wings, her beautiful face twisted in torment as tears ran down her cheeks. "Jack, I'm so sorry I couldn't save Barbara for you. We are forbidden from helping anyone except our designated charge. Please forgive me for my inaction because I had no choice. All I can do is curb your emotional distress so that you may continue to function."

Grandmother looked in confusion between me and Olivia before asking in a shaking voice, "Jack, who is this?"

"She's Olivia, my guardian angel. She first appeared the night mother had her accident and was there to save me."

"Oh my lord and savior, you have a guardian angel. The doctor told me it was a miracle that you were not injured more than broken bones. She must have been the miracle."

Grandmother looked more closely at Olivia before saying, "You don't look like an angel. Where are your wings?"

Olivia smiled at Grandmother and then spread her wings out for her benefit. "I usually don't display my wings except in action mode because it scares people who think I'm the reaper who has come to take them to the Lord."

"I can understand that. You gave me enough of a start when you appeared in my kitchen, and that scent you produce is mouthwatering. It makes me want to bake."

"What now? What should I do, just continue on as if nothing has happened?" I asked.

"Hardly! Pull yourself together. If need be, dedicate yourself to her memory. Your destiny demands that you get out of this emotional funk and continue on with your life."

"She's right. You have a few days left before school starts again. You need to center yourself and decide what you are going to do with the rest of your life that the Lord has seen fit to extend." Grandmother said with her no nonsense voice.

CHAPTER FOUR

Ten years later I'm working as an assistant prosecuting attorney for the United States District Court located in Kansas City. I graduated with a degree in political science and pre-law from KU, and earned a law degree from Yale. Grandmother is still in good health and living on the farm, while I maintain a small apartment near the Country Club Plaza in Kansas City. I'm still single and don't have a steady girlfriend despite Grandmother's urging for me to settle down.

My boss, Jessica Littleton, an older divorced woman with over fifteen years experience on the job, often refers to me as the pretty boy. She seems to respect my work as I have an over 80 percent conviction rate. My division has six other attorneys, two are women about my age, I dated each of them at least once, but never clicked emotionally with either of them.

Jessica holds a staff meeting every Monday morning to hand out assignments and offer kudos over accomplishments; however, today she was introducing a new hire just out of law school.

"People, I want to introduce Jennifer Powers who was in the top one percent of her class. Who should I assign to bring her up to speed?"

I interrupted. "Hi Jenn. It's been a long time since I've talked to you. How have you been?"

Jessica gave the two of us a questioning look, as Jennifer reacted with a bright red-faced expression.

"So, you know each other. Jennifer, do you object to Jack showing you the ropes, or would you prefer someone else?"

"Oh, Jack will be just fine with me." Jennifer said, with a lop-sided smile.

Later, I showed her around the office area and pointed out her choice of three unassigned desks. "Take your pick and drop your things before I start you on your work assignment. My office is the third down the row with my name on the door. See you later."

* * *

I watched Jack walk to his office. Somehow he looked different than she remembered. He was as handsome as before and walked ramrod straight, yet moved with the grace of a cat. He stopped at a desk outside his office and talked with the woman manning it before entering his office. She noted that the young woman followed his movement until he sat at his desk before she sighed and returned to her work. She selected her desk, stowed her purse in a locked drawer, then followed Jack into his office.

* * *

I looked up and smiled as Jenn entered my office. "Close the door and take a seat. I've just closed a case and have been given another, so your job will be to help me prepare for trial. Most of our cases are drug related, as is this one. This one involves three young men who are accused of selling drugs near a school. They had enough on them to make it our case. We attempt to make a stronger case by getting them to testify against each other. You will come with me this morning when I interview the suspects. You might find it a little different than what is taught in school. Where did you get your degree?"

"Harvard. What about you?"

"Yale, but I only made the top ten percent. But, as I recall, Barbara said you were the smart one. How is Ben doing?"

She heatedly said, "Fine. He's attending KU, playing for their baseball team. My parents are fine too. What I want to know is why didn't you ever come by to see any of us after the funeral?"

Her heated statement took him by surprise. "Jenn, I was devastated. It was all I could do just to return to KU and resume my classes. Talking to your family was just too hard for me and as time went by I took the coward's way out."

"Are you seeing anyone?"

"I think Barbara's death ruined me for any serious relationship. I have never been able to feel the way I felt about her with anyone else. How about you? Any broken hearts back home?"

"No, I've been too busy with school. How is your Grandmother?"

"The same, but she is after me to find someone and get married. I imagine your mother is after you to do the same."

Jenn nodded her head. "She says if I don't watch it I'll become an old maid."

"I can't believe that. You're as beautiful as Barbara, maybe even more so. Have you found a place to live yet?"

"No, I'm staying in a motel until I find what I want. Where are you at?"

"A new apartment building near the Plaza. It's only a twenty minute commute to work. On our lunch break I'll show you mine and you can make up your own mind."

I drove us to the downtown lockup to interview the suspects. Three hours later, finished with our interviews, I decided it was close enough to noon to justify starting our lunch break. I drove into my apartment building's basement garage, which was another plus, and headed toward my sixth floor apartment via the garage elevator.

My one bedroom apartment was small, but well appointed. The entry opened directly into the living room that featured a gas log fireplace, with Barbara's painting hanging above it. Jenn stood transfixed before the picture of her sister for a few minutes before shuddering. She looked at me with tears in her eyes. "I forgot how lifelike her picture was. How can you stand to look at it all the time. No wonder you haven't been able to move on."

"When I look at her picture it brings me inner peace and I don't long for her as a person anymore. I hope that the right person will come into my life."

Looking at Jenn, he winked, "Maybe she's already arrived."

Jenn smiled at me, then shook her head and continued her tour of his apartment. On the drive back to their office she asked about the surrounding areas shopping possibilities, including the nearest food market and restaurants. I reminded her that we were only blocks from the Plaza and all that area offered.

When we returned to the office I gave her some forms to complete from their morning interview with the suspects, while he tried to get her some time to apartment hunt. I knocked on Jessica's open door and she motioned me inside. "How's your friend doing? By the way, how do you know her?"

"She's the younger sister of my deceased fiancé, who I haven't seen or talked to in over ten years. I need to ask a favor, Jennifer needs some time off to find a apartment. Why not give her the rest of the day before she gets involved in anything."

Jessica gave me a meaningful look. "Does that involvement include you? I caught that look that passed between you and her this morning. Okay, tell her to take off, and Jack don't screw her around, she's a bright one and I don't want to lose her."

"You know me better than that. You haven't heard any complaints from the staff have you? Besides she's Barbara's kid sister. I would never do anything to hurt her."

I returned to Jenn and excused her for the day. I gave her my business card after printing my cell phone number on its reverse. "Give me a call later and I'll treat you to dinner somewhere. What kind of food do you like?"

Jenn wrote her cell number on a slip of paper and handed it to me. "If I get busy and forget to call, ring me at six. I like about anything except Indian - it's too spicy."

CHAPTER FIVE

Jenn called me as I was preparing to leave the office for the day, "Hey, I've signed a lease in your building on a furnished apartment. Would you meet me here, number 810, as soon as you can. I want your advice on some things I need to get and maybe we can squeeze dinner in as well."

I was thinking, it must be nice to have a family with money, as I pushed her door buzzer. Jenn opened the door with a flourish and invited me inside. My initial estimate of its cost went up as I looked at the furnishings. "Wow! This is really nice. Everything looks brand new and your apartment looks bigger than mine."

"I know, but I don't like the drapes and I need to buy housekeeping items. How late do the stores stay open in the Plaza?"

"Halls' is open till nine and the others follow their lead. Why not have a early dinner, then do your shopping?"

Jenn agreed and since she drove a SUV, we took her car while I guided her to a convenient parking garage near the center of the Plaza. I led the way to a nearby Italian restaurant that I liked. When we entered, Jenn's eyes opened wide in delight as the surroundings was that of sidewalk café at night with streetlights providing a soft intimate light. Once we were seated she commented, "I hope the food is as good as the décor."

I smiled. "It's better. Everything I've tried has been excellent."

"I'll follow your lead then. Order for us both and I'd like a glass of red wine."

After dinner we proceeded to shop in the nearby Plaza shops. Three hours later we resembled pack animals as we made our way back to her vehicle. We were preparing to load the SUV, when two large men wearing ski masks approached us in a threatening manner.

"Give us your money and you won't get hurt!"

We turned to the threat and moved apart enough to defend ourselves. When we failed to give them our money they both displayed knives. "Fork it over or you're going to get cut!"

They disregarded Jenn as all their attention was on me. As they moved in to attack, Jenn caught the nearest attacker's arm and propelled his body into a nearby concrete pillar. When he started to rebound she knocked his head into the pillar again where he collapsed unconscious. She turned to offer Jack any needed assistance, but relaxed when she saw that the other thug lay unconscious at his feet.

I looked at Jenn with a raised eyebrow, who shrugged and said, "You're not the only one who took self defense classes in college. Barbara told me about the classes she took with you and I thought it was such a good idea that I did it too."

I called 911 for police assistance. While we waited for them to arrive we each sat on one of the attackers to ensure they wouldn't sneak away. Two other passersby gave us worried looks as they walked to their cars. Another offered to call the police, but we assured the women we had it under control and help was on the way. Five minutes later the first police car arrived and took possession of our captives and took down our statements.

A burley sergeant made the observation, "Boy, those creeps picked the wrong victims with you two."

An hour later I was helping Jenn with her purchases and putting sheets on her bed, I asked, "Are you feeling okay, you look a little flushed?"

Jenn smiled and kissed me on the cheek. "No, I'm fine. Jack, do you always show your date such an exciting time?"

I shook my head at her, smiling. "At least it was memorable. I don't think either of us will forget it. Do you want to trade rides to work?"

Jenn nodded. I said, "I know you don't have any food. Stop by my apartment in the morning at seven and I'll make us breakfast before we leave."

The next morning Jenn and I approached Jessica's office. Seeing us approaching she motioned us inside and pointed to chairs. "Have a seat, I have a feeling that this is going to be a good story."

I flushed at her knowing smile, but started my rehearsed story. "First of all, everything's okay. I was helping Jenn shop last night on the Plaza when we were attacked by two men demanding our money. We both know Judo and disabled the men and called for the police who took charge of them."

Jessica stared at the pair before her. "By we, you mean you both took care of the attackers?" She said, continuing to stare at Jenn.

Jenn returned her stare without blinking. "We both are proficient in Judo and had no problem defending ourselves."

Jessica looked at the two members of her staff with new respect and a little awe. "My, this is a surprise. How did you both come to learn Judo?"

Jenn seemed embarrassed. "My sister and Jack took Judo together in college and I thought it was a good idea to learn self defense. This was my first opportunity to put my training to use."

Jessica turned her attention to me. "Jack, just how good are you in Judo?"

"I've got a black belt, but I've been a little lax with my training since coming here."

"Do you think that this was just a mugging attempt or might it have something to do with one of your cases?"

"I've thought about it. They were pretty aggressive for muggers, which might be explained if they were high on something. I can't think of any of my cases that would explain a hit on me."

Jenn interrupted. "You mean this might have been an attempt on Jack's life?"

Jessica grimaced. "It's a possibility we can't ignore with our job. Jack, I want you to watch yourself. Be extra careful when you are alone in isolated places, such as parking garages."

"Jennifer, this job does have its risks. I'm glad you have had self-defense training, but if threatened by a gun, my advice is to run. If there's nothing else, you people get back to work."

Back in my office, I showed her the completed interview forms she had started on yesterday. "Check these out and let me know if I missed anything."

Jenn grabbed my arm. "Jack, just how serious is this?"

"I don't know. I'm going to check on which detective is handling this case and have him check if this might be hit on me. Don't worry, I've got a guardian angel watching over me."

"Yeah sure, well I'm watching over you too." She said as she left the room for her desk.

That night as they drove back to their apartment building, Jenn broke their silence by asking, "Let's stop at a grocery store before going home. I need to pick up a few things so that I won't have to bum breakfast off you every morning."

I said "okay, but I don't mind fixing you toast and coffee if that's all you want for breakfast. Besides, you don't have a coffee maker yet."

"Maybe I can get one there when I pick up the other things. I need some personal items from the pharmacy while I'm at it."

I soon pulled my Prius into the food market lot I usually used and told her, "I need some things too. I'll meet you at the checkout area when you're done."

Thirty minutes later I was finished and waiting for Jenn to check out. As we carried our bags to the car, there was a loud engine noise behind us. Before I could react, Jenn had body blocked us down between two parked cars as the car rushed past clipping the bumper of one of cars they were between. Jenn was still on my back and by the time I got to my feet all I saw was a dark colored sedan leaving the lot with its lights off.

Jenn asked, "Did you get its number?"

I replied. "No, it's lights were off."

Jenn moaned in pain as he tried to help her stand."

"Were does it hurt?" I said, trying to see in the dim light of the parking lot.

"I think I've got a skinned knee and my shoulder hurts where I pushed you out of the way of that car."

I helped her into my car, then picked up our scattered packages from the lot, and called 911. Minutes later two police cars arrived. Jenn told them that this was the second attack in two days against us. Afterwards, over Jenn's protests, I drove us to the ER.

After tests and a few bandages for Jenn's knee we returned to her new apartment. Jenn's muscles had stiffened up, so I carried all our sacks while she held onto me as she limped to the elevator. Once in her apartment I helped her into the bathroom and told her, "Take a hot shower, then soak in the tub for awhile. Just yell and I'll get you whatever you need."

Jenn gave me a weak smile and asked. "Get me a robe from my closet." I agreed and closed the door as she started to undress.

I returned with the robe and waited until the shower was turned on before opening the door and placing the robe on its inside hook. To kill some time I decided to take care of the grocery sacks, which were now mixed together between my and her items. I soon had my items placed together in a separate sack and placed Jenn's perishables into her refrigerator. I noted that she had purchased a bottle of extra strength ibuprofen, which I set aside to give her when she finished her soak.

When the sound of running water had stopped I assumed that she was now soaking. I returned to the bathroom door and asked, "You doing okay in there?"

"Oh, this feels like heaven. Give me 30 minutes and then check back with me."

I returned to the living room to find she didn't have a TV yet, so I checked through my items for perishables and placed them in the refrigerator as well. Now that I had some time to reflect on past events it seemed likely that we had been targeted for some reason. The only thing new on the job was that drug case and the three suspects that Jenn and I had interviewed together.

Maybe someone further up the food chain was getting nervous about what they had or might relay to us in exchange for a deal. The interviews were recorded and I needed to listen to them again to see if I missed something.

I checked the time and it had been longer than the 30 minutes she asked for. I knocked on the bathroom door again. "Jenn, it's time to get out of the tub before the water gets too cold." Getting no answer, I opened the door to find her asleep in the tub.

"Jenn! It's time to get up!"

Her eyes opened in alarm, then she smiled at me. "I'm awake. Give me time to get up and you can help me into bed."

"Okay, let me know if you need help." I said as I closed the door.

Less than minute later she called out. "Jack, I've got no strength. I'm limp as a noodle. I need help getting out of this tub."

I reopened the door and looked for and found a large towel on a rack next to the tub. Jenn was covering her beautiful full breasts with her one arm while reaching for the towel with the other. She looked up at me with an embarrassed smile. "Oh Jack, I'm so sorry I'm putting you through this."

"Think nothing about it. It's not often I get to hold a beautiful naked women in my arms on a second date. Now turn your back to me and hold your arms up."

When she had her arms up I placed the towel on her shoulders and lifted her out of the tub in my arms and sat her on the commode seat. Grabbing another towel I set about drying her off while she covered herself as best as she could, but he could tell she had a drop dead gorgeous body.

I then handed her the towel. "Here you finish up while I get you some pajamas."

I handed Jenn her robe before leaving for her bedroom. I pulled the covers back on the bed and found a set of pajamas before returning to Jenn. She held the robe up against her front, her face beet red in embarrassment. "Jack, I'm afraid I need you to help me get those on. I'll help as much as I can, but I'm still weak."

I held up the pajamas. "These okay? I couldn't find any one piece slip-ons."

"Oh Jack, I don't think anyone but your Grandmother wears those anymore. Help me get my legs started in the pants and I might be able to get them over my butt."

We started on the pants, but she needed help getting off the seat so that they would slide up. Next was the shirt, which we took one arm at a time and I buttoned up the front. Satisfied, I picked Jenn up and carried her to her bed and sat her down. "Don't move, I'm going after some pills that should let you sleep."

When I returned she was still sitting as I left her, but tears were running down her cheeks.

"What's wrong, are you in pain?"

"No. You are such a good, considerate man and I'm just happy you were here to take care of me." She took the pills I handed her and a swallow of water, before swinging her legs around and laying her head on her pillow.

"I'm staying with you tonight. I couldn't sleep with you here alone, so sleep tight as I'll watch over you."

I awoke to the alarm, but was startled by Jenn looking down at me with a smile on her face. "So you stayed the night." She said.

"How are you feeling this morning? When I turned in you were fast asleep."

"I'm fine. My shoulder is still a little sore though. I woke up with an urge to pee, so I went ahead and started the coffee as I knew the alarm was about to go off."

"Do you cook, because for some reason I've worked up an appetite."

"Maybe it's because we didn't eat last night. Did the eggs I bought survive?"

"All but three survived and until I know you better, I want mine scrambled. While you get yourself ready for work and breakfast started, I'm going to my apartment to clean up. See you soon." I said as I dressed.

.

CHAPTER SIX

We arrived at work only 15 minutes later than usual and headed straight to Jessica's office. She looked up as we approached and motioned us inside where we took seats as before. "Why is it that I know you are bringing me more bad news. What happened?"

"Jenn and I were almost run down last night in Food Marts parking lot by a car without lights. Jenn saved my bacon by knocking me down between cars."

"You're sure that it was intentional and not some drunk or old lady that couldn't see you?"

"We're pretty sure. Jenn was a little shook up, but she says she's okay now."

Jessica looked questionably at Jenn, who nodded and smiled. "I'm okay."

"Damn it! What's going on that would give someone a reason to be doing this?"

"I may have an idea. It could be those three suspects we interviewed yesterday. This started the same night and it could be that someone is afraid of what we learned or might discover. I'm going to go over the recordings of those interviews with Jenn and maybe we can get some answers. It might help if you put some pressure on the detective who is handling our attempted mugging now that there has been a second attempt."

Jessica nodded her head in agreement. "I'll do that and you two should get on those interviews. Let me know if you find anything?"

Three hours later we had learned nothing more after going through the recordings twice. I looked at Jenn in frustration, then stood and started my Judo cleansing routine starting with my neck and shoulder muscles and working down my body. Jenn watched me in fascination as I went through my routine.

"Wow! I've heard that masters could do that, but this is the first time I've seen it performed. I could hear your bones pop! Would you work on my shoulder? I bet you could take the stiffness out."

"Okay." I turned her chair around and started working on her neck muscles as I asked, "How far have you gotten in your training?"

"Only a brown belt. Oooh, that feels so good. I didn't pursue it at Harvard because of the intense pressure for high grades. Oh...do that again. Yeah right there...ahh, that feels soo good."

I continued for a while longer and asked her. "Is that better?"

"Yes, much better. Can you do that again tonight...in case I stiffen up again?"

I grinned at her. "Almost as good as sex?"

Jenn shuddered. "Better!"

"You haven't been doing it right then. Let's go talk to Jessica." I said as I patted her on the back.

Jenn stood up and moved her neck and shoulders with a relieved smile. "That's much better. Damn, wait a bit. I've got to go to the restroom, I think I wet my pants."

She soon returned with a embarrassed look on her face. "I'm ready now, so lead on."

Jessica took our lack of progress with a look of disappointment, but agreed that we should take another shot at the three suspects. "I talked to Detective Sara Brooks who was assigned to your mugging case. She said that she and her partner, Sam Peterson, agree that this was not a simple mugging. For one thing, the suspects each had five thousand dollars in their pockets. They want to get together with you two as soon as possible."

"Tell them we are going to the downtown lockup to interview those drug suspects again and can meet them there."

The first suspect we interviewed was Jacob Waters, a nineteen year-old black male who had already been busted twice for drug possession with intent to sell. A third conviction would keep him behind bars for thirty plus years.

I glared at him for several minutes until he started to fidget and looked away. "Jacob, you are in a bad fix. Not only do you have the drug charge to worry about, but now you are facing attempted murder of federal prosecutors."

"What do you mean? I didn't try to kill nobody."

"We have been attacked twice by people you work for, so that ties you into the charge. If they succeed in killing us, the charge will be murder with a possible death sentence. If you want out from under this charge, you need to show us that you are acting in good faith. We need names, Jacob. Give us names and we'll even put you somewhere where no one knows you."

Jacob looked like a caged rat, looking from Jenn to me with sweat popping up on his face. "You got to protect me. They can get to me even in here. They's bad dudes, man. Bad dudes for sure."

"Take your pick. A long jail sentence, maybe a death sentence or a way to get out from under with less time and a better place to go under a different name. What's it going to be?"

Jacob looked so scared I was afraid he would break down and cry. He got control of himself and told us everything he knew. I had him write it all down and sign and date it before we started on the next suspects. One held firm, while the other broke like Jacob. He provided a little more information than Jacob, but between the two we had fifteen names to work with.

Detectives Brooks and Peterson joined us and we introduced ourselves to each other. I started to explain what we had accomplished when Sara Brooks interrupted me. "We watched the last two interviews. Jack, you surprised me at how much information you were able to pry out of that last one."

* * *

Jenn noted that Sara was about ten years older than Jack and it was obvious that she was attracted to him as she touched his arm and smiled as they talked. She was surprised at how much she disliked Sara just from this first meeting.

* * *

Jack answered, unaware of the emotional conflict Jenn had with Sara. "Jenn and I have compiled a list of people that two of the suspects had drug contacts with. Let's copy the list and you can pursue wherever it leads. I think someone has put a hit on us fearing what we might discover."

"Let me look at it, maybe I'll recognize someone." Sara said as she rubbed shoulders with Jack while looking at the list.

Jenn grabbed the list. "I saw a copy machine in the next room. I'll make you a copy."

* * *

Sara followed her into the copy machine room, where she shut the door. The two women looked at one another, a challenge in their eyes. Sara asked. "Do you have a claim on Jack?"

"I've known him since I was fifteen and I'm in love with him, so hands off!"

Sara looked at her with new understanding. "Oh. So what's taking you so long to claim him?"

"He was engaged to my sister who died, and then we were separated until I was hired here. I've just realized how much I love him, so please no distractions."

Sara nodded her head. "He's a hunk, but I'll step back for now. You better close the deal soon or I'll take a run at him."

Jenn's ire was still up, but she held out her hand. "Let's shake and try to get along. We may be working together until we get things resolved."

They shook hands, made the copy and returned to the others. As they approached the room they could hear the men talking about them and Sara held Jenn back with a finger on her lips. Sam was asking questions about Jenn, which Jack was attempting to evade.

Sam said, "Come on, you mean you haven't tried to get close to that beautiful woman."

At that comment, Jenn blushed red to the roots of her curly hair. However, she was interested in what Jack's response would be.

"Hands off! She doesn't need my defense, but I have feelings for her that I haven't quite resolved."

Sara winked at me and I smiled in relief before walking with her back into the room. "I got it." I said as I held up the copies.

* * *

I asked. "You two had lunch yet?" They both shook their heads. "Well, let's take a break and eat a bite while we discuss how we're going to handle this."

We walked to a nearby cop café, and since it was almost two hours past the normal lunch time they had their pick of a place to sit. I pointed at a large booth where Jenn and I sat opposite the two detectives. "What do you suggest?" He asked Sara.

Sam laughed. "She always gets the patty melt. I need something more substantial, so I suggest chili spaghetti." Both women cringed at the men's choice. They started discussing how they should proceed with the investigation as they waited on their orders. Their orders had arrived and were being distributed when they were blinded by a bright flash of light, followed by a loud explosion just outside their window seats.

My window was cracked, but I could see a panel truck on fire not twenty feet away. Everyone fled the café to see if they could help, but the contents of the van were being consumed by flames. I then noticed a assault rifle lying in the street not far from the van. I kicked it further away from the flames and then waited with the others for the fire department and police to arrive.

Sara pointed at the weapon. "Do you think that was another attempt on your life? I can't figure what caused the van to explode."

I just shrugged my shoulders and looked over at Jenn who had a puzzled expression on her face. Her face cleared and then with an astonished expression she grabbed my arm and pulled me away from the others. She pulled my head down close to her mouth and whispered, "you weren't kidding when you said you had a guardian angel, were you?"

"My you are smart, just from that one comment you came to that conclusion."

"Don't be a wise ass. I'm right, aren't I? It was the bright light and explosion that brought it all together. During my Sunday school classes I was fascinated by angels and how they were supposed to work and I didn't forget."

I looked at Jenn and could tell she was convinced she was right. "Okay, I'll fill you in later. Don't say anything to the others, they'll just think you're bonkers."

She gave him a self satisfied smirk before they returned to the others just as the fire trucks arrived. The firefighters soon put the fire out and Sara showed them her ID and told them not to disturb anything as it was a crime scene and they needed to wait for their forensic team to arrive and take charge of the van and the weapon.

The forensic team soon arrived and our group returned to the café to finish our lunch. The wait staff had already cleared our table, but soon brought out fresh food and despite our recent experience, we all had a good appetite. After we finished eating, Sara said, "This is the third attempt on your lives. It's dangerous just being near you. If that shooter had fired we might have all been killed."

I nodded. "You had better include yourselves at risk now. Our suspects should have special protection now too."

Sara said, "Before we left lockup I placed them all under special protection and they are being moved today to a safer location."

As they left the café, Sara stopped to talk to the officer in charge of the team. She soon returned with news. "There were three bodies in the van, all crispy critters, but they might get IDs from their wallets and fingerprints on the weapon. I'll let you two know when I find out anything. If that's all, we need to get to work."

After saying our goodbyes, Jenn and I returned to our office. Jessica intercepted us. "We are wanted upstairs. The U.S. District Attorney has taken a special interest in you two."

CHAPTER SEVEN

We were kept waiting for less than five minutes before being summoned into the presence of our boss. George Rapport pointed at a conference table where we all sat down. "Tell me what has happened during the last two days since you first interviewed those suspects in the drug bust."

Jessica pointed at me. "Tell it as it occurred and don't leave anything out."

Jenn's face was a little pale as I recited what we did and the three attempts on our lives including the one just before we arrived back in the office. DA Rapport's face grew more stiff with the reports of each attempt on our lives. Upon hearing of the latest attempt he frowned, but didn't comment until I finished.

"You say you have a list of names the suspects gave you?"

"Yes sir. I gave a copy to Detectives Brooks and Peterson and I'll attach a copy to my report when I write it."

"This is the first time I've met you Mr. Pearson, isn't it? Jennifer Powers, you were just hired and are working under Mr. Pearson. How are you holding up? This isn't how we try to break in our prosecuting attorneys. I hope you don't get discouraged."

"No sir. Since I've been here, Jack has kept me occupied and life has been very interesting."

"Well said. Do you want to continue on this assignment or would you prefer a transfer to a more sedate assignment?"

"Sir, I would like to continue on as before. I'm learning more here than I would at any other location. I'm very ambitious and I hope to be one of your best attorneys."

"Well, you teamed up with one of the best prosecutors we have here and his record is going to be hard to beat, assuming you live through this threat. Jessica, have Jack and Jennifer write their reports and then give them some time off - about a week, and let's see if this problem resolves itself while they're gone. Good work people."

We left the office at six p.m. and returned to our apartments. On the way Jenn convinced me to return with her to Coffeyville and stay with her parents. "Jack, it might be a good idea to have your Grandmother drive over as well, and if she's not able, I could make arrangements to get her."

"Jenn, we need to stay together in case we're followed and we may be placing your parents in danger by staying with them."

"We just have to be sure that we aren't being followed. If we stay on the back roads and watch our backs we should be okay." She replied.

We took Jenn's SUV because it was larger and could handle both of our luggage. She used her cell to call home after we were on our way. I could tell she was having a little difficulty in telling her mother that she was bringing me home. The last time this happened with her sister, Barbara had died within days.

After she disconnected, she sighed. "I think mom was in shock when I told her I was bringing you home."

"We can always change our plans. Let's travel to the Gulf Coast and keep a low profile. We'll have fun and no one else will be in danger."

"No, my parents already know we are together and they'll be more worried than they already are. Dad can make arrangements for protection around the house while we're there. I'm hoping that it won't even be needed if we aren't followed."

"The next time I stop for gas I'm going to check to see if anybody left a tracking device on your car. In fact I'm not waiting that long. At the next truck stop I'm going to do it."

It wasn't long before I pulled into a large truck stop where there was lots of light and using a flash light I checked under the vehicle and to my chagrin, found not one, but two tracking devices. I took them over to a nearby truck and attached them out of sight, hoping to lead any pursuers on a false trail.

To be careful, I backtracked and then changed direction several times before turning toward our original destination. When we were an hour out from Jenn's home she called to tell her parents our expected arrival time. When they heard our car, Alice and Jamison came out to meet us.

Jenn ran to her parents who fussed over her, mother and daughter had tears in their eyes when they turned to me. Jamison walked over and hugged me, something he hadn't done when Barbara and I first showed up, but times were different now. Alice kissed me on the cheek and we all carried the luggage inside. I asked Jamison if I could park the car in the garage out of sight, and he used his fob to raise the garage doors.

Once I returned to the house I said, "We need to tell you what's going on and make some plans."

After we told Jenn's parents what had happened over the last three days, they looked at us with their mouths open. Her mother said, "Jenn, you are supposed to prosecute criminals, not do battle with them. Well, no matter. You are home now and I'm sure Dad can do something about hiring some people to watch over us."

She then looked at her daughter and me with a penetrating gaze. "What about you two. There's something more going on between you than just co-workers. What's the story?"

"Mom, we have been together three days. That's rushing it don't you think?"

"Jack, how about it? Give it to me straight, are you lovers?"

I grinned at her and then laughed. "Alice, I don't remember you being this protective of Barbara when I brought her home."

"No, but she had already told me about her affair with you and here you are coming home with my youngest daughter and I don't know anything about your relationship."

"After Barbara died I didn't think I could love anyone again. When Jenn showed up it seemed like I re-awakened and I believe we are falling in love with each other, and no, we aren't lovers - not yet."

"Mom! I can't believe you are putting him through the third degree." With tears in her eyes she hugged me tight to her body. "It's true, we are falling in love. In my case I'm in head over heels. As soon as I saw him when I reported for duty I felt it, I can't describe it other than a strong attraction that gets stronger the longer we are together."

Jenn's parents looked at each other and smiled. "We were worried about you honey. Since Barbara died you didn't seem to care for any one boy or man and at first we didn't know why you wanted to go into law until we heard that was what Jack was doing. Whether you knew it or not, you were following him."

Still holding Jenn in my arms I asked. "Jenn, did you consciously pattern your life to follow me?"

Looking up into my face she nodded. "I had a secret crush on you from the first day I met you. When I heard you were taking pre-law at KU, I was determined to follow you no matter what."

"So your feelings are stronger than just a crush?"

"How can you ask that. That night in the apartment when I had trouble getting out of the tub, that was real. However, I wasn't as weak as I pretended. I wanted you, but I tested your will power in resisting having your way with me. Later, the next day when you worked on my neck and shoulder muscles, I actually had an orgasm."

Jenn looked up at me with pleading eyes. "Please forgive me, I feel badly about what I did."

"I suspected you were faking it, but I was enjoying myself so much I went along with it. Besides it gave me an excuse to stay overnight so I could watch over you." I said as I lifted her up and gave her a chaste kiss.

Alice looked at the two of us and just shook her head. "Star crossed frustrated lovers. You are worse off than Jamison and I were."

"What do you mean Mom?"

"That's a story for another time honey. It's late and I'm getting too old for all this excitement, and I'm not yet ready to put you together in the same bed. Jack, we fixed you a bed in Barbara's old work space, so good night and I'll see you in the morning."

Jenn was reluctant to leave me, but she reached up and pulled my head down for a long passionate kiss. "Maybe that will hold you until morning." She said as her mother pulled her away from me and up the stairs.

I picked up my bags and headed for the garage loft, where I found a made up bed. I was thinking, *Alice is a stronger woman than my first impression led me to believe, and that hug from Jamison, what's that about?*

I was afraid that my churning thoughts would keep me awake, but before I knew it the intercom system woke me with a demand to come down for breakfast. I hurried getting dressed and met the others in the kitchen. Jenn didn't look like she had slept much; dark shadows under her eyes told that story.

I took her in my arms and kissed her, then whispered in her ear, "Buck up, the worst is over. There are no more secrets between us, except my guardian angel and I'll tell you that today."

Jenn looked at me with a brilliant smile. Her face transformed into the most beautiful one that I'd ever seen. Alice also noted the transformation and smiled in relief. "Jenn, make yourself useful and take care of Jack and your plate. I want to see how much you've learned of his eating likes and dislikes."

Jenn took two plates and filled them and placed both on the table before filling two cups of coffee and returning to sit beside me. While her back was turned, I scraped the grits off my plate onto hers. When she looked down at her plate she noted the change and looked at her mother to see if she noticed. Alice winked at her and shook her head, but didn't say anything.

Jenn smiled as she jabbed me in the ribs. "Jack, we didn't have any potatoes or we would have fixed you some for breakfast."

"I'm sorry honey, but I knew you liked that stuff so I didn't think you would mind."

Alice spoke up. "Children, let's behave and stop playing with our food."

I laughed. "Alice, you set a good table. I couldn't help but pull Jenn's chain when we haven't eaten that many meals together."

"So, you two are just starting to get to know each other's eating habits."

"Yes, and I've just discovered that she doesn't like to be kidded where you might think she's in the wrong."

Jenn was following this discussion with increasing ire. "Hey! I'm right here. Mother, I'm sorry. I should have told you that I'm still learning things about Jack. But, I've found that he has a wicked sense of humor that I'm going to have to adjust to. How long did it take for you and Dad to get to know one another?"

"Oh honey. Even after all this time he sometimes surprises me with something new. But, we don't have any important secrets between us. That's important in a good marriage. I want you both to realize that fact."

I nodded in agreement. "Jenn and I have both unloaded secrets between ourselves. However, as soon as breakfast is over I've promised her a story she demanded to be told."

Alice looked between the two of us, but made no comment. She noted that Jenn looked relieved, but not apprehensive, so she let it pass. The meal ended and she told the couple to go take care of their business while she and Jamison would clean up.

Jenn took my hand and led the way to her dad's office, where she shut and locked the door. We sat facing each other on a couch. I started at the beginning where I first met Olivia at the car crash that killed my mother and at each subsequent meeting until yesterday, when the van exploded outside the café.

"So, your Grandmother and I are the only ones who know about Olivia? What does she look like?"

"I'm not sure everyone sees her alike. When she is in action mode with the bright white light and wings, she is awesome and beautiful to behold. When she is in human mode, she still has the same beautiful face to me, but she doesn't seem to be a angel. The other members of my judo class, including Barbara, didn't think she was anything unusual."

"So, you don't have any sexual feelings toward her?"

"She radiates love to me, but I think of her as a surrogate mother. The only woman I have sexual feelings for is you. You even eclipse what I felt for Barbara. If you should leave me for whatever reason, I don't think I would survive."

Jenn pulled herself onto my lap, putting her arms around me, and began kissing me deep and with passion. When we came up for air she sighed with happiness. "I believe we are made for each other." She said as she laid her head against my chest.

With a flash of light, Olivia was standing in the room facing us. She brought with her the familiar scent of fresh baked cookies. Jenn sucked in her breath, but made no sound as she stared at the angel.

"Jennifer, you are correct in what you say, but when Barbara was alive she was the one for Jack. Due to the accident things shifted and you became the one destined for Jack's mate. Be aware that evil forces are still out there that you both must be aware of and guard against. I can act only in Jack's behalf, so stay close to him when times are hectic. I recommend that you continue your self defense classes. Jack, as a black belt, would be an excellent instructor. Marriage would allow you to live together under your social conventions and you need to stay close together for your protection."

Olivia looked at the two of us with love radiating from her being, then she vanished with a flash of light.

"Wow! So that was Olivia. She was beautiful and her scent was just as you described. Jack, now that I think about it, you have a natural scent that draws me to you. Don't hide it under any cologne in the future."

"Jenn, would you do me the honor of being my bride?"

She looked at me with love in her eyes. "Yes, of course I will and we need to do it soon. Let's tell my parents the good news and see them freak out."

They entered the family living room where Alice and Jamison were watching the news.

Jenn said, "We have news. I've accepted Jack's proposal of marriage and we want it to happen soon, before we return to Kansas City."

CHAPTER EIGHT

Jenn's parents stared at them, mouths open in surprise. "What! Jack, what did you and Jenn talk about that caused this to happen?" Alice blurted out.

Jenn and Jack looked at each other for a moment, before they nodded their heads.

"Mom, Dad, Jack has a story he needs to tell you."

It took a little longer to retell Olivia's story because it was interrupted several times with questions from the parents. At the end, after hearing what Olivia just told Jack and Jenn, they looked at one another with concern and stood.

"Kids, we need to discuss this between ourselves. Why not discuss what kind of ceremony you want while we're gone, we won't be long." Jamison said.

Jenn looked at Jack with concern. "What's to discuss. They must believe in angels since they both are religious."

"Jenn think about it. They didn't see Olivia, so it might be hard to believe that we were visited by one. They might think I am some kind of nut and have you under some kind of spell. This is why I have never told anyone else about Olivia."

Jenn was still agitated, but shrugged her shoulders. "What kind of ceremony do you want to have?"

"I'm open to anything you want, but let's wait until they return before committing to anything. It's possible they have a surprise for us. Jamison has been acting strange ever since we arrived."

Fifteen minutes later the parents returned, ready to talk. Jamison pointed to the couch for us to sit together. After everyone was seated he smiled at us. "Kids, the night before last I had a very vivid dream. It was Barbara, who told me about the same story you just did. I thought it was just a dream until we got the phone call that you were coming home with Jack. I've told Alice about the dream and she now believes. What do you want to do?"

Jenn said. "I want a church wedding if it can be arranged, if not, a justice of peace will work and maybe a church wedding later."

Jamison smiled at us and pulled us up so he could hug us together. "Oh, I'm so happy. We are both happy that this is happening to you. I'll call the reverend and see what can be arranged."

"Jamison, don't mention anything about the dream or my guardian angel. It might cause trouble we don't need."

He frowned for a moment. "Yes, you have a valid point. I'll get right on it." he said as he hurried out of the room.

Alice came up to them and hugged them both, tears of joy running down her face. "I never expected your marriage so soon. This is happening so fast I can't get a grip on it. Honey, if it's a church wedding we need to get you a gown. What about a best man and maid of honor? Oh, there is so much to do!"

I hugged the two women. "Alice, don't worry about it. It will all work out. I have faith that this will all come together without a hitch."

She looked at me as if I was a crazy person. "Jack, I want you to call Ben and tell him to rent a tux and we'll tell him later when the wedding is going to happen, and you need to go and buy Jenn's rings."

I got Jenn's ring size, borrowed her car and was soon on my way to shop for her rings. I also had Ben's cell phone number in case I found time to call him. I was cautious of my surroundings as I made my way into downtown Coffeyville searching for a jewelry store. I made a circuit of the stores taking note of several and looking for possible trailing cars. After the third time around and not finding anything suspicious, I parked and sat for awhile before getting out and entering the first store.

I stood and watched people walking around for a bit, then decided I was being over cautious and approached the counter and started looking at rings. The door had one of those bells that rang when it was opened, which caused me to jump the first time; however, I soon got used to it and concentrated on my task.

I found what I was looking for at the second store I entered. It was a double ring set that I thought was pretty and asked if I could take it out for a trial run to my fiancé. The clerk thought I was kidding at first, then was sure I was crazy. When I told him who the ring was for, he smiled and wrapped it up for me, after taking my check for five thousand dollars.

When I got to the car I tried to call Ben and was surprised when he answered right away. When I told him my name he hesitated for a moment before answering. "You were engaged to my sister just before the accident?"

I thought, *oh boy he's going to like my next bit of news.*

"Yes. Jenn and I are engaged and are planning on getting married this week in Coffeyville, maybe on Saturday. I would like for you to be my best man and your Mother wants you to rent a tux and we'll tell you later when and where the wedding will take place."

"What's going on? This isn't a shotgun wedding is it? Why the big rush?"

"We work together in Kansas City and had to get out of town for a week while things cooled down there. I'll tell you all about it when you get here. Jenn says that you're playing college baseball. Are you doing well?"

"Fine. I'm looking forward to hearing this story. Knowing Jenn, it's got to be good. See you later. Bye."

I drove out of town and then doubled back by taking side streets while looking for any tails. Not seeing any suspicious cars I returned to Jenn's home and parked in the garage. After closing it I returned to the house, not knowing what to expect when I entered because of the several van trucks in the driveway. Jenn was wearing a white wedding gown and was attended to by three women I didn't know.

I walked up to her and gave her a kiss on the cheek. "Hon, I like these rings, but you have the final say." I said as I opened the box and displayed the rings.

"Wow! Jack, these are just perfect. Let me try them on and see how they look."

She slipped the rings on and held her hand out while moving it around to see the diamonds sparkle. Satisfied, she said, "Jack, these are perfect. They even fit. Did you get hold of Ben?"

"Yeah, he wanted to know if it was a shotgun wedding." I said smiling.

"Jack, don't say that even as a joke. Three of my high school friends had shotgun weddings and it's something that I'm sensitive about. Damn, Ben has the same kind of sense of humor that you do. You two are going to make my life miserable."

"I told him we would get back to him on the time and place. Have you heard whether we got a church wedding?"

"We didn't get the church, but the reverend agreed to perform the wedding here Saturday night. Dad's working on getting the paperwork done and wants you to see him in his office. Do you like this dress or that one on the chair?"

"I like this one. It makes you look like a princess." I said with a smile. "I guess I need to rent a tux too, so I better get cracking."

I found Jamison in his office talking on the phone, so I sat down waiting until he finished. He held up a finger while writing something down.

"All right, I got that done. Did you get the rings and talk to Ben?"

I told him of my accomplishments and how I needed to rent a tux.

"Maybe not. Let's go upstairs and see if you can fit into one of mine." Jamison said with a smile.

He had three tuxedos, each a different size. He handed me one and said, "Try it on and let's see if we need to make any alternations to it."

The waist was a little large, but the jacket was perfect. He said, "Stay there, I'm going for some help." He soon returned with a woman who looked at the tux with a critical eye. "His jacket looks good. Take it off and let me look at the pants. Yes, it's only about an inch or two off in the waist, but the length is perfect. I can handle that. Let me put some pins in it and then you can take it off."

After she left with the tux in hand I started putting my clothes back on. "I need a fancy shirt too, unless you have an extra?"

"It's lucky we are about the same size." Jamison said as he pulled a shirt out of the dresser. "I'll call Ben back and give him the details while you go down and check if the girls need anything."

I found Jenn still in the wedding gown, but they appeared to have completed the pin ups for the alterations. She was unzipped as I watched and her mother threw her a robe to wear while giving me the stink eye.

Jenn noticed this action and smiled at me. "Oh Mother, Jack has seen more of me than me in my underwear."

"Not with me present, he hasn't." She then reconsidered. "Oh, I guess a fiancé has some rights. I'm sorry Jack."

I hugged my future mother-in-law and kissed her on the cheek. "When should I make arrangements to have Grandmother come here?"

Alice said, "Why don't I give her a call. We talk to each other almost every week and are quite good friends. Just because you didn't call doesn't mean Liz and I couldn't be friends. I'll ask her if she wants to be part of the wedding preparation, if so, you can go get her today."

"Tell her to meet me in Chetopa and park the pickup in the bank parking lot. Have her call me with the expected time of arrival and I'll pick her up. I want to get there ahead of time so that I can observe if she is being followed, but don't tell her that. I don't want to worry her. Is there anything else I can do for you or Jenn?"

"Yes, go to her. I think she needs a distraction from these wedding plans, so use your charm to take her mind off it."

I gave her a kiss on the cheek and started my search for my bride-to-be. I didn't find her in the house, but then realized where she must be. When I arrived in the garage loft she was face down on my bed, sobbing. I sat down next to her and pulled her into my arms, where her sobs stopped after a few hiccups and then a long sigh as she released her breath and cuddled closer to me.

"What's wrong honey?"

"Oh, I guess it was an emotional overload and guilt over getting married to you, a man Barbara was engaged to."

"The night before we left Kansas City, I stood before Barbara's picture and told her that I was falling in love with you, her sister. I guess I wanted absolution from her. It worked, because I felt nothing but love emulating from her picture. Do you think that's crazy?"

Jenn looked up at me and smiled. "Jack, after what's happened to both of us, you can ask that? I'm glad you told me that, as I don't have a guilty feeling anymore. Now give me a kiss and let's get back at it."

I pulled her closer and kissed her until we both had to gasp for air. Her arms were still around my shoulders as she inhaled my scent one last time before we broke apart. I helped her up and we returned to the others holding hands.

Alice looked up at us when we entered the room and then winked at me when she saw the big smile on her daughter's face. "Jenn, come over here and help me pick out what flowers we are going to decorate with."

Two hours later I received a call from my Grandmother saying, "I expect to be in Chetopa at two p.m., and congrats on your pending marriage."

I asked, "Have you brought a lot of stuff with you and if so, will it fit in a SUV?"

"Now, don't give me any sass young man. You know I wouldn't bring anything I didn't need."

I laughed, and said, "I'll see you later and you better bring my favorite pie or its makings."

She replied, "You and your apple pies. Don't worry, I've got one to bring."

I looked at the time and estimated that I should leave in the next thirty minutes if I was going to reach Chetopa before Grandmother. I checked with my future in-laws and Jenn before I left town. I knew I needed to buy gasoline, so that was my first stop before going east. When I reached Chetopa I drove by the bank and Grandmother wasn't there yet, so I drove on to the Neosho River bridge at the east edge of town and parked my car so that I could observe approaching traffic.

I could see her red pickup approaching the bridge twenty minutes later. Soon she passed me on her way to the bank parking lot. The next two vehicles were pickups that looked local, then trailing them about a quarter of a mile came a new black Lincoln with Missouri tags. I waited until they were about six car lengths down the road before I made a U turn following the Lincoln which slowed, but didn't stop, when it passed the parking lot where Grandmothers truck was parked. I observed that it continued on for two blocks before stopping at the curb.

I made a right turn and backtracked to the local police station that was near the bridge I just left. I parked behind the police car and went inside to get some help. I showed the officer my Department of Justice ID and explained that I had a problem. Within minutes the officer contacted the Kansas Highway Patrol, who sent two patrol cars that arrived within minutes. After consulting among themselves, the local police and the two State cars converged on the Lincoln from the front and back. I watched as the State Police hauled three men out of the Lincoln, frisked them for weapons, and took what looked like handguns from them. They then searched the car and pulled several long guns out of the trunk. I drove up to them and talked to one of the State Troopers.

"Can you hold them at the County Seat in Oswego until I can come by tomorrow to sign a complaint?"

"Sure, no hurry. We have enough on the illegal weapons to hold them until you check in."

I thanked them for a job well done and returned to pick up Grandmother. She looked a little peeved when she got out of the truck. "I've been waiting a good half hour here and there was something going on down the street that had me a little worried."

"Don't worry they were just leaving when I drove by. Let's get this stuff transferred to the SUV and we will be on our way. Grandmother, I just had a thought. Before we head to Coffeyville, let's move the pickup down to the police station where they can watch it until you pick it up later."

"They won't give me a ticket will they?"

"No, I'll let them know who you are. They won't dare give you a ticket then."

"Okay, let's get this show on the road. I can't wait until I get to see this gal you're going to marry. Why, when I saw her last she was just a slip of a girl of fifteen."

On the drive back to Coffeyville I told her all about Jenn, her history, fears, and how much we loved each other. I then told her about our last visit from Olivia and her message.

"Oh my! So that's the real reason for this rushed wedding. How is Jennifer taking all this excitement?"

"A lot better than me. I've got a guardian angel to protect me, but those around me can get hurt from the fallout."

After driving for awhile in silence, I glanced at Grandmother who was studying me.

"What?"

"Oh, it's strange what life brings you. I was lost when your father died, and then you came to me for me to raise. It was like a second chance. You lost your first love, now you are in the process of getting married, and to her sister no less."

"Stranger still is that less than a week ago I didn't know Jenn was going to enter my life for the second time. When she showed up at the office it was like getting hit in the head by a club. She was about all I could think about, and it affected her the same as well. I agree with you in that it seems God has our lives planned and adjustments are made when outside influences occur."

Grandmother placed her hand on my arm and squeezed. "Son, just keep doing the right thing and I'm sure everything will work out in the end."

After we arrived at the Powers' home, I helped Grandmother inside and then enlisted the help of Jamison to carry inside the items she had brought with her. While doing this I informed him of the tail Grandmother had brought with her and the steps I had taken. He excused himself and walked beyond hearing range, then pulled out his cell phone and started talking. Five minutes later he returned looking satisfied.

"I called the Sheriff and he is going to send some volunteer deputies to act as security until you and Jenn leave here. He told me that if you suspect a imminent threat that you should call the highway patrol, like you did before."

"Thinks Jamison, that relieves me somewhat. Do you have any weapons in case we have a need?"

"Let's take this last couple of boxes inside and I'll show you what I have."

After we placed the boxes with the others Jamison led the way to the basement, an area I hadn't been in before. Jamison was an avid hunter based upon the number of trophy heads on the walls.

"Alice won't allow these upstairs because they disgust her friends when she has them over. I guess this is what you call my man cave." He said with a grin.

He then led me over to a locked gun cabinet which he opened and displayed six hunting rifles of varying calibers for different game. They were all bolt action and appeared to be well cared for. "I don't have any hand guns because they have only one use other than target practice, and that's to kill humans."

I looked at the rifles and considered for a moment. "We can always come down here if we come under attack. We should be able to hold anybody off until help arrives; however, let's keep this to ourselves until the need arises."

CHAPTER NINE

As we started back up the stairs I was thinking, *Olivia is my primary defense and this is just a backup in case things go south.* We found our women gathered in the kitchen inspecting the things Grandmother brought and at first I thought we hadn't been missed, but reconsidered when Jenn looked at me and motioned for me to follow her out of the kitchen.

When I left the kitchen, she grabbed me and initiated a long passionate kiss. Coming up for air, she pulled me into her father's office, and locked the door. She looked into my eyes and asked, "What happened in Chetopa just before you picked up your Grandmother?"

"She told you about the ruckus down the street from her?" I said as I gathered her into my arms. At her nod, I continued. "I left early to check if anyone followed her and when I determined she had a tail, I got the local police to call in the Highway Patrol. They hauled them off to Oswego until I stop by tomorrow to press charges."

"When were you going to tell me?" She said with a bit of ire in her voice.

"Now honey, I've been busy. I told your father and he called the Sheriff, who arranged security for us. We checked out the basement for a possible shelter and the weapons he has down there, and I was just coming up to tell you."

She looked into my eyes for a moment, then melted into my arms. "Just don't keep me out of the loop. I'm up to my neck in this, you know."

"Yes dear. How are things going for you in planning the wedding?"

Jenn smiled at me and then dug her thumb into my ribs. "As if you care. We women get the short end of this stick. All you have to do is show up."

Trying to show I was interested, I asked. "Whose your maid of honor?"

She buried her face into my chest and mumbled something. I put my finger under her chin and lifted her head where I could see her face. "Honey, what's wrong?"

She grimaced. "All my close friends have either moved away or are married."

"How about your girlfriends at Harvard?"

She looked at me as if I was a genius. "Of course, my roommates Cheryl and Sandy! I'll call them right now."

She gave me a quick kiss and pulled out her cell and punched in numbers as she muttered, "How stupid can I get."

I left her giggling on the phone and returned to the kitchen hoping to find a snack. Alice and Grandmother were admiring a colorful quilt spread out on the table. "I think Jenn has her maid of honor if she can get here in time." I said as I approached the table.

Alice looked up at me in surprise. "Oh, who did she get?"

I laughed. "She forget about her Harvard roommates. She's on the phone now."

"Assuming they can come, I think we are going to be okay." Alice said with a smile.

"Where did you get the quilt, Grandmother?" I asked putting my arm around her shoulders.

"This has been in our family over a hundred years. I gave it to your mother when she married my son. Now it is going to Jennifer when she marries you. Remind me to tell her about the curse."

"What do you mean curse?" I said as I raised a corner and felt the material.

"If she puts it on her bed there is a good chance she will become pregnant."

"Whoa! Are you saying this is a baby quilt."

Jenn entered the room just as I uttered those words. "What are you talking about?"

"Grandmother is giving us this family heirloom that has the reputation of being a baby maker."

Jenn was reaching out to touch it, but jerked her hand back when she heard "baby maker".

"Jack put that in a box labeled so we can use it when we're ready."

I winked at Grandmother and put my hand out as if to touch Jenn. "I touched it, do you think I'm contaminated?"

"Darn you Jack, stay away from me until you wash your hands." Jenn said as she backed away from me keeping the table between us. I laughed and went to the sink and washed my hands.

Jenn asked, "Elizabeth, how did you live with this practical joker?"

Grandmother looked at me with a smile on her face. "He gets it from me. I've got a low brow sense of humor and we got along fine. He'll change you or you will him."

"Jack, both Cheryl and Sandy Jackson are coming for the wedding and will call us when they have their transportation arranged. I suggested they try to fly into Tulsa and we would pick them up at the airport. They both live in Cleveland and I can't wait until I see them again."

My stomach rumbled, telling me I hadn't eaten anything since breakfast. Jenn looked at her mother and asked, "What do we have planned for dinner and when. Jack's stomach is telling me he needs something to eat."

Alice looked at Elizabeth. "How often do you feed him at home?"

"Just three times a day, but sometimes he finds snacks to tide him over. Jenn it's going to be a few more hours before we eat. Fix him a peanut butter sandwich and that should take care of him."

Jenn got the ingredients out and started fixing us both a sandwich. "You want any jam on yours?"

I came over and asked, "What kind you got?"

"Your choice, blackberry or strawberry. I'm having blackberry."

"Okay, make it two. May I have a glass of milk?" Jennifer raised her brow at me and then pointed to the refrigerator. "Help yourself and pour me a small glass too."

Alice and Elizabeth watched this interaction with a smile on their faces. Elizabeth whispered to Alice. "Good, she's starting to train him to help her."

An hour later Jenn got the call she was expecting on the travel plans of her friends.

"They're flying into Tulsa at two p.m. tomorrow, so Jack can go and pick them up."

I looked at Jenn and said with a smile, "Oh boy, I'm going to be all alone with two beautiful women for over an hour who know all your guilty secrets. This going to be fun."

"Correction, we're going to pick them up."

I pulled her into the next room and whispered, "I need to go to Oswego in the morning to file charges against those guys who were following Grandmother, but I should be back before noon. Is there anything else we need to be doing?"

She thought for a few moments, then shook her head. "No, my maids need to be fitted for their dresses, but that can't be done until they get here. Where are we going on our honeymoon?"

"I'll call the office Friday and see if we are cleared to come back. If not, we can make a quick trip to Florida."

"Oh, that would be nice if we could get a room on the beach."

"I was thinking about one next to a nice golf course." I replied with a grin. My reward was a hard right to my shoulder.

"That's not even funny. When we have the time for a proper honeymoon I want to go somewhere romantic." She said with a dreamy expression on her face.

"Yes dear." I said before pulling her into my arms and giving her a passionate kiss.

The following day we arrived at the Tulsa airport and found our party sitting on their suitcases at the curb. After retrieving our passengers and their luggage we departed for home. I learned that the young women were fraternal twins and had roomed together with Jennifer for three years.

Cheryl broke the ice by asking, "So this is the mystery man you were saving yourself for. Jack, now that I've seen you I can understand why Jenn wouldn't talk about you. Why, she didn't even have a picture, because I looked."

"Did she tell you that I was engaged to her sister for a short period before her death?"

"No!" They exclaimed in unison as they looked at Jenn."

"I told you a secret, now it's your turn to tell me one about Jenn."

"Noo! Don't you dare tell him anything or I'll pull your hair out!" Jenn almost shouted. "I'm starting to think I should have come after you by myself."

"My, he sure knows how to push your buttons. Don't worry we girls have to stick together against these pesky men." Sandy said.

Jenn sighed in relief. "He has a terrible sense of humor and delights in making me squirm. In spite of that I love him with all my heart."

The three women begin catching up on what had happened since graduation and what they were doing now. I started watching my rearview mirror for any car that looked familiar from the trip to the airport, but didn't see anything suspicious. Seeing the Bartlesville exit approaching, the women expressed a desire to go potty. I decided to fuel up while they were inside the station and watched all cars as they entered off the highway.

When the women returned they found me drinking a cup of coffee while I was waiting, and then we were on the road again. Cheryl slugged me on the shoulder before we got back into the car and I wondered what that was about, but let it go. Nobody followed us back onto the highway and I relaxed. I looked over at Jenn and she stuck her tongue out at me. I shook my head thinking, *woman are hard to understand.*

We made it back to the Powers' house without incident and I started unloading the car while Jenn took her friends inside. After setting the luggage next to the kitchen door, I drove the car into the garage and shut its doors. Jamison came outside and told me the room the twins were sharing and helped me move their luggage upstairs before leaving me alone. Cheryl followed me into their assigned room and directed where she wanted the luggage placed. I turned to leave, but she had shut the door and was standing in front of it.

"Do you love her?" She said while giving me a intent stare.

"Yes, with all my heart. Did Jenn tell you how we met after not seeing each other for over eleven years?"

"She told us, but it's a little hard to believe. Both of you, love at first sight. It sounds like a bad romance novel. She's such a good soul, I just don't want her to get hurt."

"You've never been in love?"

"Not like that. My experience was more lust than love. I want to believe that I can find that kind of love. My parents did, maybe you and Jenn, so I'm hopeful I can too."

"I'm double blessed. When Jenn's sister died, I thought I would too. Maybe my emotions died too. But when I met Jenn again, it all came back. It's strange that we have bonded in such a short time, but factors have been in play that no outsider can understand."

I draped my arm around her shoulder and gave her a squeeze. "Maybe you and Sandy will find someone soon."

CHAPTER TEN

A middle-aged man stepped off the bus from Kansas City carrying a mid-sized bag. He looked around the downtown business district of Coffeyville, frowning at its smallness. He was going to find it difficult to blend in when there were so few people. He noticed a Best Western Motel about two blocks away and headed in that direction hoping to find a room, and then he would see about renting a car. He had a lead on where the Powers family lived, but he wanted to check it out before taking any action.

* * *

I awoke to the sound of the intercom announcing it was time to get up if I wanted breakfast with the family. I showered before heading to the kitchen where I found Jenn, but the sisters were still a no show. She smiled as I entered the room, which seemed to brighten my mood. I picked her up and kissed her good morning. It was a kiss that took both our breaths.

Still in my arms, she breathed deeply before playfully biting my ear lobe. "Jack, did you sleep alright? I don't think I moved the whole night. I guess all this excitement wore me out."

I kissed her on the nose. "It must have done you some good because you look beautiful. What's for breakfast, because your man

58

could eat a horse?"

She grinned at me. "Well, we have no horse. Would pig sausage and fried eggs do?"

I asked if I could help with anything, but the women, Jenn, her mom and grandma, told me to sit down and stay out of their way. I found a morning newspaper and started reading the headlines checking if anything was happening in Kansas City. Finding nothing of note in the paper, I watched the ladies preparing breakfast. I was startled when the sisters sat down on either side of me.

We exchanged greetings and while they were both attractive women, they couldn't compare with Jenn. They both offered their help to the cooks, but were told to sit and talk to me. Sandy and Cheryl looked at each other and gave each other an impish smile, which caused me to shiver in dread.

Sandy said, "Jenn tells me that you are her boss at work and says that you have the rep as one of the courts strongest prosecutors. What are your long term ambitions?"

Both sisters were attorneys, but I didn't know where they worked. I decided to see if I could shock them. "I don't know if Jenn told you of our current problem, but the case we started together this past week resulted in," I leaned forward and whispered, "three attempts on our lives." I sat back once again. "The United States District Attorney told us to leave Kansas City for a week in hopes things would resolve itself."

"You're hiding out? Do they know where you are at?"

I glanced around to make sure no one was listening to our conversation, then turned back to the twins. "Shush! Keep it quiet, Grandmother doesn't know. I don't think they know where we are, but Jamison has arranged for security with the local Sheriff. We should be okay. I hope you two don't bug out on Jenn, because she has no one else and she was looking forward to seeing you two."

"Bug out hell! This is exciting. What kind of case was it?" Cheryl asked in a whisper.

"Before I answer, what do you two work at?"

"Oh, we are in corporate law with our father's firm. Criminal law is much more exciting, isn't it?"

"It is, but when people try to kill you, I think boring is safer. Jenn seems to take it pretty well. She didn't say anything to you?"

Jenn brought me a full plate and placed it down in front of me, watching my face for a reaction. "It looks good honey. The eggs are cooked just the way I like."

She smiled at my compliment, then said. "Now, what do you mean did she say anything?"

I whispered. "I told them about the three attempts on our lives."

Jenn looked at her two friends in alarm. Cheryl put her hand on Jenn's arm and said, "Don't worry, we aren't going to bug out on your wedding. It's quite exciting. No wonder you two bonded so fast, with people trying to kill you. Can you tell us all about it?"

Jenn looked toward the other women working and whispered, "Later, after breakfast and before the fitting people arrive for your dresses."

Jenn kissed and then bit my lip, causing me to swat her behind as she moved away. The sisters thought this was hilarious and laughed so hard they had tears running down their faces.

The older women gave us all "The Look," which caused the sisters to sober up and compose themselves. Jamison walked into the room and looked confused for a moment, then asked. "What did I miss?"

Alice shook her head. "Oh, kids will be kids. I miss them when they aren't around; however, you would think by now they would be a little more sedate."

Jamison sat down across from me and raised a brow at us. I grinned at the two sisters, who with obvious great effort both stifled another round of laughter. Cheryl said. "Jenn, Jack has a great sense of humor. I'm happy to report that your marriage will never be boring, and from what I hear will be exciting as well."

Alice and Elizabeth looked at each other and smiled at the comment. Their own observations substantiated that same conclusion. Jenn turned and looked at her friends for a moment, then smiled before returning to her tasks.

Later, after breakfast and answering the twins' questions about the attempts on our lives, we returned to what we considered our new normal condition of controlled chaos. The twins were being fitted for their dresses, so I took the opportunity to call Jessica.

She said, "There was an attempt on the lives of the two police detectives yesterday and they have a man in custody. The detectives were not injured, but were pissed off. Call me back Friday for an update and I'll call you if something happens here."

"Jessica, someone sent a car with three thugs to tail my Grandmother. I took care of that and they are in the Oswego, Kansas County Jail. Someone had access to our personnel files to find out about her and where she lives. This is getting more weird all the time. Maybe someone in our organization is tied to that drug bust and they are trying to cover their ass."

There was silence for a few moments as Jessica thought about this development. "Shit! I'm going to have to report this to Rapport and he will have to call in the FBI to investigate us. I'll get back to you."

I went back into the living room where Jenn was supervising the fitting, and getting her attention I motioned for her to follow me. We went to her father's office and shut the door. "I just talked to Jessica in the office and she said there was an attempt on Sara and Sam's life yesterday, but they are okay. I then told her about my theory that someone from our organization might be involved and my reasons, and that the FBI will get involved now."

"Wow! Do you think this is going to affect our wedding plans?"

"Who knows. We still have five days before the wedding and anything can happen. Let's not get too concerned, but we should tell the others about the FBI's possible involvement."

Jenn held out her arms for a hug, which I provided along with a kiss for good measure. "My, who would have thought meeting you would bring this much excitement into my life." She said, her face buried against my chest.

That evening after dinner was finished I stood and announced that the FBI may now be involved in Jenn's and my problems. It was possible that they could show up here anytime. I then told them about the conversation I had earlier with Jessica.

Grandmother looked at me with new understanding and then said, "Jack, you rascal. That business in Chetopa was about this wasn't it?"

"I'm sorry Grandmother, but I didn't want to worry you. It's all moot now if the FBI is involved, since it will all come out."

Cheryl and Sandy couldn't contain their excitement. "Wow, this never happens back home. Jenn, thanks for inviting us to your wedding. We are having so much fun and the wedding is still days away." Cheryl said.

The next morning started as before with the intercom wakeup, but our breakfast was interrupted by the arrival of two FBI agents. They waited until Jenn and I were finished eating and then we gathered in Jamison's office.

Special Agents Peter Jacobson and Patricia Upjohn introduced themselves and wanted to hear our story first-hand. Agent in charge Jacobson was in his late twenties and was a tall black man, built like a linebacker. Upjohn was Jenn's age and size, but appeared to be a natural redhead.

Jenn and I recounted the three attempts on our lives and the second interviews with the drug suspects where we obtained lists of their associates. I then described how I laid an ambush for anybody who might follow my Grandmother to our meeting place in Chetopa, and my steps when they did.

Jacobson asked. "Do you have a copy of that list of associates? Your report with the attached list seems to have been misplaced."

I looked at Jenn and frowned. "Well, that makes my theory of someone in our office working against us a lot stronger. I have the report and list on my computer. All I need is a printer."

Jenn pulled out a desk drawer, showing me a wireless printer. I excused myself and went for my computer. When I returned Upjohn and Jenn were discussing our relationship. They stopped talking when I entered the room and watched me print out two copies of the report and list. I then copied it to a flash drive and gave it to them along with a paper copy of the report and list.

Jacobson smiled as he accepted the copies, then said. "I understand you are planning a wedding this weekend. How long have you known each other?"

I put my arm around Jenn's waist and brought her closer to me. "Since I was nineteen and she was fifteen. However, we hadn't seen each other again until she came to work for us last week. It was love at first sight and then we were fighting together trying to stay alive. We bonded fast and I proposed after we got here."

Upjohn looked at us with her mouth open, then looked at her partner for guidance. Jacobson frowned as he considered his options. "The bad guys know where you are, which puts you in extreme danger. I'm going to recommend that the U.S. Marshall Office protect you."

"Will that be here or elsewhere?"

"You better move up your wedding because I'm sure they'll want to put you in a safehouse."

Jenn hurried out of the room in search of her parents. I smiled at the agents. "Do you want to stay for our wedding? I'm sure you will find it interesting."

Jenn soon returned looking a little frazzled. "The Reverend is on his way and Jack, you and I need to change for our wedding."

She grabbed my hand and pulled me toward the door, then turned to the agents. "You guys are invited too." She didn't wait for a response as we left almost at a run.

Jenn pointed me to my room and told everyone else to get changed as the wedding was about to happen. The wedding went without a hitch, except the three bridesmaids, which now included Upjohn, wore their own clothes and Jacobson acted as my best man. The reception was pizza and champagne and everyone had a wonderful time, including the twin sisters.

Wedding pictures were taken by cell phones and both Alice and Grandmother appeared to be in a happy daze. An hour later the Marshalls arrived and after changing clothes and packing, we were ready to travel to an unknown destination. Jenn and I were walking toward a black Suburban, when there was a flash of light, followed by a boom about 150 yards away. I turned to one of the Marshalls and said, "You better check that out. I bet it was a sniper."

When we were seated, Jenn turned to me and said, "Olivia?" I nodded and replied. "I'd bet on it."

Our drive was short as we headed to the local airfield, where a business jet was waiting. As the aircraft went airborne, Jenn snuggled up to me and asked, "I wonder where we're going?"

I answered, "Disneyland." She frowned at my joke, then sweetly said, "Honey, I'm going to make your dreams come true tonight, wherever it is."

Two hours later we began to descend for a landing, my guess was somewhere in Arizona. When the aircraft stopped near the terminal I read, Welcome to Flagstaff. I told Jenn to look at the sign, who then turned to me and said, "So this is where we hide for awhile."

After leaving the aircraft we boarded another black Suburban and ended up at a unmarked four story storefront in downtown Flagstaff. We followed a Marshall inside, past a receptionist, a long hallway, then a metal detection before a bank of elevators. The elevator took us to the top floor, where we encountered armed security. The

Marshall showed his ID and vouched for us before we were allowed to proceed.

He used a palm print electronic device that opened the steel doors into a large open office space. We were led to a side office where we were introduced to Deputy Director Alfred Burke. He was handed a folder, that had our life story, which he set aside and told us to make ourselves comfortable.

"Welcome to Flagstaff. I understand that you have been placed in protective custody because someone has placed a bounty on your heads. You are going to be with us only as long as the threat exists. You may retain your current IDs, but we have leased a house and car under the names of Jack and Jane Beckett. We will give you a $5,000 debit card that can be reloaded if necessary. The house is ready to be occupied and has been stocked with food. Any questions?"

I asked, "You said we had a bounty on our heads? How much?"

"The last information we had was $20,000 each. Why did you ask the amount?"

"I was thinking that a low amount would attract only local hitters, but a large amount would bring in professionals. What about the two KC police detectives that were attacked. Do they have bounties too."

"I'm not privy to that information. Do you know them well?"

"No, just long enough to exchange information and be part of an assassination attempt. Yesterday another attempt was made on their lives, so please check if a protection offer was made to them."

DD Burke looked at them for a few moments considering. "If they join protective custody would you accept them here?"

"You don't mean in the same house?" Jennifer said.

"No, but there is a house next door available. Having friends nearby might make your stay more bearable."

Jenn nodded at my questioning look. "Sure, the more the merrier." I said.

"You may use your cells to make calls, but don't tell anyone where you are and that includes family. What they don't know can't hurt you. Jennifer, I want to congratulate you and Jack on your marriage today. I think you'll find Flagstaff a beautiful place for a honeymoon."

We collected the debit card and car keys and followed our escort back to the Suburban where we were driven to our home away from home. It was a nice looking two-bedroom brick house in a neat neighborhood. It had an attached garage, which I assumed held our car.

I asked the Marshall as we walked up to the front door. "How cold does it get here at night? We didn't bring any coats."

"This time of year the temp ranges from a low of 45 to a high of 78, so you better get at least a jacket."

We looked the house over, checking the stocked refrigerator and the towels and sheets. Jenn said, "It looks good for now."

The Marshall handed the keys to the house to her while I checked on the car. It was a late model Honda SUV, which should suit our needs.

When I rejoined Jenn I told her about the Honda and suggested. "Let's check the bed and make sure there are clean sheets, and if it gets that cold at night we will need a blanket."

She looked at me with a little smile as she muttered, "I don't think so. It's going to be a hot time in town tonight."

Everything looked fine, so we then checked for soap in the shower and towels. Finishing, Jenn checked the refrigerator to see if she could fix dinner from what it contained while I checked the TV and what channels were available. She soon joined me and sat down beside me on the couch.

"Your choice, spaghetti and meat sauce or hamburgers?"

"What kind of sauce do we have?" I replied.

"Prego with mushrooms, and yes I have made it before. The twins and I took turns cooking, so I do know how to open a can and heat it up."

I put my arm around her shoulders and she relaxed her head against my chest. "Jack, how does it feel to be married to me. Are you sorry?"

"No, I'm not sorry because I love you deeply. I wish we had more time to get to know each other better, so bear with me if I start to rub you the wrong way. Like cooking, I had to learn or starve since I've lived alone after leaving home. I've developed habits that may conflict with what you are used to. Why don't we make a list of things we each are comfortable doing and each agree on who will be responsible for them. If we don't like something the other is doing, then we let the other know so we can change."

"Okay, but not tonight. I'll fix dinner and you can help cleanup, then we are going to break in that bed."

"Sounds real good to me." I said and then gave her a long passionate kiss.

CHAPTER ELEVEN

The next morning I awoke to find a beautiful naked woman asleep beside me with her arm around my waist. I moved enough to free an arm so that I could tease Jenn's nipple until it stiffened, then moved my finger around her breast until she started breathing faster and her eyes opened. "Hi wife. How do you feel?"

She snuggled against me, smiling in satisfaction. "I don't know yet. How many times did we make love last night, I lost count after five."

"Me too. Get up woman and fix your husband some breakfast and maybe I'll have the strength to give you some more lovin."

I swung my legs out of the bed, but when I tried to stand I groaned from overused muscle pain.

"What's the matter, did my strong handsome man overdo it last night?"

When I started to give her payback by tickling her, she too started groaning in pain. "Oh, oh, that hurts."

I helped her out of bed and we supported each other to the shower, where I adjusted it as hot as we could stand. We stood under the water massaging each other until her gasps turned into demands that I perform a more personal service. We left the shower when the water turned cold. I toweled her dry lingering a little longer on her breasts and mound than was necessary. She took a dry towel and started working down from my head, but when she got to the area she was most concerned about she failed in her efforts to get another rise out of me.

"Damn, I guess I'll have to feed you and give you some rest."

I followed her out of the shower and we dressed, each teasing the other as we dressed. She had just finished putting on panties and bra when I came over and started massaging her neck and shoulders. "Oh yes. That's it, right there! Oooh! Yes, yes, yes." She then shuddered several times and fell back against me. "You did it to me again Jack."

She then stepped out of her panties and went to the bathroom to clean up. She soon returned and we finished dressing. I went over to her to give her a kiss and she held up a hand. "Not yet Jack. I'm afraid that you'll make me orgasm again just by touching me. I need a rest too, so that I can recover."

We went into the kitchen where she told me to sit. "We have eggs, bacon, and toast. Is that okay?"

After breakfast we decided to explore Flagstaff. We flipped a coin and I was the designated driver. The car was almost at empty, so while getting fuel Jenn went inside and got a map of the city. Before leaving the service station we planned out what we wanted to see and Jenn guided us where we wanted to go. Flagstaff was on a mountainside covered in a pine tree forest. The air was clear and had the faint smell of pine. At noon we stopped at a attractive restaurant overlooking a valley.

I brought the road atlas inside with me and we looked to see if there was anything else we could see before returning back to the house. I said, "Hey, look here. Sedona is just a short drive south of here. Why not eat dinner there and then return back to the house."

"Okay, that sounds like fun. I've heard of it and the canyon ride down to it is supposed to be pretty."

The canyon ride was interesting, but the turnoffs were busy. Jenn and I were enjoying ourselves and weren't worrying about the problems in KC. When we got to Sedona we parked the car and acted like tourists shopping for items of interest. Later we ate dinner and headed back to Flagstaff.

Both our cell phones started ringing at the same time. She answered hers while I looked for a place to pull over. I could hear her talking to someone who I thought might be with the Marshall service when I found a place to got the car stopped. Jenn's face was stiff in concentration as she listened. Then she said, "Jack's available now. Please repeat what you told me."

DD Burke answered my hello. "We checked on Detectives Brooks and Peterson, but were told they were both killed last night in a drive by shooting in KC. When you left Coffeyville yesterday an apparent sniper was found burned in his car not far from where you were staying. Whoever is behind this wants you all dead pretty bad."

I thanked her for letting us know what is happening and that I would get back with her as soon as we absorbed this news. After disconnecting I turned to Jenn and placed my hand on her shoulder. "Are you alright?"

She turned to me with tears of anger in her eyes and said through clinched teeth, "I want to find these people and put them in the deepest hole we can find!"

"Let's think about what we know on the drive home. Maybe the bad guys don't know the FBI are on the case now and when they do the pressure will be off us. However, as connected as they are I don't think that's the case. Maybe they are after us because of something else. Let's think on that and compare notes later."

I pulled the car back onto the road and continued on to Flagstaff. We arrived back at the house a little after eight p.m. and sat down on the couch together. Jenn nudged me down flat and lay next to me with her arms around me. "I need to cuddle with you as we talk."

"Tomorrow I'm going to call Jessica and find out if those drug suspects are still alive. If they are I'm almost sure that this crap is caused by something else." I said with heat.

"Well, I'm sure that it has nothing to do with me as I just got there, so what have you been doing that involved the two detectives other than the drug bust?"

I thought hard for a few minutes because whatever it was also involved the detectives, or one of them. "I've never met Sam Peterson before, but it seems like Sara and I had some kind of involvement, but I can't remember what it was."

"Did you have a date with her or a double date that included her?"

"That's it! I remember now. I dated one of the secretaries at the office. We went to a bar together where we met a friend of mine who was with Sara. Sara is a man-eater because she flirted with me in front of our dates. My date, Judith, got mad and started a fight right there and I had to pull them apart before the police were called. I dumped Judith after that."

"Wow, and I thought I had it bad. You must draw them like flies. Jack, if it's her behind this does she have the money to finance her vendetta against you and Sara?"

"I don't know, but I think I'll have the FBI check her out."

She wiggled closer to me and breathed in my scent. "Jack, I'm getting horny again. Let's go to bed and forget about this until morning."

The next morning arrived early for us. It was not yet light when my phone rang and I had to untangle myself from Jenn before I could reach for it, which caused me to groan in pain.

When I answered it was Jessica. "I just wanted to make sure you were alright. I was worried after hearing about the two detectives being killed."

I assured her that we were fine and asked if she had heard that Jenn and I were now married?

"What! How did that happen so soon? You've only been together since last week for God's sake."

"Well, we knew each other from before and we've been together almost from the time we met again with people trying to kill us several times. We fell in love, what can I say."

"I'm not going to lose both of you am I?"

"That's why I was going to call you. I think we may have been looking at this whole thing wrong. Have the FBI check out Judith Albertson from the office pool. She may have come unhinged when I rejected her earlier. Have the FBI check to see if she had the financial ability to pay for hits on us."

"Oh my ever lovin saints. Please don't tell me this was the result of a love affair gone bad. Okay, I'll get right on it. Stay out of trouble until you hear from me. What am I saying, you went and got married. Bye."

Jenn was looking at me with interest and when I disconnected, she asked, "What did she say?"

"She wanted to tell us about the two detectives getting killed and to make sure we were alright. When I told her we got married, she thought you were crazy, and when I told her about Judith she might think my woman chasing caused the poor woman to go bonkers."

"You were chasing after the office help?"

"Well, I did date several of the staff, but never more than once. Remember I was an emotional cripple until you came to the office."

"I don't care about any of the others. I got you and that's all that matters. However, if I catch you stepping out on me you will live to regret it."

"Ha, you forgot about Olivia. She will protect me."

"I won't threaten your life, just one of your appendages."

"Ouch. Don't worry my love. I have eyes only for you and right now you look very attractive. Turn over and I'll give you a massage that will get you in the mood."

"Jack, you're a little slow. Where you're concerned I'm always in the mood. Let's get to it."

We were eating breakfast when I got a call from the FBI. I explained about the date with Judith that went bad and involved Sara, and then my theory. However, it needed Judith's ability to pay for the hits, everything else fit.

The female agent chuckled. "I've heard of stranger reasons for killing someone. We'll check it out and get back with you."

Later, after we cleaned up the breakfast mess I said, "Jenn, I need exercise and you need to further your Judo training. I bet you've gotten soft." At her hard look I added. "I like that kind of soft, it's your muscle tone that I'm concerned about."

We cleared a large open area in the living room and stripped down to our underwear. Barefooted we faced each other and started our warm up with a series of stretching exercises. We started circling each other looking for a opening. I elected to be the aggressor and moved into her space reaching for a hold, which she blocked and tried a leg kick, that I blocked. We moved apart and I tried a myriad of low level moves and worked up until she missed a combination that resulted in her take down.

I said, "Time out. We both need a break." I helped her to her feet, but instead of a frowning, she smiled. "That last set of moves took me by surprise. This feels good to spar with you. What level was that last set from?"

I handed her a bottle of water from the refrigerator and took a swallow from my own. "Level four plus. Have you encountered it before?"

"No, but I think it was the switch from a single move to a

combination that got me. This is fun, but I bet I'll have bruises tomorrow. Let's get some running shoes and clothes for after the next session. I like to run and it keeps the muscles from stiffening up."

We spent another forty minutes on the sets working in higher level moves until I felt she had enough for this session. I helped her up and said, "It's shower time and then I'm going to give you a full body massage."

She grinned at me and said, "Oh goody, I love your massages."

After the shower we toweled off each other and I had her lie naked, face down on a sheet on the floor. On my knees, I began at her head and started working her neck and shoulder muscles, working my way down her back. I changed position before starting on her legs, where half-way through I had her turn over on her back and finished.

Jenn lay there not moving. "How do you feel?" I asked.

"Heavenly, I don't want to even move."

I laughed. "Okay, now it's my turn. Get up so I can lie down."

She stuck her tongue out me and said, "spoil sport," before rising and making room for me. She stood and stretched before assuming the position at my head where I had started with her. She had surprising strength in her hands as she began my massage. After she finished she lay next to me on the floor and we cuddled for awhile.

I complemented her on the session and the massage and asked how she felt. "I could lie here on this hard floor for a bit longer. I like your teaching methods. I learned more in this session than a year in the others, and I liked the massage after best of all. Did I do okay?"

"I would trust you at my back any time. If you are ready, we can get dressed and go shopping for those running items and a place to run."

"Not just yet." She said, climbing on top of me and initiated making love in a position we hadn't tried before.

Later, after taking another shower we were ready to start our shopping. We found what we needed in shoes and clothing, then after getting some advice from a retail clerk we checked out a running trail through the forest. Jenn wanted to try it right away, just change shoes and run. I laughed, but agreed and we took off down the trail through the trees. It smelled wonderful, but mindful of the new shoes we took the short trail.

That night we watched TV together on the couch holding hands, Jenn's head on my shoulder. While not a planned honeymoon, it turned into one without any effort. We had agreed to alternate who prepares the evening meal, so I fixed us chicken and pasta. It was a meal I prepared for myself many times, so I knew it would turn out okay.

Later, Jenn's physical exercise caught up with her as she fell asleep against me on the couch. I carried her to the bed where I took off her outer clothing and pulled the covers over her. I then joined her after making sure the house was locked down.

I awoke the next morning with someone blowing in my ear. "Wake up sleepy head and fix me some breakfast, I'm starving." Jenn said, then nibbled my earlobe.

She jumped out of bed and headed toward the shower trailing underwear. I soon joined her and we helped each other scrub down and towel off. While we were dressing I asked, "What do you want to eat?"

"Fix me some scrambled eggs and whatever meat we have and I'll take care of the toast."

After breakfast I started a list of food items we needed to replace. We had used much of the supply that was left us. Jenn looked at the list and added several items she needed. I reminded her to call her parents as they might start getting worried not hearing from her. She nodded, then used her cell to call them. I took my own advice and called Grandmother, and then Jessica in KC.

Grandmother was glad to hear from me and nothing new was going on there. Jessica said, "The FBI has taken Judith into custody, but I don't know anything else and DA Rapport hadn't passed down any information to me. Jack, the FBI will probably talk to you before me in any case."

I thanked her and disconnected. I asked myself if there was anything else I was missing, but came up empty. Jenn came into the bedroom where I was sitting on the bed and sat beside me. "Mom and Dad are okay and were real glad to hear from me. How was your Grandmother?"

"No change, then I called Jessica and other than the FBI picking up Judith, she knew nada."

"Well, let's not mope around here doing nothing. Teach me some more Judo moves and then we can go do another run."

CHAPTER TWELVE

This routine continued for another two days before we got a call from the FBI. The Special Agent in charge of the investigation said, "Judith Albertson confessed to her part in the attacks against you and she funded the bounties from an inheritance. We think she needs a mental evaluation before we can hope to bring her to trial. When the arrest is made public you should be able to return to your life here. I'll leave that up to the District Attorney to advise you. Good luck."

I said to Jenn, "It looks like we got that problem solved. What do you want to do here before we leave?"

She came into my arms and cried in relief. After awhile she regained her composure and said, "Let's not tell my family that this was caused by a woman who became unbalanced when you rejected her advances. Let's just say a woman, who worked in our office was responsible for the problem."

"We can try that, but you know the press is going play this up for all it's worth and all will come out."

"Then let's not say anything and wait until we see how it comes out in the papers."

The following day DD Burke from the U. S. Marshal office called us and advised us to pack up and they would take us to the airport in two hours. Later that day we were back in Coffeyville at the Powers' home. Jenn and I stood outside her childhood home, our luggage stacked around us and contemplated what we should do next.

Ben stuck his head outside the door and did a double take. "Jenn! When did you get here? Is this Jack? What's going on?"

Jenn smiled at her brother. "Ben, meet my husband. You know, the guy you were going to stand up for as his best man."

Ben rushed over and hugged his sister, and then shook hands with me. "Welcome to the family. I don't know if you are aware, but you're all over the news. It came on TV last night and was in this morning's newspaper."

"What was the tone of the coverage? Just the facts or judgmental?"

"So far, just the bare facts. Boy, I bet you have a story to tell and I want to hear it. Come on in, the folks have gone for groceries and should be back soon."

Ben started to move our luggage to the garage room, but Jenn decided we would stay in her old room, so we moved the luggage into the house. We had just hung up our clothes when we heard Ben talking to his parents.

Alice came running up the stairs and threw herself into our arms with tears of happiness running down her face. This brought on the tears from Jenn as well as we stood on the landing. Jamison and Ben followed and I got a hug and handshake from my father-in-law and a slap on the back from Ben.

We made it back downstairs to the living room and they wanted to know where we had been taken and what had happened to us. Jenn told them about the trip to Flagstaff and our later side trips. She then told them that she had helped me remember an incident with a secretary I had dated and then dumped, who became unhinged and was responsible for placing the bounty on our lives.

The three family members sat with open mouths, looking from Jenn to me and back to Jenn. Alice blurted, "That's crazy! No wonder you couldn't figure out what was happening. You go ahead and visit, I've got to put the groceries away."

Jamison asked, "When do you go back?"

"We go back to work Monday, so we leave tomorrow afternoon."

Ben smiled at his sister. "Well, at least you got a short honeymoon. How was Flagstaff?"

Jenn placed her hand on my leg and smiled at me. "The place we stayed was perfect and stocked with food, so we stayed in and got to know one another better."

Ben grinned at us. "I bet you did. You both look fit and rested, what else did you do?"

"You knew Jenn was into Judo?" At his nod I added, "I'm a Black Belt, so I gave her additional training and she introduced me to running. Flagstaff had a path through a pine forest that was great."

"So you made love and exercised the whole time you were there?"

Jenn objected, "Hey, we took a short trip to Sedona that was nice."

Ben and her father laughed causing her to blush. I put my arm around her shoulders and kissed her on the cheek. "That's not bad when we arrived at a place we hadn't planned on, and it was perfect for a short honeymoon."

Alice returned from the kitchen. "What does everyone want for dinner? We've got steaks the men can cook on the grill and Jenn and I can fix a salad and baked potatoes."

They all agreed that was perfect. The men departed to get the grill ready and the women went into the kitchen. Alice said, "I called Elizabeth and she will be here soon. She was happy that you and Jack made it back without any more problems."

"Mother, when you and Dad first got married, did his touch and scent leave you weak in the knees?"

"No, but I couldn't stand to be away from him for any length of time. He still has that effect on me. So you have a strong attraction toward him."

"Oh yeah. Twice now I've had an organism while he was giving me a massage. Is that normal?"

"Normal? Not for me, but it is for you. Does he feel the same attraction for you?"

"When we met in the office for the first time since I was fifteen, it was like we were soul mates. We couldn't take our eyes off each other, and now we don't need words to communicate. A look or a touch is all we need. When we make love it's as if we become one."

"Honey, you are one lucky woman. I wonder if Olivia's influence has anything to do with your bond."

Jenn nodded her head. "I'm sure of it. She did say that when Barbara died I was his designated mate."

Grandmother arrived in her red pickup and after greeting everyone, she asked to speak to Jennifer and me alone. We went to her father's office and shut the door. Grandmother settled into a chair with a sigh. She smiled at us and said, "I didn't fear for your safety as long as you were together because I knew Olivia would protect you. Barbara came into my dream last night and wanted me to pass on a message to you. She said you should leave the job you are doing and start defending people who have been charged with crimes. She will let you know which are innocent and that you should concentrate on those cases."

I looked at Jenn and her face reflected the surprise on mine. "That's a good goal, but how are we going to support ourselves while we do this?"

Grandmother smiled at our confusion. "Jack, you of little faith. The Lord will provide so that you can achieve your goal."

We left the office and returned to the others. Jenn took my hand and gave it a squeeze. "I'm with you no matter what you decide."

I made good money, but hadn't saved much. $20,000 is not enough to open up a office of our own. We could take cases the court assigns for clients without money, but that wouldn't pay our expenses. My mind continued to explore possibilities until Ben asked me a question. "I guess you are anxious to get back to your job?"

I forced a smile and answered. "Yes, we left a case hanging when this all started."

The steaks were delicious and I immediately felt better. I guess my body needed an infusion of red meat. I noticed that Jenn had eaten all of her steak and had a satisfied smile on her face. Grandmother caught my eye and winked at me. Maybe I should just go with the flow, because it seemed that my life has been planned for me.

CHAPTER THIRTEEN

We returned to our apartments late Sunday afternoon, where we decided to move my things into Jenn's larger apartment. After moving my clothes and Barbara's picture we decided to leave the rest for later. I hung the picture over the fireplace and started on hanging up my clothes in the bedroom closet. Jenn stayed behind and looked at her sister's picture.

She stared at the picture with tears in her eyes. "Barbara you picked a good man, a better one than you realized when you were together since you didn't know about Olivia. I'm trying to take care of him the best way I know and I hope you approve."

Jenn felt a warm loving glow emanating from the picture, which seemed to answer her question. I came up from behind her and put my arms around her waist holding her close and said, "I know, I feel her love too. I'm sure she approves that we are together looking out for each other."

She turned around in my arms and started crying until she was cried out. "I miss her so much. She was my mentor as we grew up, until she left for college and met you. When she brought you home I could see the love you shared and I wanted that too. I wanted someone to love like that and I found you."

Taking hands we went into our bedroom and made passionate love. Later, she snuggled against me and said, "I'm so happy, I don't think it can get any better."

The next morning we got up early and left for work, and we still hadn't made any decision about leaving to go out on our own. We reported to Jessica, who told us that DA Rapport wanted to talk to us. Once seated in his office his serious expression told me that we were in trouble.

"You two have violated this offices no fraternization rules, evidenced by your marriage. I'm sorry to lose both of you, but I have no choice in the matter. To make it easier for both of us I'm going to give you letters of recommendation and each six months termination salary if you don't fight us on this termination."

I looked at Jenn who seemed to wink at me. "Make it one year's salary and we will leave today," I said.

One hour later we were on our own standing outside our former office building. I thought for a moment, then asked Jenn, "Do you trust me to negotiate for a deal at one of the larger firms in town?"

"Go ahead. I know you'll get us the best deal you can."

I used my cell to call a friend and explained what had happened to us and asked if he could get us a appointment so that we could give them our pitch. I turned to Jenn, "He said he would get back with me ASAP. Let's go down the street to Starbucks and wait."

We hadn't been sitting ten minutes before I got the call. I thanked him and looked at Jenn, smiling. "Our appointment is in an hour. It's with the managing partner at Phelps, Phelps, and Woodruff, LP. They are the biggest law firm in KC, and if we can get in we'll be fine. The tricky part is working a deal where we pick our clients. We need that provision to accept only innocent people. Do you have any ideas on how we should proceed?"

We were in the reception area with a half hour to spare and still working on our strategy. We weren't called for another 45 minutes, but at least we had a plan. George Phelps' office fitted his title as managing partner. It was a large corner office with glass walls on two sides offering a view of the downtown area.

We were greeted and then led to a comfortable seating area by George, who was in his late fifties and in trim shape, most likely the result of a health club, and he still had all his hair. "Walter said I should hear what you have to say. He claims you have an impressive record of convictions at the District Court here and now want to work the other side. Why should we take you on?"

I smiled at George. "Before I begin, just how much criminal work does your office do?"

"Maybe one a month and something big maybe one every two or three years."

"Jennifer and I handle fifteen a month, and if you read the papers you see that we make the news. We would like you to take us on a trial basis, no salary, but we would have use of your facilities. I think we can bring you success in this area and much more business. More business means more revenue. Your cost to try us out will be minimal."

George looked at the two of us and considered. "I can't do the no salary. I'll pay you each $1,000 a week for a trial period of three months and then we will make a determination whether to keep you on. I need to get approval for this deal from the other partners, so check back with me later today."

"One other thing. We have an aversion to setting criminals free, so we must select our clients."

George looked at us in surprise. "You want to select who you defend?"

"Yes, both of us have developed an uncanny ability to determine if a person is guilty. This also will make our win rate spectacular."

He looked at me a moment longer considering. "Very well, I agree. When do you start?"

"How about tomorrow, assuming the other partners agree. We have some housekeeping chores to take care of. You know, newlyweds and all. Who do we report to?"

"Check with Walter on the way out and he'll give you what you need to know. Welcome aboard, and I hope this is profitable for us both." He shook both our hands and showed us out.

We checked with Walter before leaving and returned to our apartment building. After consulting with the leasing agent we opted for a unfurnished apartment about the same size as Jenn's current one. The agent arranged for movers, while we went shopping for essentials. After we were in the new apartment we would worry about decorating it.

I called George Phelps back and he said, "Your deal has been approved and you are cleared to start tomorrow."

I thanked him and said, "This should be a profitable relationship for both of us."

When we returned from shopping the movers were already busy moving my furniture and our clothing. We boxed up our toiletries and I hand carried Barbara's picture to the new apartment. After the movers left we checked the old apartments for anything left behind before locking up and returning the keys to the agent.

Jenn helped me connect the TV and stereo system and she decided on the placement of my old furniture. I could see her mind working on what pieces would need replacing and what the rooms needed to be functional. I unpacked the boxes of kitchen cooking and dinnerware and stacked them on the bar.

Jenn inspected what we owned, picking up a dinner plate, then a fork to check its pattern and quality. "Jack, you did well getting a service for eight and I like the pattern. Do you think we will be entertaining people from the firm or clients?"

"Not soon, but maybe sometime in the future. We have to prove ourselves first, then when we make better money we can upgrade to a fancier apartment that would be more appropriate for entertaining."

"Okay, along with what you suggested earlier, I'll get some paper and let's start that list of household duties we each would prefer doing."

Later, we compared our lists and Jenn wrote down those items on both of our lists, which we discussed and resolved who would do the job better. We then made a list of tasks neither of us wanted to do. Some tasks were resolved only by a coin toss. We then made two lists, a his and hers of our designated household duties and posted them on the refrigerator door. Meals were a shared task, Jenn would do breakfast and I would do dinner and we would both share in cleanup. We looked at the lists with satisfaction and sealed the agreement with a kiss.

We made my old queen-sized bed with Jenn's sheets and stocked the bathroom with my old towels. Jenn took one look at them and vowed to make a replacement. Later we looked at our new apartment and were happy with what we saw, at least for now. Barbara's picture over the fireplace looked down at us with her warm love settling over us.

The next morning we reported to Walter Cassidy to learn the internal procedures of the firm. After reading the office manual, we had to sign that we had read and understood its requirements, at which time we received a copy. He then showed us our office and introduced us to the secretary we shared with two other attorneys.

"Walter, do you have an investigator the firm uses and if so, how good is he?"

"We do, and she is very good. I'll introduce you to her when you first have the need to use her."

Jenn asked, "Do you have any clients that need our services?"

"No. You are going to have to find your own clients to defend, at least not until you have obtained a reputation of winning cases where clients would then seek you out."

After Walter left our office, Jenn looked at me for guidance. I said, "We go to court and try to snag a potential client after they are indicted."

"Most of these people are indigent and won't be able pay. How much does the court pay for us to defend them?"

"Not much, but are goal is to gain a reputation of winning. Money will come later as we gain the publics' attention."

* * *

Three months later, George Phelps sent down a message that he wanted to see us in the main conference room at two p.m.. After I showed Jenn the message, she grinned. "The day of reckoning is at hand."

"We don't have anything on our plate, let's take a long lunch and enjoy ourselves. If this doesn't work out as planned we'll plan something else later."

Jenn gave me a kiss and a hug. "Don't worry, we have done quite well. I wonder if we will get a bonus?"

After lunch we returned to the office to check for messages before heading to the conference room. Walter was the only one in the room when we arrived and he pointed to the chairs where we were to sit. The room started to fill and when the door was shut, all the partners were present.

As managing partner, George Phelps brought the meeting to order. "We are here to review the efforts of two new attorneys the firm took on a three month trial basis. During the three month period they tried eighteen cases without any losses. During the last month they brought to the firm six new clients, who have a combined net worth of $400 million. These six cases show Jack and

Jennifer Pearson's value to the firm and their reputation has spread to both coasts with inquiries about obtaining their services. I want the partnership to approve their permanent addition to our firm."

There was a voice vote of approval from the partners. The meeting broke up and Jenn and I were congratulated on our accomplishments from the partners. George approached us and said, "Meet me in my office after you leave here. We still have some actions to approve."

Later, we were waiting outside his office when George arrived and escorted us inside. After everyone was seated, he said, "First of all, welcome to the firm as permanent members. Due to your efforts the firm has profited and you deserve a share. Effective today your salaries are increased to $5,000 a week and you each get a $50,000 bonus, per the partners approval."

"That's very generous of the firm." I said, then added, "Jennifer and I need our own secretary and the office we share is crowded. Perhaps you could furnish us something larger?"

George smiled at them. "I'm ahead of you on the office space. Come with me and I'll show you where you will be working."

Our new office was on an outside wall with a window, a big upgrade in the internal hierarchy of the firm. In addition, outside the office was a desk for a secretary. "Do you have a preference on which secretary you get?"

Jenn and I looked at each other and without consulting, we both said, "Constance McAdams!"

George smiled his approval. "I'll have to ask her if she wants the change. She has enough pull to work for whomever she wants. I'll get back with you."

The next day we moved into our new office which contained a partnership desk where we faced each other. This freed up additional space for a client conference seating area. Jenn was looking at the walls considering what pictures would look good in this setting. Best of all, Constance McAdams had just arrived and was smiling at our admiration of the new office.

She entered the office and congratulated us on our promotion. Jenn and I had worked with several secretaries in the past three months, but Constance was the best and had been with the firm long enough to know where all the bodies were buried.

I said, "Welcome on board. We're not complaining, but why did you decide to work with us?"

Constance, an attractive woman in her early forties, had dark hair cut fashionably short, and was in terrific shape. She smiled at us for a moment before answering. "I liked you both from the first day you started here. The way you both were shafted by that U.S. District Attorney Rapport and still were able to start here without any rancor expressed about the idiot who fired you. You followed through on your promise to George on what you were capable of and here you are, the fastest rising stars the firm has ever had. I want to be part of what's going to happen next. By the way, please call me Connie."

I walked up to her and shook her hand. "Connie, all I can promise now is lots of hard work. By the way, please call us Jack or Jenn as the case may be. Can you arrange for all our open case files to be moved here?"

"They are being moved now. I'll check for your next scheduled court date and provide you with a day, week, and month schedule."

"We have no court dates scheduled yet for our six wealthy new clients, but Jenn and I need to check their status."

A week passed and our expanded team was working together without a hitch. Connie was away from her desk, when we both became aware of a presence at our door. It was a little blond haired girl of about seven. Jenn smiled at the girl and asked, "What's your name honey?"

"Barbara, what's yours?"

Jenn's face paled and I'm sure my mouth was hanging open. Jenn swallowed to clear her dry throat and then said, "My name is Jennifer, but you can call me Jenn if you like. Are you with someone?"

Barbara stepped into the office and approached our desk. "I'm with my Aunt Sally. She's in the bathroom. She's been gone a long time and I want you to find her for me."

"Okay, we'll do that. Jack will stay with you while I go look for her. Is that alright? He's a good man and will look after you."

Barbara walked over and took my hand. I picked her up and sat her on the desk facing me, while Jenn hurried towards the ladies room. Barbara looked around the office before settling her eyes on my face.

"Jack, this is Barbara speaking through this girl. Her aunt had a stroke and will not survive. Barbara is now a orphan, without any relatives. Her parents were killed because their car brakes failed.

There have been over 100 other instances of brakes failing on this make and model. She and the other victims need compensation and the manufacturer sued."

Little Barbara's gaze left me and returned to a bird sitting on the ledge outside our office. Jenn hurried back and started to say something, but stopped when I held up my hand. "Your sister told me already. We need to determine if her aunt talked to one of our attorneys before this happened."

Connie entered our office and Jenn herded her outside and explained what happened. Connie did a double take looking at Barbara and me and then back at Jenn. She then nodded her head and hurried toward reception, while Jenn returned to the aunt to see if she had any paperwork.

Connie returned and shook her head. "No, she just got here and wanted to speak to an attorney."

I said, "Barbara, your aunt is sick and needs to be taken care of. Since you are all alone would you like Jenn and I to act as your attorney?"

"Aunt Sally is sick?" Little Barbara said and her eyes misted up. I brought her to my chest and held her close. While holding her I watched as the EMT's wheeled her Aunt out of the building. Jenn returned with a folder in her hands, but stopped when she saw little Barbara in my arms.

I motioned Jenn to me. "Do you mind if I try to get guardianship papers drawn up for us and Barbara?"

Jenn's face almost collapsed in grief for Barbara, then taking a deep breath she and Connie left to get the paperwork started. Little Barbara and I were talking to each other when they returned an hour later, with George Phelps in tow. George took one look at Barbara, and then quickly turned with his head down, tears running down his face. When he had control of his emotions he straightened up and put a smile on his face before greeting Barbara.

"Hello Barbara, I'm George. How are you feeling? Do you want a soda or anything?"

"I need to go to the bathroom."

Connie said, "I'll take you and bring you right back."

They left and George said, "I called Children's Services and explained to them what had happened and your desire to act as her guardian. They are going to send someone from their office to interview you, but I don't think there will be a problem for you to take care of her until the guardianship is finalized."

"Did you hear why her aunt was here?"

"No." George replied. I looked at Jenn and she nodded her head for me to continue."She was here to bring suit against an automobile manufacturer she believed to be responsible for the deaths of Barbara's parents. Would the firm support this suit? Over100 accidents have been reported of this make and model because of bad brakes."

"Let me see what you come up with and we'll go from there."

CHAPTER FOURTEEN

We left work early and went clothing shopping for Barbara. We also returned home with a collapsible bed for her. When we entered the apartment Barbara's eyes were drawn to the picture over the fireplace. She stood there with a teddy bear in her arms looking up at the picture. "She's a pretty lady. Who is she?"

Jenn smiled at her. "That's my sister. Her name is Barbara too."

"She makes me feel safe here."

Jenn stooped down and placed her arm around Barbara. "She makes me feel safe too."

I was cooking dinner when Jenn called her mother. "Mother, I have news. We are in the process of getting the guardianship of a little seven year-old blond haired girl named Barbara Messing. She's an orphan now after her aunt died of a stroke in our office today. Mother, when she showed up in our office and said her name was Barbara, both Jack and I were speechless. Then our Barbara spoke through her telling Jack how her parents died and that her aunt would die of a stroke. I didn't hear this as I was hunting for the missing aunt."

"You have the girl now? Jenn! How are you going to take care of a little girl. A seven year-old girl."

"Well, you did. Not only one girl, but two girls and a boy. Jack and I can manage. She's school age, so we have to find where she went or transfer her to a school near us."

"We're coming up there tomorrow and we'll help you get things arranged. I know you don't have room for us in that little apartment of yours, so we'll stay at a hotel. Take care, bye."

Jenn came into the kitchen and said wistfully, "Mom and Dad are coming tomorrow to help out."

"Thank God. I hope we didn't bite off more than we can chew." I said.

"What are we having and did you ask Barbara what she likes?"

"I did, and she said she likes chicken and pasta."

"I guess we are going to have to learn what she is used to eating and we need to talk to Children's Services about getting the rest of her clothing and school supplies. I'm glad now that I called Mom. She already knows how to do all this stuff."

The next day I left alone for work, leaving Jenn with Barbara. Her parents were expected to arrive about nine or ten a.m., and she needed to wait for Children's Services to check out the apartment. I arrived on time and Connie ribbed me about leaving the little lady to take care of the mess. I stuck my tongue out at her and asked if I needed to do anything important.

* * *

Alice and Jamison arrived at the apartment and rang the bell. The door was answered by little Barbara, who took both of their breaths away. "I'm Jenn's mother, can we come in?"

Little Barbara looked at them silently, sizing them up, then smiled and let them enter. This was the first time they had visited the apartment and they both were stopped in their tracks by their daughter Barbara's picture over the fireplace.

Alice said, "Ooh. I've forgotten how beautiful this picture was. I haven't seen it since Jack left with it. I can't get over how her eyes seem to look right at me and I'm getting a warm fuzzy feeling."

Little Barbara said, "She makes me feel safe."

Jenn walked into the room and greeted them. "I see you've met Barbara. Sorry I didn't answer the door, nature called."

"Honey, you might not remember seeing pictures of Barbara when she was that age, but she's the spitting image of your sister."

"I know we were destined to meet her from the moment Jack and

I first saw her. That was reinforced when Barbara talked to Jack and told us to sue the company that made the cars with faulty brakes that caused Barbara's parents to die."

"Barbara didn't ask you to be her guardian?"

"No, but both Jack and I bonded with her. I have even thought about adopting her. She needs a guardian to file a lawsuit against the car manufacturer and be responsible for her safety and wellbeing."

"Can you as her guardian appoint someone else to take care of her?"

Jenn looked at her parents for a few moments as she thought. "Mom, that's a lot of responsibility to take care of a little girl you've just met. You and Dad need to discuss this further. In any case we haven't gotten her guardianship yet, only approval to take care of her until its finalized."

"Barbara, do you know the name of the school you go to?"

"Horace Mann and I'm in the second grade. Can I go back to school? Mrs. Littlejohn will worry about me."

Jenn looked at her mother and smiled in relief. "I'm going to call your school and see if we can get you in. Mother, while I'm doing that would you take Barbara into the bedroom and see if the clothes we bought for her yesterday are appropriate for school."

When they left the room I used my cell to find the phone number for her school. After a few false starts I got its principal and told her about Barbara's situation and her current residence. The Principal told me to hold while she looked at the schools district map, then responded. "You're in luck. You live in this school's district. Why don't you bring her here with your documentation from Children's Services."

I asked her for the address of the school and said we would see her soon. Jenn looked at her father with relief. "Well, that's taken care of. Let's check on Mother and see what they are doing."

* * *

Later that day, as I was driving home from work, I was wondering what was waiting for me. Jenn had called earlier and asked if she could arrange for a larger apartment. I told her to use her own judgment, but it should be at least three bedrooms. I entered the apartment to find Jenn's parents helping box up our things for another move.

Jenn hurried over and kissed me. "Honey, I hope you like this new apartment. It was furnished and I worked out a deal for its purchase, rather than have them move it all out and store it. Mom, Dad, Barbara let's all go look at it together."

We took the elevator to the tenth floor, which was the top of the building. When Jenn opened the apartment door, I was impressed by the view through the wall of glass. We were looking south toward the Plaza, which at night would be all lit up. "Wow! This view alone sold me."

Jenn grabbed my hand and led me through the apartment, showing me the three bedrooms and an office. The master bedroom held a king size bed, while the other two bedrooms were vacant of furniture. The office had a fancy desk and chair with walls lined with bookcases. The living room's furniture was expensive and all was arranged to take advantage of the view. The separate dining area had a large cherry table with seating for ten. To cap it off it also had two full baths, one attached to the master bedroom.

Alice and Jamison looked at us with their mouths open. "Can you afford something like this?" Jamison asked.

Jenn looked at me with a smile. "We can now. We've received a big raise and a bonus for our first three months on the job."

I asked Jenn, "How much will this cost us since we bought the furniture?"

"It's been vacant for over a year, so we got a deal of only $2,000 a month."

Jamison smiled at Jenn. "That's pretty good, but you should consider buying. Rent is like throwing money down a rat hole. You never get it back."

Jenn smiled at him. "Dad, I've heard that comment from you so many times that I insisted on a lease/purchase plan."

I put my arms around Jenn and gave her a kiss of appreciation. "That's my wife. I knew you were the smart one when I married you."

Barbara asked, "Which one is my room?"

We took her to the two vacant bedrooms and asked, "Which do you like best, you pick."

The two rooms were almost the same size and either would accommodate the queen-size bed we used. The temporary bed we purchased for Barbara would have to be replaced.

"I want this one." She said. The room she chose was the closest to our master bedroom.

Jenn took one last look around. "The movers will be here tomorrow, so let's go finish while Jack fixes us dinner."

While we were walking toward our old apartment I asked everyone what they wanted to eat. They either took pity on me or didn't trust my cooking, because they all wanted pizza.

The next morning we delayed our departure for the office until Barbara got on the school bus that had stopped in front of our building. Jenn's parents were going to stay another day and spend the night in our new apartment. They were going to shop for a new bed for Barbara and get it set up before Barbara and we returned home this afternoon.

When we got to the office we looked through the information Barbara's aunt brought with her. It contained the police report of the accident, which included a forensic analysis of the mechanics of both cars involved in the accident. The reports noted that the brakes on the Messing car had locked up on the left side, which caused the car to veer into oncoming traffic. There was a notation that this analysis was done because of two other recent accidents involving similar make and model vehicles.

Barbara's aunt had also gone to the library and done a search of newspapers from other large cities searching for accidents involving the make and model of her car. She had found fifteen different accidents involving similar vehicles. Jenn started calling the police departments that investigated these accidents while I went to the library searching for more accidents across the country.

Later that day I returned with twenty more suspicious accidents and joined Jenn in calling police departments. By the time we were ready to call it a day we had at least twelve vehicle accidents caused by faulty brakes and the police were taking another look at the accidents where no analysis was done.

We checked with Connie and we had nothing scheduled for the rest of the week, so we headed for home. We found Jenn's parents looking at something Barbara brought home from school and asked what they were looking at. Barbara proudly held up a pencil drawing. "Look, I drew everyone. See, this is Jack, and this is Jenn, and this is Jenn's Mom and Dad."

I was expecting stick figures, but instead everyone in the sketch was recognizable.

Tears were running down Alice's face as she said. "She is so much like my Barbara that it is uncanny. She was drawing pictures like this at her age too."

Little Barbara looked at Alice, then at the picture above the fireplace. "The pretty lady in the picture could draw too?"

Jenn had tears in her eyes as she replied, "Yes, she painted that picture of herself. It's pretty isn't it."

Little Barbara walked over to the picture and examined it. "I want to draw as good as this someday. Do you think I'll be as pretty as she is?"

Alice and Jenn went and stood beside her and looked at the painting. "I have a feeling that you might be even prettier," Alice said.

I checked the bedrooms and noted that the beds needed to be set up and my old furniture was scattered throughout the apartment. "Jenn, why don't you and Alice look at my old furniture and decide which we want to keep. The others we can have goodwill pick up. Jamison, let's put these two beds together so that the women can make them up."

It didn't take long before we finished and I had a chance to see what the women deemed not needed any longer. I wasn't attached to any of items, but I thought we could still use one end table and I carried it into the master bedroom. Jamison helped me carry a easy chair that was being retained into the master bedroom. I looked at him and said, "All I need now is a lamp to put on the table and I have a place to read."

The women looked at me and shook their heads. "What?" I said. Jamison grinned at me and herded me away from them before I got into trouble.

"Jack, decorating is one of the things women take seriously. The thing to do is ask them if this looks right before you move furniture."

"Thanks, I wish you had told me that before now."

The next day Jenn and I consulted with George. "We can't bring suit against the car manufacturer yet because we don't have legal guardianship of Barbara. However, do we have a legal or moral obligation to inform the company of their problems with the automobile?" I asked.

"Have you checked to see if other suits have already been filed?"

At my nod, he continued, "There is no legal obligation. That starts with the suit being filed. Morally, maybe. However, that applies only to public safety and we can be sued for bringing this matter to the public's attention without the proper basis. Let's continue to build our case, at least until you get you guardianship in place."

A month later the court ruled in our favor for our guardianship of the financial and personal welfare of Barbara Messing. Jenn and I had documentation of the brake failures involving thirty accidents caused by the same make and model vehicle. We had also compiled a list of over 100 victims, of which twenty-two were dead.

We asked for a meeting with George where we outlined our evidence and the number of victims. He looked at us and smiled. "Good work. Now that the guardianship is in place we can proceed with the lawsuit. I'll bring this before the partners today and I'll inform you of their decision."

When we returned to our office, Jenn called home. "Mom, we received the guardianship approval today. What have you and Dad decided about Barbara?"

"We've already cleaned Barbara's old room. I know she's not our old Barbara, but she's close enough that Jamison and I want to experience watching this new Barbara grow up and we already love her."

"Jack and I have discussed this and we think we should wait until the end of the school year before we transfer her into your care. Little Barbara already knows that you are going to take care of her, but she doesn't want to leave the picture of Barbara. Jack had a photo reproduction of the picture made and framed just like the original, that will travel with her when she comes to Coffeyville."

"Oh my! She has a connection with the picture too. This is so spiritual. It's only a month more until school's out. We kept her room just as she left it, but we'll let the new Barbara decide how she wants it."

The weekend after Barbara's second school year ended, we packed Barbara's possessions into the SUV and headed toward Coffeyville and a new life for Barbara Messing. Jenn called ahead as we neared her old home and her parents were waiting outside when our car pulled up.

When Barbara got out of the SUV she ran to them and they all hugged each other. Ben came outside and was introduced to Barbara.

She looked up at him in surprise. "You are Jenn's brother?"

Ben grinned and stooped to her level. "Yeah. Can you believe I'm her little brother and you're my new little sister?"

"You're not very little."

"No, but I'm younger than her, like you're younger than me. Welcome to the family."

Ben took her hand and led her into the house and to her room. She looked around the room and then asked, "This was Barbara's room and this is all her stuff?"

"Yeah. You can keep what you want and we'll move what you don't."

"Okay. I want her picture above my bed."

Ben was about to ask what picture when I brought it into the room. "Wow! I forgot about this picture. Let me help you get that up."

We all stared at the picture after it was hung. I noticed that it seemed to have the same effect as the original. Barbara smiled at the image of Barbara looking down at her. "She seems to be happy and feels at home. I'm glad I brought her here."

Ben could feel a glow originating from the picture and felt his sister's love. "I can feel her love. Am I crazy?"

"We all feel the same thing. Somehow her essence is in the picture, even this copy."

Jenn said with her eyes bright with unshed tears.

Barbara looked at the posters on the walls. "Can you take those posters down. I don't even know who they are."

We all laughed and soon she had blank walls and we helped her put away her clothing in dresser drawers and in the closet. Barbara looked at her room with satisfaction. "Can I see her workshop. Jack told me about where she painted."

Later, we ate lunch and discussed what art classes Barbara would attend. Ben was fascinated that this Barbara shared his sisters art talent and looked at her speculating what other similarities they shared.

Grandmother arrived soon after lunch and met little Barbara, whose experience with much older people was limited and was fascinated with Grandmother. We had already told her about the similarities with my former fiancé and of Barbara speaking through her, so she and little Barbara went off to a quiet area and got to know one another. Little Barbara didn't know her grandparents, as they had all died before she was born. She now had a great grandmother to talk to.

We left the next afternoon for KC. Little Barbara kissed us and we promised to return as soon as we could to see her. With tears in her eyes she waved goodbye to us as we left. I glanced over at Jenn as she wiped her eyes. "Barbara has a double hold on us, doesn't she?"

She replied, "Yes. She's such a lovable little girl plus there's the connection with my sister. There seems to be a unreal connection between our families that seems to be growing."

"We are living in interesting times, as a great man once said."

The next day at work we reviewed our responses from inquires with other victims of the accidents caused by the bad brakes. Fifteen wanted to join our lawsuit and fifty others inquired about a possible class action suit. The remaining victims we contacted made no response, which meant they were going to initiate their own suits, or do nothing at all.

The morning news, paper and TV, reported that the car manufacturer had initiated a recall of the vehicle responsible for the accidents. I made an appointment to meet with George at two p.m. to discuss the matter. Jenn and I had to get ready for court tomorrow for the first high roller we gained as a client. It was a one car accident involving the man's son, and a female passenger was suing for damages.

That night after eating out for dinner and stopping for groceries on the way home, we both felt the need for exercise. After clearing a large area in the living room and putting down pads we had bought for this purpose, we practiced Judo. Jenn was now wearing a black belt, having earned its beginning rank. I had a higher rank black belt, but was now eager to test her abilities as we circled, each trying to discern a possible weakness in the other. It was my turn to act as an aggressor and as I moved into her zone she reacted, taking me down. I stood, gave her a bow, which she returned, and then I waited for her to attack. We traded take downs for forty minutes before calling it quits and storing the mats.

We placed our gi's in the dirty laundry and entered our large shower. It was a full body shower with temperature control. Jenn ratcheted the temperature to its highest safe setting and set the shower heads to the needle flow. As the spray pummeled us, we rotated, allowing the hot stream to massage us. She then adjusted the shower heads to a gentler flow and we washed each other's bodies until the hot water began to ebb. We got out and rubbed each other with towels until we were dry.

Jenn took my hand and led me into the bedroom where we made passionate love. "Ooh, it's much better when we don't have to keep the noise down," she said as they lay together sated from their lovemaking. We kissed and were soon asleep.

At work the next morning, we went over our plans for our court appearance, then had Connie send out documentation to the fifteen victims who wanted to join our suit against the car company. We would amend the suit later to include them when we got the paper work back.

CHAPTER FIFTEEN

The following week we amended the suit to include the fifteen new clients who wanted to join us in the suit against the automobile manufacturer and increase the damage amount to reflect their losses. The suit was now worth $55 Million. George also authorized us to advertise on the majority of TV stations across the U.S. for additional victims to join our firm in a class action suit. In addition, we acquired three more clients because of the notoriety of our court actions without any losses.

A week after the ads began airing the firm received an inquiry from the attorneys representing the auto manufacturer. They wanted to meet and settle the suit, which was encouraging news for the firm. The meeting was scheduled for Monday at 10 a.m., three days from now.

Our TV ads produced ten more claimants, but documents from them had not yet been returned nor could they be added to the suit before the Monday meeting. George called a partners' meeting for 3 p.m. today to discuss strategy.

At the strategy meeting George was appointed lead attorney with Jenn and I acting as backup and responsible for preparing charts and other documents. When we returned to our office we called Connie in and told her what we needed to do. We worked until nine that evening, stopping only for a quick Chinese dinner delivered to the office. We all met again Saturday morning and worked until five that afternoon until we were satisfied that we had everything in order.

We took Connie out for a dinner at her favorite Italian restaurant. The following afternoon we met with George at the office and reviewed our presentation with him. He was happy with our efforts and only suggested a few minor changes, which we took care of.

That night Jenn and I relaxed at home together on a couch watching TV. We both fell asleep on the couch watching an old movie until I awoke and carried her into the bedroom. I remembered to set the alarm before undressing both of us and then collapsed, completely wiped out.

The next morning we arrived at the office refreshed and ready to take on the enemy. Connie helped us set up our displays in the large conference room and place our handouts at each of the expected attendee's seats. George said that he thought that there would be at least five attorneys from a large NY firm representing the manufacturer and we would have six from our side, including George, Jenn, myself, and Connie who was there to run errands. The meeting was to be recorded and the opposing council would receive a transcript.

Our guests arrived fifteen minutes early and the six opposing attorneys took advantage of the coffee and tea we provided. George called the meeting to order and we all sat, each team on opposite sides of the table.

George started the discussion. "We have another ten claimants that have not yet been added to the suit. When adjusted, the number of individuals included in the suit would increase to 26 and the amount to $75 million. Please refer to the handout which contains information regarding the forensic analysis conducted by the various law enforcement agencies who conducted a review of the accidents and their findings."

There was silence for about ten minutes as opposing counsel reviewed the information, and then the lead attorney stood and said, "I need to make a call for clarification on the extra ten claimants. I need a fifteen minute break."

George granted the break and fifteen minutes later everyone was back into place. The opposing counsel's lead attorney nodded his head to proceed. George continued, "Some of those who died in the accidents had no dependents left in their family, but many did. In addition, many of the accident victims survived, but have substantial medical expenses. These victims should receive amounts sufficient to cover current and future expenses, and damages for lost income. What are you authorized to offer to settle this suit?"

The lead attorney stood and said, "We are authorized to settle the full amount of your current suit, but not the additional ten clients. These are all relatives of the victims who were not directly involved in the accidents. We are authorized to award each of them $10,000 to drop their claim."

George looked at Jenn and me for guidance. I stood and motioned for George to join Jenn and me outside the room. George smiled at the others and excused himself for a side meeting.

When George joined us, Jenn said, "He's right about those last ten clients. They were not directly harmed by the accident, but they do have a claim."

George thought a moment, then nodded his head. "Let's go back inside."

After returning to the table George appeared to come to a decision. "We won't add the ten to the main suit, but they should receive $20,000 each. If they don't take the settlement, they can always sue on their own and I think the larger amount will convince them to settle."

The lead attorney said, "Done. As soon as we make changes in the settlement papers and everything is signed, we will send you a wire transfer."

Later that day, after the NY attorneys departed, George came by our office to show us what a $55 Million wire transfer looked like. The firm's cut was twenty percent or $11 Million. Not a bad payday.

George said, "I want you two to come up with a fair division of how much of the $44 Million goes to each of the sixteen clients. I want to see your reasoning in each case to see if I agree. Tonight at six p.m., you three are invited to a celebration at the Top of the Crown, and you are the guests of honor, so dress accordingly."

Later, Jenn asked Connie, "What do you dress for an occasion like this?"

"Black tie for the men and sleek gowns for the women. I bet neither one of you has anything like that." At our blank faces she said, "Never mind, let's go shopping!"

That evening as we were getting dressed I walked up behind Jenn and kissed the back of her neck. She arched her back into me and sighed. "Honey, that gown you have on looks divine, but I think I've got something here that will make it look even better."

Jenn turned away from the mirror, gazing at the diamond necklace I held in my hand. "Ooh, please put it on me!" She said, pulling her hair away from her neck.

After I laid the necklace around her neck and fastened the clasp, she fluffed her hair back out and adjusted the necklace slightly, while watching the light dance on the diamonds.

"You're going to be the most beautiful woman in the room tonight," I said.

She turned and kissed me. "Correction, we are going to be the most beautiful couple in the room."

She turned us toward the mirror and we struck a pose. "See, no one can beat that."

I hugged her closer and laughed. "You might be right. I want to remember everything about tonight. I'm even going to take pictures to send home to your parents."

We took a taxi to the Crown Plaza and after we exited our vehicle, we saw George Phelps and his wife Marilyn, waiting for us just outside the hotel's doors. "We just got here ourselves and I thought we could arrive upstairs together." George said.

When we stepped off the elevator the party appeared to be in full swing, with many of the guests already present. The band stopped playing and then begin with the tune, *For he's a jolly good fellow.*

George and Marilyn stepped aside and then we realized the tune was for us. Jenn and I blushed with embarrassment as we wished for the music to end. We then received a round of applause from everyone present, including George and Marilyn, who stepped up beside us. George held up his arms for quiet and when there was silence he said, "Now that the guests of honor have arrived we can party!"

There was a roar of laughter and applause before everyone continued dancing. George and Marilyn escorted us to the bar as the band started a new tune. Jenn and I both ordered drinks and then followed them to a reserved booth where we sat. Marilyn stared at the new gown and necklace Jenn was wearing. "Jennifer, is that gown a Vera Wang, and that necklace is perfect for it."

"My friends call me Jenn. Connie and I went shopping today and she helped me find this gown. I think it's a knock off, because I didn't pay full price for it. Jack got me the necklace today as well. He knows how to take care of me, doesn't he?"

George winked at me, then we were joined by another partner and his wife to congratulate us. Later, Connie and her date showed up and commented on Jenn's necklace. This continued on for a time until Jenn pulled me out of the booth to dance with her. It was well that the music was slow as my dance experience was minimal. Jenn melted into my arms and we danced as one on the dance floor, with me thinking, *how much better can it get for us.* We went to the buffet table and filled our plates before returning to the booth. George and Marilyn had already been to the buffet and were eating when we sat. Jenn used two napkins to make sure she didn't spill anything on her new gown. Marilyn followed Jenn's lead and added another napkin for her own protection. My new tux was going to have to rely on my careful eating habits because I wasn't going to add another napkin around my neck.

I looked at Jenn and shook my head and she asked, "What?"

"You look ridiculous with that napkin around your neck."

"I don't care. I'm not getting this gown dirty."

Marilyn frowned at George and me. "You men just don't appreciate what we women have to do sometimes. These gowns are not easy to clean if they get dirty and they are expensive, so buzz off."

"Well, I guess that tells us off. They are trying to save us some money." I said with a smile.

When everyone finished eating I volunteered to clear the table to avoid future spills and took drink orders. When I returned Marilyn and Jenn were deep in discussion about something as I set the drinks on the table. After the drinks were distributed to everyone's satisfaction, I asked Jenn if she wanted to dance.

On the dance floor I asked, "Are you having fun?"

"Oh, I am enjoying this. Marilyn wants me to join a group she heads that places children at risk in good homes. My part would involve legal expertise when the occasion arises."

"Do you like Marilyn? She seems very friendly."

"Yes, both George and Marilyn are easy to like. She told me that George was very emotional when he first saw little Barbara because she reminded him of his granddaughter who died last year."

"This get's weirder the more we learn. How is Barbara getting along in Coffeyville when you talked to your mother today?"

"She's doing great. She was an only child with no living relatives and now she has parents, siblings, and a living great grandmother who all dote on her. She wants to know all about the other Barbara and has spent a lot of time looking at her old paintings. She is starting a art class next week that she's excited about."

"Well, after we get the settlement distributed you and I are going to have to decide what investments we should place it in. She is going to be a rich young woman one day."

We danced a while longer and then returned to the booth, taking a sip from our drinks. George and Marilyn soon followed us off the dance floor and took their seats. George sighed in relief as he sat. "I'm out of practice, but that was fun, wasn't it Mare?"

"Yes it was and I'm getting you out there again before we leave tonight." She said with a giggle.

"Jack, you and Jenn are newlyweds aren't you?"

I smiled at Jenn. "Honey, how long has it been now?"

"It's been 106 days and you better not forget our anniversary either."

My face paled as I tried to remember which anniversary she was referring to. I cleared my throat. "Honey, are you referring to our six month or one year anniversary?"

Jenn turned to Marilyn and asked, "Should I tell him or should I make him sweat?"

George spoke up. "Jack, do both, but do more on the first year anniversary. Mare knew how absent minded I was and reminded me every week the last month before the date. She got an extra reward for that."

"Jenn, take heed. A wise wife knows how to get the best reward for her efforts. Besides, I think you got short-changed on your wedding and I was thinking of doing it over on our anniversary. What do you say?" I asked with a raised eyebrow.

"Ooh Jack, that would be wonderful. I'll talk to Mother and have her get the ball rolling so we can have it at the church this time."

Marilyn looked at us in speculation. "This sounds like a good story. Tell me all about it." When we finished with our tale, they both looked at us in awe. George shook his head. "I remember the newspaper story, but there was nothing in it about you being placed in protective custody. Has the woman ever been charged?"

"Not that we are aware of. The last we heard she was placed under psychiatric observation. It may be years before she is brought to trial, if ever," I said.

"I want to hear about the wedding you had. Who did you get for bridesmaids and best man?" Marilyn asked.

Jenn looked at me and smiled before replying. "Two of my friends had already arrived for the planned wedding. They were twins that I roomed with while I attended Harvard. My brother was going to be best man, but he hadn't arrived yet, so we drafted the two FBI agents into our wedding. One as best man and the other as a bridesmaid. An hour after the wedding, we were on our way."

Marilyn looked at us wistfully. "You two have led very interesting lives, so much excitement and it's still happening."

I thought, *you don't know the half of it.*

We were home exhausted and in bed by one a.m.; however, we had a wonderful time at our first office party. The next morning we were back at work on the task of figuring out how to distribute the settlement.

Four victims had severe injuries requiring additional medical services, maybe for the rest of their lives. These we gave a blanket $5 Million each, or $20 Million. The remaining twelve victims we allotted $2 Million each for a total of $24 Million. We double checked our figures for the estimated future and present medical costs of the injured clients, before Connie put it into a form we would present to George and the partners.

Jenn and I handed the documents to George, who looked at the disbursement figures. "I'll take this and analyze how you arrived at your figures and then get back to you."

We decided to take an early lunch and invited Connie to join us. We asked her to pick the restaurant and we ate at a barbecue place we heard about, but hadn't tried yet. This was one time that I didn't hesitate about using a bib to protect my clothing. The food was excellent and we returned to the office stuffed.

Jenn and I were going over a court case that was going to trial in two days involving a young adult female with no priors who was accused of shoplifting. It was a case appointed by the court for us to defend. We reviewed the stores video showing a woman stuffing something in a shopping bag and the store clerk's testimony that our client was stopped at the door with an item from the store without a receipt.

Our client stated that she had just entered the store to exchange an item when she was stopped and her bag searched. By carefully observing the video we determined that the woman was dressed differently than the one who was stopped. In addition, the exit video showed the guilty woman leaving the store several minutes before our client arrived. We were confident that we would win our case and maybe even get some money from the store for our client.

The next day George stopped by our office and said, "The partners agree with your division of the settlement proceeds. In addition, the partners authorized you a bonus of $250,000 each and one of $50,000 for Connie."

We thanked him and the partners for the generous bonuses and after George left we called Connie into our office and gave her the good news. "Boy, O'boy I can think of several things I can use that money for. I sure made a right choice when I agreed to work with you two."

CHAPTER SIXTEEN

A month later we met with a potential client in our office. Sharon Gilbert was the CEO and major shareholder of Gilbert Electronics. Gilbert Electronics was being sued for patent infringement on one of their biggest selling products that would cost them millions in lost sales and penalties if they lost the suit.

Jenn said, "We've got a copy of the lawsuit, but we need the history of the R&D on this product. Before we accept you as a client we want to do some research of our own."

Sharon looked at us in speculation. "I've heard that you only accept clients that you believe are innocent. Maybe that's part of how you achieved your high success rate. How much time do you need?"

I answered. "We will let you know within a week. However, if you are guilty you better start looking for another attorney."

Sharon nodded in satisfaction. "I was right. I'll give you a week and I'll send over the other information you requested by messenger."

Jenn took our copy of the suit out to Connie to make two copies. When she brought them back, we started reading and making notations of interest. After finishing we compared notes and then started a line of inquiry for Daisy McGrady, the firm's investigator to follow up.

Connie gave her a call and she was in their office an hour later.

Daisy appeared to be in her early forties and was attractive in an understated way. She was dressed conservatively with nothing that drew your eyes to her, in short a perfect person to tail someone without drawing any attention to herself.

Connie introduced Daisy to us and we invited her to sit in our small conference area. She was studying us as we were introduced and when we sat, she asked, "You two were in the news about six, seven months ago. Something to do with two police detectives getting killed?"

I answered. "Yes, we were with the U.S. Attorney's office then. You have a good memory."

Daisy smiled slightly. "I do. How can I help you?"

"We have a potential client who is being sued by Peter Umberger for patent infringement. The date of his patent is April 23, 2003, and his current address is Paola, Kansas. We want to know what he has done and where he has lived for the past ten years. We need it ASAP as we need the information to help us make up our minds on whether to take the case," I said.

She grinned. "Piece of cake. I'll get right on it." She got up and left, stopping only long enough to say a few words to Connie at her desk.

I turned to Jenn. "I think Sharon Gilbert is speaking the truth, but there may be someone within the firm who is the culprit."

Jenn nodded her head. "I agree. Maybe Daisy will turn something up."

Early the next day we received the R&D history for the electronic device in question. Sharon Gilbert also included a list of all the employees and the dates of their employment on the project. We started a timeline for each employee and then called Sharon to determine if any of these employees were terminated or had quit the firm and the dates of termination.

Three days later Daisy McGrady returned with the information we requested. She handed Jenn her written report, then said, "Peter Umberger did not exist prior to April 23, 2003, the date the patent was filed. The address listed on the patent filing was the same as the address in Paola, Kansas that you gave me. The tax records for that property is for a Mrs. Joyce Summers. She is shown as its owner for at least the past ten years. I could not find any documentation for Peter Umberger other than a social security number issued in 1938 and a Kansas drivers license that shows his birth date as June 23, 1968. The picture appears to be a man of about forty, so this date might be correct. I've made a copy of the picture in case you might be able to compare it to someone of interest."

"Daisy, you do good work. Thank you for your efforts and we may have use for your talents on this case later," I said.

She gave us a small smile and wished us good luck before leaving.

We scanned the employee names for anyone named Summers and found a Roscoe Summers. Jenn and I looked at one another and smiled in satisfaction. I then called Sharon Gilbert. "Sharon, if you are still interested in retaining us as your legal counsel we would be happy to accept your firm as a client."

"That didn't take long. What did you learn that convinced you that I was telling the truth?"

"Jenn and I already were convinced of that. We just wanted some additional information to support our trust in you. Do we get the job?"

"Of course. What's next?"

"I'm going to fax you some documents that will give us the authority to act as your legal counsel. Sign those and email or fax them to me ASAP. I'll get back to you as soon as I receive them."

The next morning the signed documents were waiting for us when we arrived at the office. Jenn got the honor of calling Sharon Gilbert. "Sharon, we need you to e-mail us a picture of Roscoe Summers. He was terminated on December 16, 2002. If we are correct, maybe we can get this suit to disappear."

There was dead silence on Sharon's end for a few moments, then she exclaimed, "You've got a lead! Great, I'll get that picture right to you."

After comparing the two pictures it was obvious they were the same person. Jenn called Sharon back and asked her to come to our office for a conference. She agreed to meet us tomorrow at 10 a.m.

Sharon Gilbert arrived at our office a few minutes early and her first comment was, "I hope you've got some good news on this lawsuit because I don't think I can take any more bad news."

Jenn explained what we had discovered about Peter Umberger and how we discovered that he was Roscoe Summers.

"That scumbag was caught trying to steal our R&D plans and selling them to our competitors. Are you telling me he's the one behind this whole thing?" Sharon asked.

I answered, "Yes. We need some input from you on how we are to proceed. He's committed fraud; not only against you, but also against the U.S. Patent Office. We can bring a countersuit against him, which is going to cost you more money. We can notify the U.S. Patent Office, which will investigate and bring charges against Summers. We also can have them set aside the patent until their investigation is finished. Another option is that we can notify the Attorney General of the State of Kansas of the fraud against your firm."

"What do you recommend?" Sharon said.

"We recommend contacting the law firm bringing this suit and see if we can get it dropped. Depending on their reaction we can then proceed several different ways against Mr. Summers."

"Let's try it your way. I like the idea of them dropping the suit."

"Okay, we'll give them a call and see what develops. We will let you know what the results are of our conversation."

Sharon left our office with a smile. I had Connie contact the law firm of Hooper, Goodell, and Baker and arrange a meeting as soon as possible. She soon reported that the meeting is set for 1 p.m. tomorrow. Jenn and I then went to George's office to see if he was available for a consult. He was talking to his secretary when we walked up and he showed us inside.

After retelling the fraud story and our idea to try to get the law firm to drop their suit, he agreed. "I don't think you will have any problem with them dropping the suit. If I was them I would be worried about Gilbert Electronics bringing suit against their firm. I can't believe that they didn't do a better background check on their client. When is this meeting scheduled?"

"Tomorrow at 1 p.m."

George used his intercom to call his secretary and asked what his schedule was for tomorrow afternoon. He smiled at the response and replied, "Cancel all my afternoon appointments and reschedule if possible. I'm going to Jack and Jennifer's One o'clock meeting at Hooper, Goodell, and Baker."

"Let's have an early lunch tomorrow. There's a great restaurant just a block from their office. I wouldn't miss seeing the expression on Jason Hooper's face for all the tea in China when you drop this load of crap on him."

When we arrived at the firm we were shown into their conference room. When George followed us into the room, one of the senior staff rose to greet us. "George, no one told me you were going to be here. I would have made arrangements for a better spread than coffee and tea."

"Jason, it's good to see you again. I'm here with Jack and Jennifer Pearson. Who's the attorney who has the lead on the Umberger case?"

Jason's face turned blank sensing something bad coming his way. "That would be Robert Madison. Stand up Bob and let's see what we missed."

George said, "Go ahead, they can take it. They brought the suit, so they're going to have to live with it."

Bob seemed to stiffen his spine, as if he was expecting bad news. "Bob, what kind of background check did you do on Peter Umberger before you took him on as a client?"

"He told me that he was disabled and couldn't drive and all he had was his Social Security Card for ID."

"You should have dug deeper. There is no Peter Umberger. The person is actually Roscoe Summers who was fired by Gilbert Electronics in December 2002. You are representing a person who is attempting a fraud against my client. What do you intend to do about it?"

Jason interrupted. "I assume you have proof of this?"

George said, "Show them."

When we finished describing the timelines and the photo likeness between the drivers license of Umberger and the Summers Gilbert personnel file, they were convinced. Bob's face became even paler, if possible. Jason's hand hit the table with such force that it caused everyone to jump, except Bob who fainted.

Jason looked at Bob's prone form on the floor and said, "Shit! I can't even yell at him. You all know what the correct procedures are for getting ID from our clients. This is the reason we do it. George, I'm sorry for the screw up and we'll drop the suit against your client. We'll even join you in bringing charges against this Roscoe Summers. Let the Gilbert people know we'll even consider paying damages to them."

"I will let Sharon Gilbert know what you offered. She has been in a lot of stress because of this lawsuit. Can I have her call you and see if you can work something out face-to-face. I personally don't want to sue another law firm if it can be avoided." I turned to George. "Can we give him a discount on our fee if he can arrange a settlement?"

George thought a moment. "Jason, for you I'll only take fifteen percent."

Jason gave him a lopsided smile. "You don't pay those two enough. Have them get with me on the charges we want leveled against this prick, the sooner the better."

When we got back to the firm, George asked us to meet him into his office.

"You both have continuously surprised me since you've joined the firm. Not only by your insight in finding the solution for your clients' problem, but how you handled the situation at Jason's firm. I didn't want to sue his firm either and you had the perfect solution. If you keep this up you may be the firm's youngest partners. Keep up the good work."

CHAPTER SEVENTEEN

Jenn called Sharon Gilbert with the good news about the lawsuit being withdrawn. She then gave Sharon the telephone number of Jason Hooper and said, "Jason wants to express his apologies for his firm's error in bringing the suit and they are open to paying damages. The attorney who brought the suit went against the firm's policy about checking their clients background and may be terminated."

Sharon gave a satisfied sigh and then asked, "How much should I ask for?"

"Don't be too greedy. After all, he's been hurt too. When the word gets out about this fiasco, it's bound to hurt his reputation. If I were you I would start at $500,000 and settle for not less than $250,000. That would come close to paying our fee. Even better, if you don't get the $500,000, try to get him to pay our fee."

Sharon laughed so hard that she got the hiccups. After regaining control of her emotions she said, "I like the way you think. It's been a pleasure doing business with you and Jack and I'll pass it on to others. Talk to you later."

When Jenn put down the phone I said, "Great idea for them to pay our fee. After all, it was their fault we got involved in the suit. Who should we notify first about the fraud?"

A week later as we were readying another case for trial, we heard a disruption at the reception desk. We looked outside and spotted

Roscoe Summers knocking the receptionist to the floor. He was carrying a rifle of some kind, which he started firing into the main room, yelling our names. I grabbed Jenn and Connie and pulled them into our office where we crouched behind our large desk. We could hear him approaching our office from the sounds of his gun fire, where he paused to reload.

He must have read our names on the door because he started laughing and said, "I've got you now!" Before he could resume firing there was a sudden flash of light and a loud bang.

Looking up over the desk I saw Olivia in full fighting form, spread wings and sword in hand. Summers was lying smoking on the floor, just like all the others she had incinerated. Olivia gave me a small smile and vanished with a slight pop. I turned to check on Jenn, but she was right beside me and it was obvious she had seen Olivia too. We helped Connie stand and we all went outside to help anyone who might be hurt.

Within minutes the police and EMTs arrived to take care of the people hurt and try to make sense of what happened. Jenn and I retrieved a first aid kit and were treating those we could help. There were two dead and six wounded during that first clip that Summers fired, all from people who were in the main room.

The condition of Summers body dumbfounded the police. His rifle was partially melted, becoming part of the burned body. The police had no idea who he was until Jenn and I gave them his name and explained that he was there to kill them. George arrived to substantiate our story and explained Summer's apparent motive for his actions.

After the police and EMTs left, George told everyone to take the rest of the day off and spend time with their family members. Jenn and I had already called our family letting them know we were alright and that Olivia saved us from a terrible fate. That night we visited the six wounded at the hospital. Four were secretaries and two were new attorneys. None of them were seriously injured and were expected to be released the next day.

We went to bed that night, holding one another while Jenn cried for the dead. The next morning we felt wrung out and forced ourselves to get ready for work. We arrived an hour late and were still the first ones there. I called Jason Hooper and asked, "Have you heard what happened at our office?"

"Yes, it's all over the news. I've tried to call Bob Madison, but I couldn't reach him. I think I'll call the police to go check to make sure he's alright."

"Yes, that's a good idea. However, I don't have a good feeling about his condition. He must have been the one that gave Summers our names."

Jason didn't say anything for a few moments. "It just gets worse, doesn't it?"

Two hours later Jason called back. "The police just called and said that they found Bob dead in his apartment. That's all they would tell me, but Roscoe Summers is suspected of killing him. I wish Bob had followed procedure and maybe none of this would have happened."

George had arranged for a cleanup crew to come into the office and remove all the blood and gore, so we didn't have that to contend with this morning. Memories of the event were going to be harder to get rid of. Jenn and I continued with the review for a court case that was interrupted yesterday.

We were interrupted again when two detectives arrived to take our official statements. Detectives Mary Cullen and Peter Jackson listened to our memory of the events and how we recognized Roscoe Summers from the pictures we acquired while putting the case together. We then told them about reporting the fraud to the KBI, the United States Patent Office, and the U. S. Attorney General. They then interviewed Connie and the other members of the staff. Before leaving the office the detectives asked, "Are you the lawyers working for the Attorney General that was targeted for assassination?"

At our nod they shook their heads, then Detective Mary Cullen said, "You guys are either very lucky or unlucky, depending on your viewpoint. People around you are getting killed."

Jenn looked a little angry as she replied. "I guess we shouldn't call you the next time we get a death threat."

The two women looked daggers at each other for a few moments, then Detective Cullen's expression changed as she reconsidered. "I'm sorry, that was uncalled for. You were not even present when Brooks and Peterson were killed. Sara and I were good friends and I miss her."

Jenn nodded. "We were becoming friends too and Jack and I

tried to get them into protective custody as well, but they were killed before it happened."

Mary said, "I doubt they would have taken it. They were both hard headed and thought they could take care of themselves. Thanks for the thought anyway and if we can help on anything in the future, just let us know." She handed Jenn her card and they left.

That weekend we returned to Coffeyville to calm our families' fears. I stopped and picked up my Grandmother before continuing on to Jenn's home. Her whole family came outside to greet us as we pulled up to the house. Little Barbara appeared to have grown a foot since we last saw her. She hung back as her new family greeted us, then she ran into Jenn's arms with tears of happiness.

When they disengaged, Barbara ran to me and hugged me too. She then looked up at me and said, "I've got something I want to show both of you!"

She then grabbed our hands and started pulling us toward the garage. The transformation was amazing, little Barbara had turned the upstairs back into a work studio. It was obvious that she was working in watercolors as her pictures were stuck on all the walls. "Start looking here and then go to your right to see how the pictures get better."

Jenn and I did as she asked and the first picture did look primitive, then each new one showed improvement until we reached the last one, a landscape. I hugged her and said, "Can we take your first and last picture, so we can show our friends how much you have improved?"

Barbara looked closely at us to be sure we liked her work before she smiled. "Well, the last one is over here on the easel," she said and removed the cover from the picture.

We took in a quick breath of surprise and awe, because she had painted a self portrait in the same style as the picture above her bed of our Barbara. It was done in watercolor and looked like a younger version of the older Barbara. Tears were running down both of our faces as we gazed at the picture.

I laid my arm around Jenn's shoulders and hugged her closer to me. "Can we take this back home with us?"

Barbara knew from our emotional reaction that we wanted it and she ran over and hugged us with tears in her eyes. "I hoped that you would like it, and I want you to have it."

We then became aware that the rest of the family had followed us into the studio and they all had tears in their eyes as they looked at the painting. Alice was looking at the picture with pride before saying, "I knew she was improving as she gained experience, but this is just outstanding. We are going to have to save all her work from this point on because it is going to become valuable."

Barbara ran to her mother and hugged her.

I asked, "Barbara, when are you going to start learning oils?"

"Not for a while yet. I'm still experimenting with water colors. My instructor thinks a good background there will help me when I start in on oils."

I took the two pictures and asked Barbara how best to protect them for transport. She took care of that task and we carried the package with us to our bedroom. Later, we gathered in the living room and everyone wanted to know about the shooting in our law office. Jenn told the story from the time of us accepting Gilbert Electronics as a client to the eventual shooting.

During the telling, Ben and his girlfriend arrived and they were enthralled by the story. Judy Ellsworth, who was a student with Ben at KU, was wide-eyed with excitement at the end of the story. "Ben's been telling me about all the adventures you and Jack have had in KC since you graduated from Harvard. How you met Jack and it was love at first sight, and got married about a week later while hiding from people trying to kill you. That's almost unreal."

Jenn and I looked at each other and smiled, while I thought, *if she only knew the rest of the story, then it would be unreal.*

Jenn asked her. "What grade are you in and what are your plans for the future?

Judy blushed. "We're both half way through our second year and I haven't yet decided on a major. However, if being an attorney is this exciting maybe I should consider that."

"You still have time to decide and we're not normal attorneys, so don't use us as a guide on how an attorney's life will become. We were prosecutors who morphed into defense attorneys. This is more exciting than if we were corporate lawyers, but everyone has their own ideas of what constitutes excitement. When people are shooting at you, that is more excitement than I want."

"Amen!" I said.

Jenn asked her mother, "What's the status of our plans for a redo of my wedding in a church?"

"Reverend Reynolds has reserved us a spot at 9 a.m. on Saturday, May 5th. It's not the one year anniversary of your first marriage, but it's as close as we could do it."

"Mom, I better go check my dress and see if it still fits. I'll just die if I can't get into it."Alice looked at her daughter and laughed. "Jennifer, if anything you've lost weight since you got married. You and Jack are not eating or you have been doing some serious exercise."

Jenn's face blushed scarlet and she exclaimed, "Mother!"

"Oh, I don't mean sex. I mean exercise! You've been doing Judo and running haven't you?"

"Oh. Yeah, we have." She then patted her flat tummy and checked her trim butt in the mirror and smiled. "You might be right. Let's go try it on."

"Can I come too?" Asked Judy.

Jenn nodded and the women went upstairs leaving the men behind. Jack asked Ben,"How long have you and Judy been together?"

"We've known each other since high school, but have been dating only since we started KU together. At first it was only as a convenience for us, but now we care for one another."

"Do you have any long term plans for your future?"

"I'm considering going into law despite what has happened to you and Jenn. Do you recommend going into prosecuting first, then defense later like you and Jenn did?"

"It worked for us, but that was not planned. I did get some good court room training while working for the Attorney General. Others go directly into a large law firm and work their way up according to their abilities. We were different. Do you have any idea how smart your sister is?"

Ben looked at me, surprised. "Why do you ask? We all knew she was a brain and could outthink anyone in school."

"You know Harvard Law School is the best school we have. She finished in the top one percent of her class. She won't tell me what her actual rank was, but it has to be in the top ten. She followed me to KC to work for the Attorney General when she could work anywhere she wanted at a much higher salary. I was in the top ten percent at Yale, which is no slouch, but it doesn't compare to

Harvard. I'm the luckiest guy in the world to have her as my wife and working together we are a hard team to beat."

We were watching a game on TV when the women returned. Jenn came over and sat in my lap with her arm around my neck. "Jack, my dress fits me better now than when I was married in it. Isn't that wonderful?"

I squeezed her waist and replied, "Yes dear. Are you going to get the twins to come back for the replay?"

She stiffened and then left my lap on her way to her cell phone, muttering to herself, "I'm going to have to make a list before I forget where I left my head."

That evening after dinner Jenn and I were in her old room where she was making her list of things that needed to be done for the wedding that was only five months in the future. She was to get commitments for bridesmaids from three of her high school friends and the twins she roomed with from Harvard. One of them would be her maid of honor, to be decided by a coin toss according to Jenn. The maids would wear their own clothes as long as it was a dress with a full skirt.

I stood looking over her shoulder at the list and smiled. "Honey, what are we going to do about the ring ceremony since you are already wearing your wedding ring?"

She turned and looked at me in confusion. "I don't know. I'm not taking these off. That first wedding was our commitment to each other. This one is just for show."

"Maybe I could place that diamond necklace around your neck, which will match the diamond ear rings I'm giving you for our anniversary."

Jenn jumped up and hugged me around the neck. "Oh, that sounds perfect. Have you gotten them yet?"

"No. Do you want to help me pick them out?"

She nodded and kissed me. "You're the best husband I've ever had."

"I know and thoughtful too," I said before picking her up and carrying her to bed where we made passionate love.

CHAPTER EIGHTEEN

The next morning I was up before Jenn, who appeared to be worn out. I found Alice and Grandmother in the kitchen starting breakfast and I asked if they needed any help. "Where's that lazy daughter of mine?"

"I think I wore her out last night. She sends her regrets."

Alice and Grandmother looked at each other and smiled. "When are we going to get some grandchildren out of you two?" Grandmother said.

"We have been on the job only for a short time and I think we need at least three years before we think about kids, besides Olivia told us to stay close to each other so that she could protect Jenn."

The two women seemed to be in sync. Alice's face cleared as she had a thought. "Jack, does your office have a daycare for its employees?"

"No, but you have a great idea. I'll talk it over with management and we'll see what can be arranged."

Jenn walked into the kitchen and asked, "What can management be talked into?"

I hugged Jenn and said, "A day care for our office. These two were getting tired of waiting for us to give them grandkids."

"Whoa. I'm not ready for kids yet. Are you?"

"I was thinking about how we were so attracted to little Barbara.

If your parents hadn't wanted to raise her I'm sure we would have stepped up. I told these two that we wanted to wait three years, but with a daycare, maybe sooner."

Jenn looked intently at me and then her mother before speaking. "I'm going to have to think on this for awhile, but we can go ahead with the daycare idea. I've heard the women in the office complaining about the high cost of day care. Let's brainstorm this before going to George with it."

Jenn and I helped getting breakfast ready before Jamison, Barbara and Ben came down to eat. Judy was staying with her parents, but came in when we were finishing up the dirty dishes. She sat down beside Ben with a cup of coffee and started asking us questions about what classes she needed to take to qualify for pre-law later. Jenn asked Judy what her GPA was.

"Last semester it was 3.9, but I had a real hard class that brought it down." Judy answered.

"Judy, you need at least a 4 to even be considered at a good law school. Do some research on the various schools requirements and then plan accordingly. I didn't have a social life when I attended Harvard because I was studying all the time."

Ben placed his hand over Judy's. "Hon, Jenn's the brain in our family and she graduated Harvard in the top one percent of her class. Can you imagine how hard it would be for us just to get into the top 50 percent."

Judy said, "I think I'll look elsewhere for my career goal."

When Ben and Judy left the table to go to his room, Barbara took their place and gave them both a big smile. Jenn asked, "what do you want to be when you grow up?"

"You mean besides being an artist?"

We nodded and she replied, "I don't know. I'm just a little kid."

We all laughed at her response which brought a smile to her face. "Maybe a mommy like Alice." She volunteered.

On the drive back to KC Jenn and I discussed several ways to broach the subject of a daycare to George, but first we needed to determine how much the cost was going to be and how many children would be cared for. That night after arriving home we unpacked the self portrait of little Barbara and I set it on the mantel next to the larger one of our Barbara. We stood back and admired the two paintings, one in oil and the other in water color. Somehow they complimented each other.

I took the water color down and pressed it to keep it from curling and told Jenn we would have it framed tomorrow. When we arrived at the office the next day we asked Connie to join us as we had a question.

Jenn said, "We want to get some data together for a possible daycare in the office. Do you know how many children of the staff that are of that age group?"

Connie smiled. "So maybe you are planning ahead for the eventuality of children in your future."

Jenn nodded her head. "If we have children it would be convenient to have a daycare here. Has it been brought up before?"

"Not that I'm aware of. I'll take a survey and get back with you, but it's going to be about twenty and that's not including the attorneys' kids. We have room for one in the back corner, but it would have to be enclosed and soundproofed."

After Connie left I asked Jenn, "She did say twenty plus didn't she? Why that would require a staff of at least two or three to operate it. Do you know what the start age would be for such a center?"

Jenn started calling day care centers and asking what ages they accepted children and what was their staffing number verses the children they care for. I called a building contractor I knew who was a former client we defended successfully. I told him what we had in mind and the outside dimensions of the room and asked for a rough guess on what it would cost. He told me that with soundproofing and plumbing, it would be about $50,000, depending on how far they needed to go for water and sewer connections.

"This is going to be expensive and we need some inside help if we're going to get this done. Let's host a party at our apartment for all the partners and their wives. Maybe we can get the wives and the women of the firm to back our idea, especially if we can get Marilyn behind the effort." I said.

Jenn had Connie prepare a memo to the partners about our party, which was to occur the next Saturday at six p.m.. That would give us time to cater the snacks and buy booze for an open bar.

Jenn and I had just finished up the final preparations when the first guest arrived. George and Marilyn Phelps brought us a housewarming bottle of expensive wine, that I started chilling, while Jenn showed them the apartment. All the window drapes were open to show our guests the view of the plaza lights. When Marilyn walked up to the window she was enthralled.

"Oh my! This view is fabulous. How in the world did you find this place?"

"Jack and I already had an apartment here and we needed something larger when we started to care for Barbara. Speaking of Barbara, I must show you the self portrait she gave us on our last trip home."

George and Marilyn were struck speechless when they stood before the two portraits. Marilyn inhaled deeply and asked, "Who's the beautiful woman? She is so captivating that I can't seem to take my eyes off her. That water color portrait can't be by Barbara. Why it's even in the style of the larger picture! There has got to be a story here."

I smiled at Jenn before telling our family story. "The oil painting was done by Jenn's older sister, Barbara, who gave it to me before her death. Little Barbara seems to have great talent as an artist and was captivated by this self portrait by Jenn's sister. If you look at the faces of the two portraits you can see a strong resemblance. Jenn's mother tells us that her Barbara looked just like little Barbara at this age and demonstrated the same talent."

Marilyn looked again at the two portraits and shuddered. "That's just plain spooky, but then you two have a strange history as well."

Our other guests started arriving and we were kept busy until everyone had arrived and were shown the apartment. Before we hit them with our idea for a day care we wanted them in a mellow mood, so we waited until everyone had at least two drinks. Jenn had separated Marilyn from George and tested the water first with her, who thought it was a great idea. She then asked, "Jenn, are you and Jack preparing the way for a place to keep kids of your own?"

Jenn blushed, then smiled. "We want children, but not quite yet. I want to continue to work and this seemed the best way to achieve my goal with the least amount of time off. Besides, I'll be able to keep tabs on them if they are in the office. Also, the staff has a real need for such a service. I bet we can attract and keep the best people with this as a benefit."

"George told me that they have lost some of the staff because of that shooting. Maybe this benefit would be something the firm needs at this time."

The two women joined the others and mingled, each retelling the Barbara story to those who expressed an interest. When I deemed the time was right, I approached Jenn and together we stood before the bar and I rapped on a glass until we had everyone's attention. Jenn and I then made our case for the establishment of a daycare, stressing the high cost of daycare that the staff had to pay and the need to attract good people, which this benefit would bring.

I knew we had a chance when every woman in the group turned to their spouse and started speaking. Marilyn had been speaking to George before we gave our talk to the others. He let the other partners discuss this with their spouses while he joined us at the bar.

George waited until he thought the others had finished discussing this topic with the others, then he held his hand up for silence. "It's somehow appropriate that this request has come from our newest hires. Most of the partners have already had all the children they intend to have, but the real need is from our staff. They can't afford day care on their salary and I agree that as a benefit, it would be a tremendous draw for a new hire. Jack, I want you and Jenn to give me an estimate of what the initial and subsequent operating costs will be. When I have that data I will present it to the partners for a vote on whether to establish such a daycare."

Based upon the applause from that statement I thought we stood a good chance of getting the daycare. Later, Senior Partner Clarence Woodruff, as he was preparing to leave said, "Those paintings on your mantel fascinate me, especially the small water color. It shows promise and I would like to see more as she progresses."

I replied, "I'll send you photos and if you want a closer look at any that interest you, I can make arrangements to get them here."

After everyone departed and the remaining snacks put away, we sat together on the couch and enjoyed the view while relaxing in each other's arms. Jenn's head was on my shoulder as she softly said, "That was nice of Clarence to show an interest in little Barbara's water color. Do you think he was serious?"

"George told me that he had a very good collection of water colors, so he was serious. This validates our own opinion of how good she is."

CHAPTER NINETEEN

Time passed and we were back in Coffeyville for our church wedding. When we pulled into the parking area at Jenn's home, Cheryl and Sandy Jackson came outside to greet us. The twins and Jenn hugged one another with loud exchanges of laughter and giggles as they entered the house, leaving me with the luggage.

Ben came outside with a bemused smile on his face. "Those women are crazy. Here, I'll help you with that stuff."

"Is Judy here yet?" I asked.

"Yeah, she and the twins are bridesmaids. The other maids should be arriving soon and they are getting Jenn dressed and ready for the ceremony. You better hurry upstairs and get dressed too. I'll bring these bags up for you."

I was looking into the full length mirror at myself in my tux, when grandmother appeared beside me. "My, you look handsome. Just like your father did when he got married. Turn around, I've got something for you."

She pinned a white carnation on my jacket and said. "Now, that looks good."

"Did Mother and Dad have a nice wedding?"

"Yes, it was wonderful and your mother was a beautiful bride. My son and your mother were very much in love with each other. When he died, we both died a little too. You were our salvation. She lived for you and when she died I got to raise another son."

I hugged her to me and kissed her on the cheek. "I know Grandmother and I love you too."

We both went downstairs and joined Jenn's father, brother and little Barbara. Jamison stood and gave me a big hug, then Barbara grabbed me around my waist and hugged me tightly. She looked at me with tears in her eyes as she said, "Those mean women wouldn't let me hug Jenn!"

I stooped down to her level and wiped a tear away. "I know. They wouldn't let me in to see her either. Do you know why that is?"

Barbara looked at me in surprise. "They won't let you in either? They are mean!"

Grandmother chuckled, which caused Barbara to look at her in surprise. "It's not funny! They won't let Jack in either."

Grandmother sat down and pulled her into her lap. "Barbara honey, Jack's the groom and he's not supposed to see the bride until they arrive at the church. They kept you out because they were afraid you would muss up her bridal gown. Aren't you the flower girl?"

Barbara's nodded, and Grandmother said, "Why you have an important job to do in spreading flowers down so that the bride can walk on them. You are the only one that has been given that task because they knew you would do a good job."

Barbara wiped her nose with the back of her hand and smiled. "They weren't mean after all?"

"No, they just had a lot of work to do. How about you, have you gotten your instructions on what to do?"

Barbara smiled at Grandmother and picked up the basket of flower petals. "See, they're all here."

The wedding went without even a small hitch and Jenn and I renewed our commitment to each other. She was wearing the diamond ring and necklace I gave her, so instead of a ring this time I gave her the matching diamond earrings she helped pick out for her wedding anniversary gift.

Back home we welcomed guests at our reception where we saw former high school classmates from both our schools, many we hadn't seen since graduation. Our notoriety had reached even here, as they wanted to know all the details about the shooting at our law firm.

Little Barbara stood next to Jenn in the greeting line, which caused some speculation from Barbara's former classmates who noticed the resemblance between the two, and later when the greeting line broke up and little Barbara followed Jenn where ever she went. It didn't help matters when I picked little Barbara up, taking her to the cake and giving her the first piece.

Jenn joined me at the cake and took a little of the frosting off of little Barbara's piece with her finger and tasted it. "Umm good. Okay folks help yourself." She said.

I stooped down and whispered in Barbara's ear, "Go to the kitchen and eat this. I bet Grandmother will put some ice cream on it if you ask her."

Catching Grandmother's eye, I nodded my head towards the kitchen where Barbara was headed. Grandmother smiled and followed behind. Alice and Jamison seemed to be happy hosting their daughter's wedding party as they greeted old friends. Ben and his girlfriend, Judy Ellsworth, were busy talking with old classmates and renewing acquaintances.

Later, after all the guests had departed except the twins and Judy; Jenn and I had changed clothes and were sitting together on the couch relaxing. Barbara was helping Alice and Grandmother clean up and the twins were talking to Ben and Judy about career choices.

Jenn was leaning her head against my shoulder and sighed in happiness. "Jack, one of these days we need to take off and have a proper honeymoon."

"What do you consider a proper honeymoon?"

"Oh, I don't know. I guess go somewhere where other young people go after they get married."

"As I recall, we went on an all expense paid trip to Flagstaff for our honeymoon. We did what other people do on their honeymoon, and as I remember we both enjoyed ourselves. What would we do different if we had a chance to do it over?"

"Nothing, it was the threat of somebody trying to kill us that contributed to the frenzy of our lovemaking. I was wondering what it would be like if it had been normal."

"Honey, we are not normal. Not by any stretch of your imagination. The honeymoon you want to try would be boring after what we experienced."

Jenn turned and looked into my eyes for a moment, then she hugged my body to hers while staring at me with lustful eyes. She then started kissing me passionately until we were both breathless. I picked her up and started carrying her toward the upstairs bedrooms, while the other people in the room stared in surprise.

* * *

Judy looked at our backs in wonder. "Ben, you better be that passionate with me when we get married."

"Jenn is lucky with this one." Cheryl and Sandy said together.

* * *

We were in our apartment celebrating our second wedding anniversary. I gave Jenn a diamond bracelet that went with her necklace and earrings and she was showing her appreciation by kissing me passionately and then cuddling up against me while we sat gazing out at the glitter of the Plaza lights.

"I have some wonderful news." She said.

I said, "Oh?"

She hugged me even closer to her. "I'm pregnant."

I looked at her in surprise, then smiled as I pulled her into my arms and kissed her."Are you sure?"

"Yep, I tested two days in a row with the same result. I'm seeing my doctor next week to confirm."

"That was quick. We've only been trying for a month. I'm glad the daycare is now in operation because we're going to use it."

"Not for awhile. I checked and they only accept children who have been potty trained. We're going to have to hire a nanny until that happens."

We told Connie about the baby after the doctor confirmed the pregnancy. She looked at us in surprise, then exclaimed, "You're pregnant! When are you due?"

Jenn smiled at her. "I'm barely pregnant, so about nine months from now. Maybe we better keep this quiet for awhile in case something goes wrong."

Connie's face sobered. "Okay, but three months from now I'm going to give you a baby shower."

That afternoon we interviewed a potential client, James T. Kratts of Kratts Manufacturing. Kratts was primarily the manufacturer of children's toys under the well known brand name, Sunshine. He arrived with a woman he introduced as his wife and CFO, Elizabeth Kratts.

James deferred to his wife, who seemed to calm herself before speaking. "I'm being threatened with blackmail from someone who claims to have had an affair with me. He or she claims to have pictures of me in a compromising position and sent a sample picture with the demand for money."

She then handed over the picture for us to view. Both the picture and demand for payment were enclosed in clear plastic. I looked at the picture while Jenn took the written demand. We then exchanged the items for review before setting them down on the table.

"Is that you in the picture?" I asked.

"No! You can't even tell who it is because all you can see is her back. However, that person has some kind of mark on her shoulder that I don't have."

Jenn spoke. "Why us and not the police?"

"We don't want the publicity that the police investigation and trial would bring. It could cost us millions in lost sales. However, if we paid them off we would never be off the hook. We want these people found and pressure exerted to keep them off our backs." Elizabeth said.

I looked at Jenn and she nodded. "Very well. When we find these blackmailers we will consult with you on the proper action to take place. Is this agreeable?"

The Kratts held hands, and James asked his wife if she agreed. At her nod, he turned to us and said, "Do it! Give us a weekly status report and if you haven't found them in two weeks, we will need to reassess."

After they left our office I had Connie contact Daisy McGrady and have her meet with us. Daisy arrived that afternoon and we told her about the attempt to blackmail our newest client. She took possession of the two items left with us and departed.

Three days later Daisy returned smiling. "We got lucky. Both the letter and the picture had fingerprints that belonged to people who have been arrested in the past. They belong to George Preston and Lilly Shepherd. Lilly's rap sheet shows a mole on the back of her left shoulder, which appears to match that in the picture."

Jenn asked, "What kind of pressure can we use against them

without bringing charges?"

Daisy asked, "The client doesn't want any publicity?"

"They just want them to go away and disappear."

"Well, they both have two strikes against them and one more conviction will mean 30 plus years. That threat may be enough, but these people are dangerous and have used violence in the past. Maybe, rather than us bringing charges we can find something else they have done and sic the police on them."

I nodded. "I'll give you a week to work that angle and if it doesn't pan out we'll go with the threat from us."

Daisy grimaced. "I'll try. Wish me luck," she said as she left the office.

Jenn called Elizabeth Kratts and told her that we found out who the blackmailers were and were now trying to determine the best way to get rid of their threat. Two days later Daisy returned with a possible solution.

After we were all seated Daisy said, "These people are a real piece of work. Not only do they have the blackmail scam going, but they deal drugs on the side. We can let the police know about the drugs and hope they bust them, but I think they are already watching them with the intent to build a bigger case."

I looked at Jenn thoughtfully. "Honey, what if we wrote them a letter to appear before us to answer to a charge of attempted blackmail?"

"On our letterhead?"

"Sure, otherwise they wouldn't know who we were."

"That would be risky. We don't want another shooting episode here in the office. We should meet somewhere not so public, yet not remote."

Daisy looked at us as if were crazy. "You can't do that! I told you that they were violent people and we can't be sure what they might do."

"I'm counting on that. Let's have the meet place be the courthouse at one p.m., two days from now and send the letter by messenger today. Unless I'm completely wrong they will attempt to meet us in the garage here or our apartment tonight."

Daisy's face was pasty white in shock and disbelief. "You are both crazy as loons. You can't go up against them, you're just attorneys!"

Jenn smiled at her. "Maybe, but we both have a black belt in Judo and if that is not enough I plan on having some police protection nearby."

She looked at me and asked, "Detectives Mary Cullen and Peter Jackson?"

I nodded, whereupon Jenn dug out their card and gave Mary a call. When all was arranged she called Connie in and dictated a letter to the blackmailers. After we signed it Connie was told to messenger it to them today.

Daisy watched all this activity in rapt fascination. "You two work together as if you were of one mind. No wonder you are so successful. Well, if you need me you know where I can be reached," she said as she left the office.

We left the office a little later than usual to let the garage clear out and give us a better view of the surrounding vehicles and people. We got off the elevator into the garage and hesitated a moment, looking around, before walking toward our car. A man and woman stepped out from behind a supporting column just in front of us.

The middle aged man was built like a linebacker and looked to be over six and a half feet tall. The woman looked small beside him, but she was taller and heavier built than Jenn, and they were both scowling at us. I stepped slightly away from Jenn to give us both room to move if we were rushed.

I said, "George and Lilly, I presume?"

George frowned at me. "Smart ass. What's your play on the Kratts?"

"It's simple. You fold up your tent and leave town and we won't press charges against you. The Kratts hear from you again, then the police get involved. I understand that if you are convicted of another felony, then your next stay in jail will be several decades."

"What if we make you disappear?"

"Assuming you can do that, we have the charges all documented and then you have murder charges to contend with. Get smart and leave town."

Lilly screamed a profanity and rushed Jenn, who grabbed her clothes and falling back threw Lilly ten feet, where she slid under a SUV, knocking her unconscious.

George seemed the more cautious of the two, because he hadn't moved as he watched Lilly fly through the air. At seeing Lilly knocked unconscious, he said, "You two have had martial arts training. Okay, help me get her into my car and we'll be gone. The Kratts won't hear from us again."

After George and Lilly left the garage, Detectives Cullen and Jackson walked up. Cullen smiled at us ruefully and shook her head. "When Lilly went for Jennifer I thought she was going to wind up as a wet spot on the floor. Imagine my surprise when Lilly started flying. What was that move?"

Jenn said, "Judo. We are both black belts."

Jackson muttered, "Shit, and I was worried about you two."

I patted him on the back. "We were worried that they might bring guns, so everything worked out okay. Thanks for your help and if we can repay the favor just let us know."

The next morning I called the Kratts and told them that the blackmailers had agreed to leave town, but to let us know if they should contact them again. Not only did we gain a new client, but one that seemed anxious to spread the word about how good we were.

CHAPTER TWENTY

I left three new watercolor photos of paintings of little Barbara's with Clarence Woodruff's secretary. Two hours later he appeared at our office with the pictures in hand and a big smile on his face.

"I'm interested in all three of these watercolors. Can you have them shipped here so that I can make a decision if I want to make an offer?"

Jenn asked me, "Which pictures are those?"

Clarence handed the photographs to her. In each case a twelve inch vase stood next to the picture to give it scale. To Jenn, the landscape was the most striking of the three. The other two were a still life of a bowl of fruit, and a picture of Jenn's mother kneading dough at the kitchen table.

"Jack, I didn't see this one when we were last home. Just look at it. It's almost as if we were there."

"I know. I was going to bring it home and frame it for you until I saw one that I knew you would want."

I reached inside the foot space of my desk and pulled out a framed watercolor and handed to her. It was a seated portrait of her mother looking at herself in her vanity mirror, with our wedding picture next to it. As Jenn looked at the painting her face was wet with happy tears. She put the picture carefully down before hugging and kissing me. "That's the best present you've ever given me."

Clarence was examining the watercolor. "You know, this is even better than the self portrait she did. I'm anxious now to see all her paintings. Tell her to hold them aside and every quarter I'll make a trip down to Coffeyville to see what she has done. You can bring back the ones I want to make a bid on."

"I'm just curious, but what would you have bid for this one if it had been for sale?" I said.

"You understand that she's an unknown. However, I believe she has the potential to be a great artist. I would have bid $5,000. These other three, maybe $3,000 for the one of your mother, and $1,000 each for the others."

"Wow! It's too bad my sister never got a chance to sell her work."

"Your sister, is that her oil self portrait over your mantel?"

"Yes, she gave it to Jack just before her death. Mother has dozens of her other paintings in storage."

Clarence looked at us in speculation for a few moments before seeming to make a decision. "When are you going to make your next trip home?"

"We go home once a month, but if you want to go see the paintings, we can go this weekend."

"May I go with you, I'll probably get lost if I drive outside the city?"

I looked at Jenn, who nodded. "Sure, why not. Mother and Dad would be happy to meet someone from the office. Did you ever meet little Barbara when we cared for her?"

"No, but I've seen her self portrait over your mantel."

I chuckled. "She looks more like the larger Barbara now since her last growth spurt."

"You know, that story of the two Barbara's is quite interesting."

I looked at Jenn, who shook her head, as we both thought, *if he only knew the whole story.*

The next Saturday, on our drive to Coffeyville, we got to know Clarence Woodruff much better. He had been a senior partner for more than twenty years and was one of the original organizers of the firm. He lost his wife ten years ago and they never had any children. When his wife died he developed an interest in paintings, with his water color collection being well known as one of the best in the Midwest.

When we were about thirty minutes from Jenn's home she called to let her parents know of our expected arrival time. Alice asked if our guest had any special diet restrictions, which Jenn then asked Clarence. He replied, "At my age anything good is bad for me, but I'm not on a special diet."

Jenn passed that information on to her mother and then asked, "Is Elizabeth going to be there? If not, I can call her."

Alice laughed. "She's been here for over an hour and brought Jack's favorite apple pie with her."

Jenn thought, *I've got to get that recipe from her before it's too late.*

I pulled into the parking area and honked the horn, alerting everyone that we had arrived. Clarence got out of the car and gingerly stretched his muscles, while looking around at his surroundings. We were soon joined by Jenn's and my family, who welcomed us and were introduced to Clarence.

Clarence and Grandmother were close in age and he seemed taken by her smile. She invited him inside while the others took care of the luggage. When Jenn and I returned from our room we found everyone in the kitchen. Little Barbara had developed a special relationship with Grandmother, and now she was interested in the man we brought home who was closest to Grandmother's age.

Clarence seemed fascinated by little Barbara as well and was telling her how much he liked her paintings. He asked, "Have you completed anything since the water color of the woman looking into the mirror?"

She smiled at him, then looked over at Jenn and me. At my nod, she answered, "You mean the picture Jack took to give to Jenn. I have another that you might like. Alice thinks it's even better."

Grandmother spoke up. "I don't know about the rest of you people, but little Barbara and I are about starved. Let's eat and then go look at those pictures."

Clarence smiled at her and said, "That's a good idea. I've been smelling something that has been making my mouth water. What is that?"

I laughed. "That's Grandmothers special apple pie and I hope she brought more than one for all of us."

Later, after everyone had satisfied their appetites; Jenn, Barbara and I showed Clarence all the water colors in Barbara's collection. She had them arranged in date order and that was how they were presented.

"My most recent ones are on that west wall and then go left to the ones I first saved."

I motioned Barbara to join Jenn and me over next to the oldest paintings, where we took seats and waited. Clarence stood and stared for a long thirty minutes at the west wall before turning to Barbara.

"The one you mentioned in the kitchen. Is it the one of Jack and Jenn looking at a angel?"

"Yes. That came in a dream. It is pretty isn't it?"

When our names and angel were mentioned, we quickly stood beside them looking at the picture. Without a doubt the angel was Olivia and the vision came to Barbara in a dream. Jenn and I looked at each other in speculation. At first I didn't recognize the surroundings within the painting, so maybe the scenario hasn't happened yet. I took a closer look at our positions in relation to Olivia and then looked at Jenn. She just shrugged her shoulders.

In desperation I asked Barbara, "Do you remember anything else from the dream?"

Barbara looked at us in surprise. "You were there, don't you remember?"

"It's your dream, maybe it hasn't happened yet."

"Oh… The angel was real pretty, but kind of scary too. She said Jenn and your daughter were now under her protection too. What does that mean?"

I cleared my throat. "Jenn and I will tell you later. Did she say anything else?"

"No. She just spread her wings and disappeared in a bright flash of light."

I looked at Jenn and smiled. "We're going to have a daughter."

Jenn rushed into my arms, crying happy tears. Barbara came over, hugging us, while Clarence looked at us in awe. He gasped out the words, "You've got a Guardian Angel!"

Barbara asked, "What's that?"

Jenn said, "Oh boy!"

I had Barbara and Clarence sit down while Jenn and I repeated our history with Olivia. When we finished, Barbara said, "Cool. I wish I had one too."

Clarence, still looking a little shook, said, "Me too."

I patted Barbara on the head. "Barbara, you are special since angels have spoken through you twice now."

"Clarence, it would be best if you didn't repeat anything about our Guardian Angel. People would think that you were starting to lose your marbles." I said.

"Barbara, the same goes for you too. You can talk about it with family members except Ben, who doesn't know yet. Grandmother has seen Olivia and I'm sure that she can answer any questions you might have later. Now Clarence, I think you were looking at these water colors."

Clarence asked. "How about the angel painting. Do you want to keep it?"

Jenn answered. "No. It's message has been delivered and we don't need it anymore."

Clarence took the painting from the wall and handed it to Barbara, and then did the same with four other paintings on the west wall. He scanned the other walls and added three more he liked. He spread the eight water colors on the table and looked at them considering their value.

"Barbara, I think that you are going to be a great painter sometime in the future and I want to help you get started. I'm going to offer you what you may consider a fortune, but if I'm correct it will only be a pittance of their future value. Jack and Jenn are your financial guardians and will make the final decision on whether to accept my offer. Do you understand?"

Barbara looked at Clarence with wide eyes, then turned to us. "He wants to buy some of my paintings and you're going to decide if it's okay. Does all the money go into my trust or can I keep some for myself?"

"How much do you want to keep for yourself?" I asked.

"Jenn, your parents have been paying for my lessons and supplies and I want to pay them back if I can."

Jenn hugged her tightly before replying. "They were happy to do it, but we'll discuss it after we find out how much you will receive for the paintings."

Clarence offered $10,000 for the angel painting and the others averaged $3,000 each, for a total of $21,000. Jenn and I walked away and quietly conferred about the offer before accepting.

Clarence smiled and shook hands with Barbara. "You might want to make a copy of this check to remind yourself of your first sale. Now, Jenn where are you keeping those oils of your sister?"

The oils were stored in three large wooden crates, which I opened for him. Later, Clarence reviewed his notes for each painting and made a swift calculation. "Let's have your parents come up here and we'll discuss my offer with them."

* * *

When everyone was gathered, Clarence said, "Your two Barbara's are talented artists. I think little Barbara may become a great one as she gains knowledge and experience. Once I have enough of her work accumulated I intend to enter all of them in a water color showing, which may result in a demand for her work. Your elder Barbara's work in oil I have just reviewed and I want to make an offer for all three boxes that contain 28 pieces. Have you already saved from her work those pieces you want to keep?"

Alice and Jamison nodded their heads, and Jamison said, "Yes, we've kept back four that we like."

"Good for you. My offer is $280,000 for the contents of those three boxes. At the present time she's an unknown painter, but after a show I plan on having after returning to KC, I hope everyone will know her name."

Jenn hurried over to her parents who appeared to be in shock. Jenn said, "Now Barbara may get the recognition she deserves."

Her parents, after some discussion, accepted Clarence's offer. Jamison and I replaced the top of the crates and arranged for their shipment to Clarence's address. It wasn't long before we each had a large check in our hands, Jamison's quite a bit larger than mine. Later, we took little Barbara into our bedroom and started to discuss her financial future.

First we asked her how much she wanted to keep from her first sale. She replied, "How much have my lessons cost since I've been here?"

"You've been taking them for what, about two plus years?"

"Almost three years, three times a week."

"Let's say fifty weeks times three, or 150 lessons at $50 per lesson is about $7,500. Plus supplies would bring it to about $8,000. Is that what you want to hold out?"

Barbara thought about it, then said, "I think $10,000 would pay that and give me extra spending money for clothes and whatever I might want."

"Okay, how do you want to handle giving this money to Alice and Jamison? You know they love you like a daughter and they may think you didn't want to accept their help."

Little Barbara looked at us for a moment before tears started coming and then she started crying in earnest. Through her sobs she said, "I know they love me and I just wanted to pay them back for how much they have done for me."

Jenn hugged her and kissed her forehead. "Barbara, I think they would like for you to call them Mom and Dad, rather than for you to give them money. Their older Barbara just gave them a huge amount of money from the sale of her paintings. They would have preferred to have her here to give them a hug and a kiss."

Barbara sobbing grew even louder as she held onto Jenn. When she was cried out, Barbara wiped her eyes and used the cool wet cloth I gave her to wash her face. "Okay, I think I'm alright now. Forget about what I said before, just put it all into my trust. I'll think of something to give them later that will show them how much I love them."

Barbara left our room with her back straight with some inner resolution within herself. I looked at Jenn and said, "I think we did good. I've been worried about Barbara's apparent inability to think of your parents as hers. We now need to tell everyone about our new expected daughter before Barbara spills the beans."

Jenn led the way downstairs where we found everyone in the kitchen. It was apparent that Barbara had said something that had made everyone smile. Jenn said, "What's going on?"

Her mother said, "Barbara wants to do a family portrait, so we need to take a photograph that she can use as a guide."

"What about Ben?"

"Oh, I can paint him into the background. I'll just use an old photo."

"That should work. Jack and I have some good news for everyone. Barbara just told us that in her dream that she used as inspiration to paint Olivia and us together, that Olivia told us that she would now protect me and my daughter, which I'm now pregnant with."

Her mother said, "What! Oh my gosh, you're going to have a little girl. We're going to have another girl in the family."

Jenn rushed to hug her mother and father, while Grandmother sat with tears of happiness in her eyes. I stooped down and kissed her on the cheek. "Grandmother, you're going to have another child to help raise."

"I wish your mother and father were here to see your first born." She then smiled and said, "Maybe they will at that. When angels are involved, anything can happen."

CHAPTER TWENTY-ONE

Late Sunday, after returning to our apartment, Jenn and I were relaxing on our couch in each other's arms contemplating the changes in our lives. Jenn was looking at the portrait of her sister, when she had a sudden thought and left my arms to stand in front of it with her arms around her body.

"Barbara, you already know about Jack and my daughter who will be with us in about six months. I hope that you are as happy about this addition to our family as we are and I want you to give us your blessing."

I stood beside Jenn as she finished her request. We had always felt Barbara's love emulating from the portrait, but now she was there in front of us, as if she had stepped out of the painting.

"Jenn, you know I will always love both of you, and your daughter will be as mine. I spoke for adding you both to Jack's protection as you will be central to what is to come. Never doubt my love as you are one with me."

When her image returned to the portrait, unshed tears were bright in both our eyes as I held Jenn close to me. When we went to bed, neither of us believed we would sleep because Barbara's words kept swirling about in our minds. However, once we put our arms around each other we were soon asleep, and found ourselves still in each other's arms when the morning alarm sounded.

We arose refreshed and completed our morning routines before arriving at the office. We found that Connie had not forgotten her promise, as our office was filled with staff members bringing presents for Jenn's baby shower.

Marilyn Phelps soon arrived, representing the partners of the firm, and gave Jenn a $5,000 Hallmark gift certificate. Jenn was so surprised and grateful at the generosity from the partners and staff, that she broke down and cried. The women all rushed to comfort her and after she had regained control of her emotions, Connie said, "This is the staff's recognition of your efforts to get them a daycare for our office. It has been a financial life saver for most of them."

After everyone left to return to work, Connie gave Jenn a card with a name and telephone number on it. "My sister-in-law does nanny work when she can get it. She's good at it and has two of her own. I think she'll be free about the time you need her, so keep her in mind."

That evening after we had brought all the gifts into the apartment, Jenn took a good look at what she received, while I fixed dinner. I checked on her when I could, knowing how emotional the pregnancy was making her. She had started making a list of who brought what, and a separate list of items so that she would knew what she still needed to obtain. At one point I found her crying into a pretty baby blanket.

I took her into my arms and kissed her, then just holding her until she was cried out. "Ooh honey it's all so pretty. They gave me such nice things."

I told her dinner was about ready and she should come and sit down. I gave her a glass of sparkling water and finished cooking dinner. Keeping a watch on Jenn, I filled her and my plates and placed them on the table. Before I sat next to her I gave her a lingering kiss on the neck, which initiated an entirely different emotional state as she gave me a smoldering smile. I don't think either of us tasted our food, before she abruptly stood up and pulled me into the bedroom, where we made passionate love among all the baby shower gifts.

Jenn and I continued to work together until late in her eighth month. She was so large that it was uncomfortable for her to continue at the office. We asked her parents to come and stay with her while I was absent from the apartment, which was perfect because they had been calling daily for updates in her condition.

Two weeks later, her water broke and an ambulance took her to the hospital, where she soon delivered a seven pound girl. I was there beside her throughout her delivery and when Jenn was handed our daughter, I gave them both a kiss. After holding our creation for a short time, she looked at me and asked, "Well, what are we going to name this little angel?"

I looked at Jenn with a surprised expression, which she understood. "Should we name her Angel?"

I thought about it and looked at her parents for their input. "Why not? It might give her problems when she starts school, but I think it's appropriate."

Jenn handed me our daughter and smiled as I gingerly took her in my arms. "I wanted to see if the name fits her and I believe it does. Angel Pearson, welcome to our family."

The new grandparents crowded around to see our own angel. Three days later we were back into our apartment with our daughter. Alice started teaching Jenn all the things new mothers had to learn. Jenn didn't make enough milk to feed Angel, so she was forced to use formula. We both learned how to change diapers, but the new ones were a breeze to use.

Alice said, "Jenn have you noticed this birthmark on Angel's back? It's shaped like a small cross."

"No. Let me see! Oh my gosh that's really something and we named her Angel."

After two weeks, Jenn's parents went home and our new nanny started caring for Angel. Connie was right about her sister-in-law, Betty Upjohn was a great nanny. Jenn planned to stay home another two weeks to observe the nanny in action, but after a week she was back at work.

Jenn was still wearing maternity clothes because she hadn't lost enough weight yet to get into her regular clothes. On the drive to the office she told me she wanted to start our exercises again. I was glad to hear her resolve, but I was not going to rush into it as she needed time to heal.

George and Clarence came by and wanted to take us out for lunch. We agreed, but I told them, "Jenn has placed herself on salads until she loses some weight."

They laughed and George replied, "That's okay, as long as we don't have to eat that too."

They took us to the Crown Plaza where they reserved a small room. We men all ordered steaks, while Jenn ordered a large salad. Clarence said, "This weekend they are going to have the annual Art Festival here at the Crown. I'm displaying both Barbara's work; however, the water colors and oils will be in different locations. I was hoping that you would answer any questions about the water colors, while I cover the oils."

"Oh, that's wonderful. I was wondering when you were going to show the paintings." Jenn said.

I asked, "What time of the day is the show. We may need to make arrangements for a nanny for Angel if there's a conflict."

"The show is from one to five p.m., with a break, then from seven to ten p.m. for both days."

"That lets me out unless Jack and I take turns each day." Jenn said frowning with disappointment.

I said, "Honey, why not call your mother. I'm sure that she and your Dad would be happy to come up for the weekend."

Clarence smiled at her. "I have a thought. I can arrange for a plane to pick them up in Coffeyville and fly them here and then back home Monday. It would save them the four hour drive each way."

"That sounds a little expensive to me. Are you sure you want to do that?" Jenn asked.

"With you two there to answer questions about the artists, is more than enough justification."

"I'll call them now and ask if they want to do that before we make any more plans." Jenn said.

After she disconnected, Jenn's face lit up with a big smile. "They agreed and I told them I would call back with the details."

Friday night Jenn's parents arrived and they were still excited by their flight in a twin engine charter aircraft. Alice said, "They landed just across the river from downtown and the taxi here was less than half an hour."

Angel was a good baby according to Alice, who only fussed when she needed to be changed or was hungry. Jenn and I competed for her attention, each rushing to be the one who took care of her when she needed our attention.

Alice watched us competing for Angel's attention and nudged Jamison. "Who does that remind you of?"

"Us, with Barbara our first. By the time Jenn came along we weren't as frantic, but we loved all our children equally. However, I don't think we were quite so competitive in caring for Barbara."

The next day after lunch, Jenn and I went to the Art Festival and received our official badges, before finding Clarence. He explained what he wanted from us and gave us a list of the paintings with their posted price. After we sold a painting we would place an orange sticker on the frame and our list.

Before returning to the water color section I found a chair that Jenn could use if she became tired. The exhibit soon started filling with people and we watched their faces as they viewed Clarence's water color collection, which little Barbara's was only a small part. I thought her bright colors caught more attention. By the break time, four pictures were sold including one of little Barbara's.

We checked in with Clarence and gave him the checks we received for the sold paintings. "That's not bad for the first period, but we should do better this evening. I sold two of Barbara's oils. Would you bring her self portrait here this afternoon? I'll put a purple sticker on it to signify that it's not for sale, but I think it's presence will draw buyers for her other works."

"If we hang little Barbara's self portrait next to it, would that help your water color sales?"

Clarence's eyes got a little bigger as the possibilities occurred to him. "Yes! That would be perfect and the two together would be an ever greater draw. I'll get it approved so that when you bring them here you won't have any problem."

That afternoon we arrived early so that the oil display could be rearranged to include the two Barbara's. The idea of having a water color as part of the oil painting collection, brought many viewers. Once there, they were enthralled by the Barbara's, people standing three and four deep looking at them.

The Sunday morning *Kansas City Star* had a big article and pictures describing the two Barbara's. I showed the article to Alice and Jamison, who were fascinated with the coverage and the speculation about the two Barbara's.

We arrived early that afternoon expecting a bigger than normal crowd and were not disappointed when we had to skirt around people waiting in line for the doors to open. We found Clarence in the oil section looking at the two Barbara's.

He looked at us with a smile. "My idea about the oil was good, but combined they are the big draw. I've raised my prices on all the Barbara's and expect to sell them all today. I think you will get some large offers for these two as well. You better get an insurance rider and additional security for your apartment because of the publicity these have gotten. "

He gave us a new listing of the water colors with the revised prices before we returned to our post. The noise volume increased, heralding the opening of the doors. The first person to our section was a reporter, who wanted pictures and the story behind the two Barbara's. Jenn handled the other inquires, while I answered the reporter's questions. He was soon joined by two others. They left to continue their quest for a story in the oil section.

At the mid-day break we returned to Clarence giving him a update on sales and asking how the oils were selling. "I only have eight of Barbara's paintings left and I'm considering pulling them for the sale next year, when I'm sure their value will be higher. I've recovered my purchase price of the group twice over."

"All of little Barbara's water colors sold. The publicity did everyone a favor. I talked to other vendors on the walk over here and they all had good sales."

"Jack, I want you and Jenn to take the Barbara's back home with you. They have done their job and I appreciate your help. I won't need you to return this afternoon unless you just want to."

Jenn and I wrapped the paintings, and with an escort we took them to the garage and returned to our apartment. On the drive, Jenn called our insurance agent and got a verbal rider for the Barbara paintings.

The next morning, Jenn's parents made their return flight to Coffeyville and we returned to the office. I arranged for our wood outer door at the apartment to be replaced with a reinforced decorated steel door. I also purchased a state of the art alarm system that included our ability to view inside the apartment through our cell phones.

Our Nanny, Betty Upjohn, called that afternoon to let us know that the new door had been installed and that it had a digital keypad for unlocking the door, and a video monitor to view anyone wanting entry.

When we returned home that night, the security people were still there installing the system. Betty showed us how to set the door lock before leaving. The lead installer showed us how to set the alarm at night or when everyone was leaving the apartment. He installed an application on our cell phones that allowed us to view the inside of the apartment thru small video cameras. All rooms were covered except our master bedroom and bath. The feed from the cameras were saved on a wireless hard drive hidden inside the couch. The hard drive was automatically wiped once each week.

While he was still there we experimented with the cell phone and went through the selection of cameras for each room covered. Jenn exclaimed, "Wow! This is a clear picture and there is a camera positioned looking right at the two Barbara's. Jack, this was a great idea and I can check to see how Angel is doing. What's the range on this? Can I check here while I'm out of town?"

The technician said. "If you can get a cell signal then you can call from anywhere."

The next morning, when Betty arrived we gave her the key pad code to enter the apartment in case she wanted to take Angel outside for fresh air. While I was driving to work, Jenn was watching Betty take care of Angel. After she put her phone away she sighed and said, "I enjoy the opportunity to check on Angel at my leisure."

CHAPTER TWENTY-TWO

Jenn and I had interviewed a potential new client this morning. Morning Glory Enterprises, a conglomerate of fast food businesses all under their own names. Jessica Walker, currently the CEO, was elected by the Board this year after her husband died in an aircraft crash.

When Jessica arrived, Connie showed her into our office and we invited her to sit with us in our little conference area. I introduced ourselves and asked, "How can we help you?"

"I'm in a fight to retain my position as head of Morning Glory. A major shareholder, Greg Stories, is trying to garner enough votes to take over. I was hoping to delay the next board meeting long enough to win more votes to defeat his bid to take over the business."

Jenn asked, "has the NTSB investigation into your husband's crash revealed the cause yet?"

"No. It may be another six months before they reach a decision. Bob and three other officers of the business died in that crash. It took the NTSB over a month to get all the pieces together in a hanger."

"Has Stories indicated what he plans to do when he gets control?" I asked.

"He wants to dismantle the business and sell it piece by piece. Stories tried to get Bob to do this before he died, but he refused."

"That sounds to me like a good motive to remove Bob from the picture." Jenn said.

"When is the next board meeting scheduled?" I asked.

"Two weeks from tomorrow. Do you think you can get it postponed?"

Jenn nodded. "Leave it in our hands for a few days while we consider how best to proceed."

I said, "I bet we can get a court ordered Stay to stop any further board action until the NTSB makes a ruling on the cause of the crash. I'm going to ask George if he knows who to call at the NTSB to let them know about our theory that sabotage might have brought the plane down."

"Okay, and I'll start my research on what I need for a Stay."

George gave me a Washington, D.C. number and I called to get the IIC of the Walker aircraft crash. I spoke with Robert Jacobs, who was working out of Independence, Missouri, near where the plane crashed. I called his number and introduced myself and gave him the background information concerning the possible motive for sabotage of the aircraft. "Have you made any progress in your investigation?"

He laughed. "That plane came apart in the air and debris was scattered for about a square mile. We got most of the pieces, but all we can say at this point is that there was some kind of an explosion that brought the plane down. You say someone has a motive for doing it. Fine, prove it and save me some work."

I thanked him and then sat for a few minutes marshalling my thoughts. I asked Connie to call our investigator, Daisy McGrady, and have her come by our office. I looked at Jenn and said, "The NTSB says that a explosion brought the airplane down, which fits our theory."

Jenn smiled. "I think that will be enough to make a Judge sign off on my Stay Order. When I finish I want your input before we send it over to the court house."

We were discussing the first draft of the Stay Order when Daisy arrived. Jenn and I told her our new client's story, and our theory about Greg Stories arranging the explosion that brought down the aircraft, killing the former CEO, Bob Walker. Daisy got all the names and relationships pertaining to the case and after asking a few questions she left the office.

I said, "She's a woman of few words. It's kind of refreshing."

Jenn asked. "What's that supposed to mean?"

"Nothing. I was just making a joke."

Jenn looked at me considering, while I attempted to look innocent.

"Okay, but next time give me a warning when you make a joke about women."

"Yes dear." I said as she came over and kissed me.

We went back to editing the order and when satisfied we had Connie put it into its final form and emailed it to the Court House. Two days later we got a email from Judge Brunner, who asked several questions before saying he would sign it. Minutes later I had Connie messenger a copy of the Order to all the Morning Glory Enterprises Board Members.

Jenn called Jessica and informed her of the Stay Order and asked, "Is there anything else you need from us?"

"Upon reflection, I'm concerned about me and my children's safety. Do you know of anyone you could recommend that provides protection?"

"No, but I know someone who does, and I'll have them call you to make arrangements."

Jenn called Daisy and asked for her opinion on who would be best for that kind of security service. She said she would call around and have them contact Jessica. After disconnecting from Daisy, Jenn told me about Jessica's request and that Daisy would handle it.

A day later Jessica called and thanked us for the security help. "They foiled a attempt to break into my house, but fled when they realized I wasn't alone. You might be careful as well because your names are on the order."

I asked Jenn, "Is there anything else we can do to protect ourselves? I'm not sure what Olivia's protection threshold is, so we better be careful. Maybe take a cab to and from work for awhile until we get a feel for what sort of danger we're in."

That evening I was careful as we approached our car in the office garage. I even looked under the car for a bomb before we opened the doors. Driving home I watched for anyone tailing us, but detected nothing. Arriving in the apartment garage we drove around inside looking for anything suspicious before parking.

When we got to the apartment we informed Betty, "One of our clients has been threatened, which might spill over to us and you should be very careful with anyone who might want to enter the apartment. If in doubt call us before letting them inside, and don't take Angel outside until we tell you otherwise."

Betty looked a little concerned as she left and we were afraid that she might not want to return. It was Jenn's turn to cook and she started looking for something to prepare, while I was taking care of Angel. Standing in front of the Barbara paintings while holding Angel, I felt an increased flow of love from the older Barbara. Angel must have felt it too as her hands reached out to the outpouring of love.

I whispered to Angel, "That's your Aunt that you feel. I wonder if you're going to look like her. Your hair is so much like hers."

Angel twisted in my arms to look at me and giggled, as if she had understood what I had said. I carried her into the kitchen and told Jenn what we felt from her sister's painting.

"Ooh. I wish I had been there. Jack, I can't find anything here I can fix. I'll call for something delivered?"

"Okay, but it's still your turn to cook next time." She grimaced, but then asked, "Is Golden Dragon alright?"

"That sounds good."

She called in our usual order and then joined us in front of the mantel.

"Ooh, I can feel it too. We have the strangest family and I hope nothing changes. Jack, I've never been this happy before I married you. Did you tell Barbara how well her old paintings sold at the Art Festival?"

"No. You do it."

"Barbara, Clarence Woodruff, one of the senior partners at our firm bought most of your old paintings from our folks for $280,000. At the Art Festival he sold all but eight paintings, which he held back, for over twice what he paid for them. He says that you have become famous in the art world and the value of your works keeps going up. He told me that this picture of you is the best of your work and is worth over $500,000. That's the original reason for the increased security here. Now we're worried about some nut trying to get back at us because of our new client."

Barbara's picture started to glow with a white intensity that was so bright that I had to turn away and cover Angel's eyes. Jenn's mouth dropped open in surprise and amazement as Barbara stood in front of her.

"Tell me about this person you believe threatens you and your family!"

The bright light faded and I turned around facing Barbara's glowing figure. Angel was not afraid of her as she held her arms out toward Barbara. Barbara's serious expression turned into a smile as she took Angel into her arms and kissed her forehead, then handed her back to Jenn.

I told Barbara about our client, and Greg Stories, who we suspected of arranging the bombing of the aircraft carrying our client's husband. "There was an attempted attack today against our client, who warned us we may be in danger."

Barbara smiled at us for a moment, before looking up at the ceiling and raising her arms, then her image was back into the painting and we could feel her love reaching out to us again. Jenn turned to me and we embraced, with Angel caught between us.

We stood in each other's arms for several minutes, holding Angel against our chests, when the door bell interrupted our thoughts. I checked the video screen to verify it was the delivery man from Golden Dragon, before opening the door and paying for our dinner.

I put water on to heat for our tea, while Jenn placed Angel in her recliner seat between our chairs at the table and then warmed up her formula. By the time Angel's meal was heated, I had set the table and our tea was ready. We had been married long enough now that this routine was second nature for us. Jenn made sure the formula was not too hot before giving it to Angel, and we started our meal.

Dipping my egg roll in hot mustard sauce, I asked, "I wonder if Barbara is an angel or something else?"

Jenn thought a little before responding. "If she's an angel, she's not like Olivia, who's a warrior. Maybe she's some kind of messenger. Whatever she is, she loves all of us very much. She picked up our Angel and kissed her. Angel is double blessed."

We were awakened at about three a.m. by our security alarm. Jenn ran towards Angel, while I checked the front door. I replayed the door video feed and saw three men trying to get through our reinforced door. When the alarm sounded they ran for the stairs. I used my cell to report the attempted break-in, and while I waited for the police to arrive, I downloaded the attempt on a flash drive.

When the police arrived minutes later, I let them inside where we all examined the damage to the door, which was slight. I explained my security system to the officers, and handed over the flash drive I made that showed the faces of the men who attempted breaking into the apartment.

CHAPTER TWENTY-THREE

The next day at work we were visited by two police detectives, Mary Cullen and Peter Jackson. They greeted us with rueful smiles, with Mary saying, "You guys must lead interesting lives. We've looked at the flash drive you gave us and we recognized all three of the perpetrators, who have long criminal histories. What were they after?"

Jenn said, "We have a valuable painting done by my sister, or it could be because of a new client with a vengeful enemy."

"Let's start with the enemy. That sounds more interesting."

I spoke up. "We can't divulge information about our client, but do you recall that private aircraft that went down near Independence about three months ago."

They nodded. "Well, NTSB investigated the crash and told me they thought it was caused by a mid-air explosion. We have a theory it was caused by Greg Stories. At this point it's only a theory because we don't have any direct evidence."

"Why would he come after you?"

"We served him with legal papers two days ago."

"Okay, now about the painting. How much is it worth?"

"Clarence Woodruff, one of our senior partners, who is also an art expert, thinks it could be worth over $500,000."

The detectives raised their eyebrows at that amount of money.

"You're putting me on!" Mary said.

Jenn smiled at her. "You guys didn't catch those articles in the *Star* about my sister's self portrait?"

Mary looked surprised. "That's the painting?"

Mary looked at her partner and said, "Well, it looks like we have two avenues to follow up on."

Mary turned to me and asked, "Which do you think is more likely?"

"If I was you I'd sniff around after Greg Stories. He must be guilty of something."

"Gee thanks. Can you give me a copy of those legal papers you gave Greg?"

Jenn thought a moment before she turned to her computer and printed it out. Before giving it to Mary, she said, "You didn't get it from me. If you need a copy for your evidence file, get it from the Court House."

Mary smiled at Jenn and said, "Gotcha." They left the office.

I called the leasing office for our apartment building and made arrangements to repair our damaged front door. I then called Betty and told her to expect someone soon to repaint the scratches on the front door, but don't let them inside without first contacting us.

Jenn and I made a list of grocery items we needed and she called in a order to be delivered at six p.m. We had traveled to the office by taxi, so it was inconvenient for us to pick it up ourselves. We arrived at our apartment at the same time as the grocery delivery man, so we escorted him to our apartment where we paid and tipped him generously. When we arrived at our door I noted that it looked flawless again.

Betty left us a list of items we needed to get for Angel, and then we were alone with our daughter. Jenn looked after Angel, while I put away the groceries. When I finished that task, I checked on my two girls and found Jenn changing her clothes while watching Angel play with her toys. I followed her example and was looking after Angel while Jenn started dinner.

Later, after dinner and with Angel asleep, we sat together on the couch looking at the Plaza night lights. Jenn was snuggled tightly against me, with my arm around her shoulders, while we let the tensions of the day evaporate. We were so comfortable that we both napped until the front door exploded off its hinges, the force of the blast turned the couch over onto us, and blew out the window we had been previously gazing out of.

Luckily, Angel was in her crib in the nursery, well away from the blasts effects. I crawled out from under the couch and was lifting it off Jenn, when Olivia arrived in a flash of white light. She looked magnificent with her wings spread in warrior mode, and then she stopped all four men in their tracks with a lightning bolt that engulfed them all in a flash of light too bright for my eyes to absorb.

My eyes were still registering spots when the bright light disappeared, but my first thoughts were for Jenn and Angel and as I turned, Jenn collapsed into my arms asking about Angel. We hurried into her room and found her awake in her crib, but strangely quiet as she held out her arms for us. Jenn picked her up, but could find nothing wrong with her as she smiled at us. I looked at Jenn, checking to see if there was any visible cuts or other damage. Finding none, I used my cell to call 911 to report our problem. I must have been a little loopy, because I called our leasing agent to get someone to fix the damages.

The police and fire department were both there within minutes to take charge. EMTs soon arrived and checked all three of us out, but could find no injuries. I guess the couch saved Jenn and me from the blast effects. Before the firemen left they covered the broken window with plastic and masking tape and reset the front door, although the lock was busted.

The police marked off the area inside the apartment where four dead men lay just inside the door. The CSI people did their jobs while we stayed in the master bedroom, with occasional trips to the nursery for items needed for Angel.

Detectives Cullen and Jackson arrived and after looking at the crime scene, knocked on the master bedroom door. I invited them in and they took our testimony. Mary wanted to see our video of the attack. I looked at Jenn who grimaced and then shrugged her shoulders. I reversed the video until I saw the explosion, then stopped the action where we were sitting on the couch before the explosion, and inserted the flash drive. I resumed the video and watched the door explode into the room and seconds later, four men appeared in the doorway. One man points at me getting up from behind the couch, then the video picture goes white for about twenty seconds. When a picture next appears it shows the burned husks of the four men on the floor and shows Jenn and I embracing before heading toward the nursery.

I pulled the flash drive and handed it to Mary. "I was blinded by a flash of light, which took out the video as well. It took several minutes before I could see something besides spots."

"Crap! We didn't get to see what happened to those men, only that something burned them and left the room unscorched. It looks like you didn't have anything to do with it though."

I told them to follow me into the living room. "See that big picture over the mantel. It's very valuable and our front door no longer locks. Can you leave some police protection in the hallway, so that we can get some sleep?"

Mary said, "Sure, why not. We need to protect the crime scene anyway. After everyone left I looked up at Barbara and winked, then went back to the master bedroom to look after my girls. I called Betty early the next morning and told her about the break-in and that we were caring for Angel today, and then called Connie to tell her we wouldn't be into work today and the reasons why.

"You poor people. I'll let the others know and I'm happy to hear that you weren't hurt."

The security alarm people were next on my list to have the system checked after our break-in. The leasing agent soon had people on the scene to replace the door and facing, and the broken window. The CSI people had removed the dead bodies and the burned carpet around them. Since the carpet was too old to find a replacement to match what we had, I convinced Jenn to go for tile to replace the burned area cut out by the CSI.

Later that day, after all the service people left, we decided to take a long weekend. I carried our bags and Jenn held Angel as we approached our SUV. I realized that I had not checked the cars for a bomb. I told Jenn to take Angel and stand behind a concrete column while I checked the vehicles. Finding nothing, we loaded up and drove toward grandmother's house near Baxter Springs.

Once we were heading south on the Interstate, Jenn called Grandmother to let her know we were coming for a short stay. When Jenn disconnected, she said, "Your grandmother was excited that we were coming and mentioned looking for an old crib in case we needed it."

"I remember seeing Dad's old crib in the barn, but we'll have to check it out before we use it. My Grandfather made it and it's a rocker."

Dusk fell as we drove up the long lane to the farm house and parked near the kitchen door in the back. Grandmother came outside, drying her hands on her apron, as she greeted us. She hurried over to offer help as Jenn removed Angel and the car seat, but seeing Jenn needed no help, she led the way up the steps and held the door for her.

Jenn set the car seat, which doubled as a portable crib, on the kitchen table. It was Grandmother's first look at Angel, other than photos. "Oh my, she is a beautiful baby and I can see why you named her Angel. Does she need anything that I can help with?"

Angel, fascinated with Grandmother's white hair, held out her hand to touch it. Jenn asked Grandmother to sit down, and she laid Angel in her arms. Grandmother held Angel tenderly in her arms while Angel looked at her and smiled, causing happy tears to trickle down Grandmother's cheeks. Jenn brought a bottle of warm formula to Grandmother and watched how she carefully positioned it.

I photographed them on my cell phone and then we watched how they interacted. When Angel finished the bottle, Jenn placed a cloth on Grandmothers shoulder and helped her position Angel so she could burp. When Angel belched, Jenn asked Grandmother where she could change her, and they both left the room with Angel. I went back to the car and brought in our luggage, which I set it in my old bedroom.

I was looking around the room, noticing keepsakes I accumulated while growing up here. Something new was on the floor next to the bed, the crib Grandmother mentioned. It was cleaned and polished so that it gleamed. I nudged it with my foot and it gently rocked. It was made of hardwood and there was a carving on the headboard of wheat stalks and the name, Jackson Pearson, my father. I picked up the crib and inspected it for how well it was made and turning it over on its bottom, I saw the name, Clyde Pearson, my grandfather who I never met.

I heard voices back in the kitchen, so I replaced the crib on the floor and returned to my family. Grandmother was in a very good mood until we told her of the attack on our apartment and Olivia's arrival. Jenn also told of our conversation with Barbara a day before the attack.

Grandmother was puzzled. "You have had conversations with Barbara too? An actual physical presence where she held and kissed Angel?"

At our nods, she said, "Barbara now appears to be an Angel too. Olivia is still the Guardian Angel that now protects all three of you. Jack, what in the world does God have in mind for you, for all three of you?"

I shrugged my shoulders, "I assume that when the time is right, God or his messenger will let us know."

Grandmother looked at me in disbelief. "You seem to be lackadaisical in your attitude. Don't you care?"

"When you are dealing with God's will, what can I do different? All I can do is try to protect my family from evil and follow God's instructions. My attitude is that of an open vessel as I await his will."

Grandmother looked at me with tears in her eyes. "Honey, you have had tragedy in your life, losing both your parents as a child, and later your first love. But you have also gained a new love and now your first child. Not an even trade, but you appear happy with what life has given you. I suppose most people don't have that, love of family and God."

By this time the only people in the room with a dry face was Angel. She made a loud noise that brought everyone's attention towards her. Jenn said, "She can't be hungry, I just fed her."

I grinned. "Maybe she heard my stomach growl, because I can eat a cow I'm so hungry."

Grandmother gave a shudder and said, "Oh my. I hope you like beans and cornbread because I already had them started when you called."

Jenn wrinkled her nose, but replied, "I'm game. Jack mentioned that he was raised on beans and cornbread growing up, but we've never had it since we got married."

"Well, I make it from scratch and it takes longer, but it tastes better too. Others use canned beans and just heat it up. It's not as good and everyone pays for it later when they start farting."

"Grandmother has a way of reducing the gas attack, and it does taste good too. Do you want me to cut up a onion?"

I was helping Grandmother fill our plates and I asked Jenn, "Do you want your beans on top of the cornbread or beside?"

"I'll do it your way, but don't give me very much. Remember I'm trying to get rid of this extra weight."

I dug in with gusto, as it had been years since I'd eaten beans and cornbread. Jenn asked, "What kind of meat is this that you're using for flavor?"

I grinned at her and replied, "Salt pork. It's mostly fat, so don't eat it. Try a slice of onion with that, it brings it all together."

CHAPTER TWENTY-FOUR

Later, that night I showed Jenn the crib that Grandfather made for my father.

"Ooh it's beautiful. Do you want to try it tonight for Angel?"

When she placed Angel in the crib she said, "Look, it rocks too."

When we got into bed, Jenn snickered. "I bet you never thought you would be sleeping with your wife in this bed while you were growing up."

I hugged her close to me and kissed her on the nose and then passionately on the mouth.

"I had the usual dreams, but I never thought beyond my current fantasies. I miss our king-sized bed, so if I start to squash you, wake me up."

"You mean like this," She said as she dug a thumb into my ribs.

"Yep, that'll wake me up."

The next morning Grandmother fixed us a big breakfast, and as we were eating asked how the crib worked out. Jenn answered, "Angel got me up once for a feeding and change, but I put her back into the crib and rocked it with my toe for a few minutes, and she was asleep again in no time."

Grandmother smiled at me. "Jack, your mother used the crib for you too. Angel is the third Pearson child that has slept in that crib."

Jenn asked, "Can we take this home with us. I don't want to

break a family tradition, besides I think it may be useful."

While Grandmother watched Angel, I took Jenn on a tour of the farm. I showed her the inside of the barn and told her of my childhood here after my mother died. Jenn pointed to a little building with a crescent moon on the door and asked, "Is that an outhouse?"

"Yes, but I've never used it. Grandfather updated the house before I started living here. Grandmother said she got stung by wasps while using it and made him bring the toilet inside."

Jenn asked, "Was it lonely living out here with no other kids to play with?"

"I had my bike and sometimes I would ride into town to meet some of my friends. It's over two miles into Baxter, so I didn't do it very often. Besides, I had chores to do here. I don't remember being lonely."

The free roam chickens Grandmother kept were curious and started to gather around us, clucking, which made Jenn nervous. "Jack, what do they want?"

* * *

Just then a rooster ran through the chickens, flapping his wings, heading straight for me. I screamed and ran for the house, with the chickens on my heels. When she got inside she looked back at Jack and discovered him laughing so hard that he had to grab a post to keep from falling down.

Grandmother came up behind me and asked, "What's going on?"

I replied, "That mean ole rooster chased me into the house."

"Oh, I bet he thought you were going to feed the chickens and he wanted first dibs. That Jack is such a jokester. You need to give him a good dose of the same medicine."

"I know he is, but I don't have his talent on the spur of the moment."

"Jenn you are a smart cookie. Plan one out that will get him good. However, be aware that he'll come back at you when you don't expect it."

I thought, *what can I do that doesn't appear to be planned?*

* * *

I came inside and apologized to Jenn for laughing at her. "But honey, it was so funny watching you run from Big Red. He's a bully, but wouldn't hurt you or I would have wrung his neck."

I put my arms around her and whispered into her ear, "Am I forgiven?"

Jenn pulled me closer and kissed me, then looked into my eyes and smiled. "I forgive you, but there will be payback."

Oh lord, I wonder what she has in mind for me. I thought.

We made a quick overnight trip to Coffeyville before returning to Kansas City Sunday afternoon. Inside our apartment we found a note from the security company saying the system was working and that we should change our entry code. I did that and called Betty, telling her the entry code had changed and we would give it to her after she arrived tomorrow.

Jenn and I toured the apartment, looking it over for anything that needed to be fixed. Jenn pointed at the tile floor that replaced the burned carpet. "That looks better than I thought it would and your idea to put in an angel design sets it off."

We inspected the furniture in the living room for wear or tears from the explosion, but thought they only needed a good cleaning. Angel was asleep when we arrived, so we placed her into the rocking crib in front of the couch, while we took our usual position on the couch looking out at the Plaza lights. Falling asleep in each other's arms, we were awakened by Angel, who wanted her bottle.

The next morning we met with George and brought him up to date on what had happened in our apartment and that we needed to contact our new client, Jessica Walker, on further developments from her end. George nodded his head, then asked, "You feel certain that the attack was tied to your legal action for the Walker account?"

"Yes, but when the police positively identify the bodies from our attack, we will have proof."

"If you have proof they are tied together, then charge the Walker account for any damages incurred in the attack. There's no point in you eating that expense."

Later, Clarence Woodruff stopped by our office and after hearing our recap of the attack, smiled ruefully. "I assume those four were taken out by your Guardian Angel. Have you heard anything from the police yet?"

I looked at Jenn and then shook my head. "No, and we're

concerned. This is not the first time our attackers have become burned out husks. I bet someone is scratching their heads trying to figure out what happened."

"I wouldn't worry too much. The cause is too incredible for anyone to believe it. They are more to think you have supernatural powers than a Guardian Angel."

Two days later Detectives Cullen and Jackson returned to our office. Mary said, "I've got some good news for you. The DNA tests confirmed the identities of all four of the bodies in your apartment. Three were the same people who tried to get into your apartment before and the fourth was Greg Stories, who was the ringleader and the one with explosive's knowledge. I've already sent samples of the trace materials to Robert Jacobs of the NTSB, and he verified that the explosives used to bring down the Walker aircraft and on your apartment door are the same."

Jenn and I smiled with relief. "Did you find out what caused the deaths of those four when they entered our apartment?" I asked.

Mary looked at me in curiosity before replying. "No. That's still a mystery. We're taking another look at those bodies recovered from the burned out van that was used in a previous attempt on your lives. People who try to harm you don't fare well, do they? We've asked the FBI to check for similar deaths in an attempt to discover a cause."

The detectives left after wishing us well, while Jenn and I contemplated what the FBI might bring into our lives. I called Jessica Walker and informed her of the death of her enemy, Greg Stories, and how he had died. There was silence from her end for a few moments, then she started crying hysterically until she disconnected.

I looked at Jenn and said, "I made a mistake. When I called Jessica she lost it and hung up on me. We should have had a face to face meeting with this news. Would you call her back in about a half hour and ask her if she would like to meet with us?"

Jenn nodded her head in agreement and then placed her arms around me. "Jack, you had no way of knowing she would react that way. We both learned something today. When we deliver good or bad news to a client, we should do it in person."

Jessica arrived at our office early the following morning. She seemed to have recovered from my phone call yesterday as we sat in our conference area. Jenn asked her how she was feeling and she gave us a small smile as she replied. "It was a shock to discover that my guess that Stories was behind my husband's death was true and that his death has been avenged. I've conferred with the other board members, who all agreed that I should continue as the CEO. Please have the Stay released so that we can move on with the business."

We agreed and I asked, "Is there anything else that our firm could do for you?"

She looked at me for a moment, while thinking. "At our next Board Meeting I'm going to officially switch legal firms. I'll send you a copy of the resolution, which you may use in your letter to my old legal firm, J. K. Meadowlark, informing them that you now represent Morning Glory Enterprises, and to send you the files of all outstanding legal actions. After you receive them, let me know and I'll tell you how I want to proceed in each case."

After Jessica Walker left, Jenn started drafting a letter to the court that would end the Stay on Morning Glory's Board meetings, while I drafted a memo to George on Morning Glory's expected move to our firm. Later that day Jenn and I reviewed a pro bona case that would go to trial next week.

CHAPTER TWENTY-FIVE

Five years later my two girls and I arrived at the firm, where we dropped Angel off at the day care, before walking a few steps to our office. Angel had been using the day care for over two years and had made several close friends. The other children were from staff parents, except two from firm lawyers, including Angel.

The children didn't care who their friends' parents were, they just enjoyed playing with each other. Angel seemed to draw certain children to her, even some who were a year or two older. Angel's hair had lightened in color to almost a pure white, which was striking even for one of her age. Her name hadn't yet caused her any problems with the other children, but the daycare staff couldn't keep their eyes off her.

Angel was a happy child and when she smiled at you, it seemed to draw you towards her. It wasn't long before we were hosting play dates for many of her friends. Two of these friends were special to her, Josh Richards and Mary Ortega, and they were always at her side. Josh was a year older and her self-appointed protector, while Mary was her age and confidant. Angel and Mary were almost opposites in appearance, with Angel's white hair and light skin complexion, to Mary's dark hair and light brown skin color. Josh was a red headed boy who towered over both of them.

This Saturday play date was attended by ten other children and their mothers, most who had been at the apartment before. I stayed in the kitchen and made sure that snacks were available and served drinks in covered cups with straws. Sometimes some of the mothers helped me, while Jenn supervised games. I looked up once and noticed that Angel, Mary, and Josh were standing in front of the mantel gazing up at Barbara's picture.

I eased my way closer until I could hear what was being said. Angel pointed at the two Barbara's. "That big picture is Barbara, who I'm named after. Can you feel her love coming from the picture?"

Josh and Mary both nodded, while Mary said, "It's strong, even stronger than when Mom hugs me."

Angel smiled, still looking at Barbara. "She's my Aunt and sometimes she comes out of the painting and talks to me. The small picture is a Barbara too. Mommy and Daddy told me that she looks a lot like my Aunt and has her talent to paint. My Aunt is pretty, but Mommy is beautiful, don't you think?"

Her two friends looked between the picture and Jenn several times before agreeing with Angel. By this time several more of Angel's friends had gathered and voiced their agreement. I smiled and returned to my duties, and the children resumed their play.

That night as Jenn and I lay in bed, I told her what I had overheard Angel and her two friends discussing. "Oh my. Do you think we should have a talk with Angel?"

"Not yet, but it's interesting that Barbara is talking to Angel, who thinks Barbara is an angel. She said Barbara is her namesake - an angel. What can we say at this point?"

"We can tell her not to tell others she speaks to an angel, especially when we go to church. People will think she's mental. At this point, because of their age, adults will pay little attention to what children say. As Angel gets older we need to make sure she understands the problems she'll face in talking about this."

"Okay, let's caution her tomorrow on the way to church. What do you think of the kids saying that you're more beautiful than Barbara?"

"I'm more interested in what you think. Do you think I'm prettier?"

"Honey, there's no contest. You're the most beautiful woman in the world to me."

"Good! Just for that you get a reward." She murmured in my ear before kissing me passionately.

The following Saturday we took Angel to the Ortega's for a play date. Gabrielle, Mary's mother, wanted to pay us back for all the times we hosted the play dates. Josh, Angel, and Mary were the only children present for this date because their house and yard was small. The weather was sunny and warm, so the children were allowed to play outside in the Ortega's fenced back yard.

The adults were sitting under a large tree enjoying a glass of lemonade, when we heard Josh yelling for us. A child's scream for help is a parent's worst nightmare as we all ran towards Josh. He was wringing his hands as Angel was trying to stem the flow of blood from Mary's head by pressing her hands against the wound.

Angel's voice got louder as she said, "Stop, Stop, Stop!"

At her last word, the blood stopped flowing and Angel wiped the blood away from the two-inch gash on Mary's head. Angel leaned over and kissed the wound and said, "There, I kissed it to make it better."

As we watched, the wound started healing before our eyes. I ran back to the bucket of ice and wet my handkerchief, before returning to Mary and started to wipe the blood away from the wound, which was now only a red mark that soon faded to nothing.

Josh, with tears in his eyes said, "Mary tripped and fell against that rock. She just lay there until Angel turned her over and we saw the blood. That's when I yelled for you."

Mary looked up at us and blinked, then said, "What happened? Am I hurt?" Placing her hand to her head, she rubbed it before noticing the blood.

"Mommy! What happened to me?" She said as she sat up and looked around at the expressions of the adults surrounding her. She then saw Angel on her knees next to her, smiling at her.

"Angel, what happened?"

"You fell and hit your head on a rock, but I fixed it. Does your head hurt?"

"No, but I feel funny. I'm a little dizzy."

I said, "She bled a lot of blood before it stopped, maybe she needs to drink some juice and eat something."

I helped Mary up and we took her inside where Jenn cleaned the blood off her face and neck, while Gabrielle fixed her something to eat and drink. The children soon returned to their play, although at a slower pace. The adults were a different story as our minds tried to make sense of what we observed.

I placed my hand over Gabrielle's as we sat at her table. "Please don't repeat what happened here. If the wrong people hear about this it will make Angel's life a living hell. She will never have a normal life again."

Gabriel nodded. "I agree. Besides there is no proof to support that Angel cured her injury. I'm just glad that she did it. I'm not even going to tell her father what happened."

Jenn called the children over to their table. "Kids, you must not tell anyone what happened here today. It's our secret that Angel fixed Mary's head wound. See Mary's head - there's not even a mark on it and other kids and adults will think you are making up a story. So to keep you out of trouble, don't tell anyone. How about it? Are you going to tell anyone else?"

"No, Mrs. Pearson."Mary and Josh said, while Angel said, "No, Mommy."

Jenn looked at them intently for a moment, then smiled. "Okay, go play."

I said, "Gabrielle, if I were you, I'd get rid of that rock in the yard."

Later, after we returned home we started a conversation with Angel. Jenn asked, "Angel, did you know that you could heal Mary's head before you tried?"

"Barbara told me that I had been given healing powers, but I hadn't tried them before."

"How long ago did she tell you this?"

"Last week. Did I do something bad Mommy?"

"No honey, but the next time Barbara tells you something, will you tell us what she said? We might have to make preparations."

"Barbara wouldn't tell me to do something bad, would she?"

"No dear, but maybe we can help you do something better that needs to be done."

I asked Angel, "Did Barbara tell you that Mary was going to be hurt and that you should fix her?"

"No, she said I could now heal people if I judged that they needed it to get better."

Jenn and I looked at one another for a moment. Jenn said with a little catch in her voice, "Mary's injury must have fit that need?"

"Mary's my bestist friend. She was bleeding awful bad and I didn't know how to stop the blood, so I just told it to stop. Mommy, you always kiss my hurts, so I kissed it to make it better."

Jenn hugged Angel, kissing her forehead. "You did good. Keep making those kind of decisions. If they are not in immediate danger of dying, let the adults handle it."

Angel smiled at her. "Okay Mommy."

I asked. "Are you hungry? I can fix you something if you want it."

"Can I have pancakes, even if it's not breakfast?"

"Sure. Do you want anything else with it, like bacon or eggs?"

"I want both, but Mommy doesn't like to eat bacon because she says it has too much fat."

I leaned over and spoke softly in Angel's ear. "That's alright. I'll cook just enough for the two of us. That way she won't be tempted."

Angel looked at Jenn and asked, "Is that alright Mommy?"

"Fine, but I may take a bite of Daddy's."

Later, after we had eaten and Angel was watching a children's movie on TV, Jenn and I sat on the couch together with our arms around each other while lost in our thoughts about the day's revelations. *What will Angel's healing powers mean for our future. God gave her this power for a reason. We will have to be careful that Angel realizes the responsibilities of this gift. She is still so young to make these kinds of decisions.*

"Jenn, are we going to be wise enough to guide Angel through the next years?"

She tightened her arms around my waist. "We will have to be. We can always ask for guidance if we are stumped. I don't think God would ask anything of us that we couldn't handle."

The next day at church, we prayed in earnest for guidance. Afterward, we both felt better as we drove to our favorite restaurant.

* * *

Life continued for another two years with no new challenges. Angel had another growth spurt and was looking more like her mother, except for her hair color. Jenn had cut her soft white hair to shoulder length with bangs in front. Angel was now attending second grade and most of the other children in her class were drawn to her, although Mary was still her best friend. Josh was now in third grade and was now drawing away from their close relationship.

Little Barbara was now a teenager and painted in oil most of the time. Clarence bought every piece she was willing to sell and demand for her work had caused prices to escalate. Last year she added over $400,000 to her trust fund. A month ago at our last visit to Coffeyville, when we first saw little Barbara exiting the house to greet us, we were struck speechless by the close resemblance between her and the picture on our mantel of Jenn's sister.

It had been six months since little Barbara and Angel had seen each other, and both had grown and changed appearance. Little Barbara ran into our arms and greeted us as she normally did, but when the two girls realized who the other was, they just stood and stared at each other trying to adjust to what they saw.

Angel ran into her arms saying, "Barbara, you look just like my Aunt Barbara."

Little Barbara held her close with tears in her eyes. "Angel, it's so good to see you again. You've changed too." She said as she touched Angel's face.

She then took Angel's hand and asked if she wanted to see her workshop, and they hurried off. Later, little Barbara found Jenn alone and asked, "I don't know if you realize it, but Angel emits a glow of energy. It's not quite the same as what Barbara's picture does, but is similar. In Angel I can now see and feel it. The last time I saw her I could only feel it, but she is now much stronger. I want to paint her so bad that my fingers tingle. May I, please!"

Jenn placed her hand on little Barbara's shoulder and smiled. "Of course you can. Do you want to take a photo to work from when we leave?"

"Yes, I want to take several, some with you and Jack together with her. At this point I'm not sure how I want to portray her. I may try several poses before settling on the final one."

Jenn found me later and whispered that she wanted to talk to me alone. After we were in her old bedroom, she told me what little Barbara had told her about Angel.

I said, "Maybe, we have been too close to her to see or feel it."

"I think it's because little Barbara is so sensitive that she's aware of it." Jenn said.

"I wonder if Angel is capable of other things besides healing?"

"I don't think so or we would have been told by an angel." Jenn replied.

"Well, we always knew she was special. I guess we have to keep a open mind and be alert."

During our return drive to KC, Angel said, "Mom, Barbara is so much like Aunt Barbara. Not only do they look alike, but they feel the same."

Jenn's hand gripped my leg as tears ran down her face.

CHAPTER TWENTY-SIX

Two months later we were returning to Coffeyville in response to a call from Jenn's mother. She said we needed to see little Barbara's latest painting of Angel. When we arrived, little Barbara was the first out of the house to greet us, but this time she headed towards Angel.

She helped Angel out of the car and gave her a smile and a big hug, before turning to us and giving us both a hug. "I finished it! I hope I caught Angel's true potential."

Before we even unloaded the car, she wanted us to look at the painting. Little Barbara took Angel's hand and led her up to the studio. When we were all standing before the covered painting, she removed the covering with a flourish. We stood spellbound by the painting. It was a portrait of Jenn and I standing behind a seated Angel, her hands folded in her lap. Jenn and I were smiling, but Angel's smile seemed to light the room from a glow of multicolors radiating from her head. Her eyes seemed to reach deep into our souls, making us want to step closer so that she could whisper into our ear.

Angel stepped closer to the painting looking at the picture of herself. She turned to little Barbara and asked, "Can I make a change. The colors radiating from my smile should be blended rather than separate, like this."

She than touched the painting and the colors shifted to reflect what she said. "Is that better, if not I can put it back."

Little Barbara was surprised at first by what Angel had done, but soon realized who was talking. "Barbara, I believe you're right. The composition flows from the smile, where it belongs. I like this better. Thank you for your help."

We all realized then that Barbara was present in Angel's body. Angel stepped back from the painting and then looked at little Barbara. "You are better than I was at your age. You will be a master in your lifetime. You have captured Angel nicely, and in the future, this will be a wonderful attraction for others to view. Have Clarence Woodruff loan this painting to the art museum in Kansas City, with the understanding that if it is removed from display that it reverts back to Angel."

When Angel next spoke we knew she was back. "I've got a funny smile in this picture, but Mom and Dad look good."

Alice and Jamison hugged little Barbara, with tears in their eyes. Jenn joined them and placed her arms around them all. Later, we returned to the house and Jamison and I unloaded the car.

During dinner that night, Jenn and I told the family about Angel's gift of healing. Little Barbara smiled, "I knew it. I knew Angel had some kind of power by the way she radiates."

Jenn cautioned them. "We can't tell anyone outside the family. I'm sure that our secret will come out when she uses her power in some public way, but please not for a few more years."

Later, Alice brought me a book on the human body that showed cross sections of the body down to the bone structure. "Maybe Angel can make use of this book if she ever uses her healing power again."

As I thumbed through the pages, Alice asked, "Do you think it's too graphic for her age?"

"No, she didn't seem to be bothered by copious amounts of blood when she healed her friend. This might be useful, depending upon the type of injury she attempts to cure. I'll check with Jenn and see what she says."

Jenn gave her blessing on the book and on our return trip to Kansas City, Jenn sat in the backseat next to Angel and answered her questions as she looked at the pictures. Angel could read simple words, but technical terms she needed help with. Angel seemed fascinated with the bodies circulating system of blood arteries and vessels. How the heart pumped blood throughout the body. How the lungs added oxygen to the blood and the kidneys removed waste from it.

"Why, it's like a big self sustaining biological machine. If a part goes bad, if you could repair or replace it, then it continues to work."

She picked a page showing the heart, then placed her hand over her heart feeling it beat, then did the same with her other major organs. "Mom, this is a very interesting book. Would you get me more books on the body. I'm interested in how to transplant organs and limbs."

I caught Jenn's eyes in the rearview mirror and nodded my head. Jenn thought a moment before answering. "I think I can get you what you want, but I can show you how you can get all kinds of information on the computer when we get home. If you run into something you don't understand, I'll help you."

Angel smiled at her mother and seemed satisfied as she continued looking through her new book. When we got home Jenn showed Angel how to log onto the computer and the web addresses of several search engines where she could seek information. Angel was soon able to select different search engines and access information that she wanted without further help from her mother.

* * *

I did put limits on Angel's computer timer and informed her of the risk of getting a computer virus from sites she opens and how to avoid many of the risks. Her hand was so small she soon started using the two finger method on the keyboard. I watched her go through several sites until Angel asked, "Mom, how can I get a copy of this section?"

I showed her how to use the wireless printer, cautioned her to make sure it was loaded with paper and showed her where extra paper was stored, and how to instruct the computer how and what to print. After watching Angel complete the task, I joined Jack in the kitchen.

* * *

I asked, "How is she getting along using the computer?"

"I think she is smarter than you and I combined. She's never used one before, but is now using it like it's second nature to her. She even added two search engines that I didn't know existed. Tomorrow we need to buy more printer paper and ink. I have a feeling that she is going to go through what we have in short order."

Thirty minutes later we called Angel to dinner and while eating, I asked her how she was getting along with the computer? Angel gave us an excited smile. "I wish I had started earlier. I didn't know all that information was there for the asking. Did you know that MU and KU had courses that you can take on the computer? I'm making a list of the courses that look interesting from the listed briefs, but I'll need your approval and credit to begin."

"Jenn looked at me and silently mouthed, "I told you so."

"Your mother and I will take a look at the courses and go over them with you to make sure that is what you want. Before we sign you up for multiple courses, let's see how you do on the first one you complete."

"Okay Dad. The lessons at school are boring, but I don't want to leave Mary behind if I jump a grade. This way I can learn something interesting and still stay with Mary."

That night in bed, Jenn and I discussed Angel's obvious problem of wanting to stay with Mary while her lessons were too simple to hold her interest. We decided to wait until the end of the school year before discussing it with the school principal.

The next morning we took little Barbara's painting of Angel with us to work. Connie followed us into our office and watched as we unwrapped it. When I propped it on our desk and stepped away, Connie inhaled audibly in surprise and awe. We looked at her and saw her close her mouth and slowly exhale, while gripping a chair back for support.

"Wow! That picture has power. It draws you right into Angel's smile. Is that another of Barbara's paintings?"

Jenn answered. "Yes, I think it's her best work yet. Please call Clarence's secretary and let him know we have another of Barbara's paintings to discuss with him."

Minutes later, Clarence hurried into our office and seeing the painting propped up facing away from him, he looked at us and asked, "Is this it?"

At our nod, he joined us where he could observe it with full light from the windows on it. His eyes widened and he took a hesitant step toward the painting before stopping. He gazed upon the painting a full minute, before turning to us.

"She's outdone herself with this one. What do you want done with it, surely you don't want to sell it?"

I buzzed Connie to hold all calls, then shut the door and gestured toward our small conference area. Clarence tore his eyes away from the painting and joined us. We told him about our trip to Coffeyville to view the painting and what happened, including the message to loan the painting to The Nelson-Atkins Museum of Art in Kansas City.

"I wonder what the intention is for placing it there?" Clarence said with a raised eyebrow.

"It's not clear, but can you do it? We must have the stipulation that if the painting is ever taken down from viewing that it comes back to Angel."

"That means to you and Jenn until she becomes of age. I can do it, but what is going to be the draw for people to go view it?"

Jenn looked at me with a question in her eyes, before we both nodded our heads in unspoken agreement. "This is a secret that Jenn and I have kept for several years now. Angel has the ability to heal and we think this is going to become known in a very public way soon."

Clarence looked at them with his mouth open in surprise. "Oh my! You two and Angel are going to be very famous. How can the firm help you survive the publicity and demands from the sick?"

Jenn spoke up. "We'll need the expert advice from a good PR firm, but not until after Angel becomes public. I'm not sure yet, but this painting has some direct relationship with Angel's healing power. To reach the masses there has to be a method Angel can use other than direct contact between her and patients."

Clarence looked at us for a moment considering. "You're going to have a security problem too. Just think of the nuts out there and the desperate people who will want to get close to Angel. Your apartment is isolated at the top of your building, but you will still need security to keep people away from your front door. There is one other penthouse apartment on your floor. Is it occupied? If not, buy it and lock down the elevator to only accept a key code, and then have security at the elevator doors on your floor."

We discussed several other items including whether to notify the

Board at this time. Clarence considered it and then shook his head. "Many would think you were nuts and then there is the problem of the news media getting word of Angel's healing powers. George needs to know and I can vouch for you. Stay here and I'll go and get him and bring him back here."

When Clarence left I said, "I had no idea that this was going to be so complicated and we haven't even started yet."

It was over forty minutes before Clarence and George arrived. George looked at us with new understanding of our background as he said, "Clarence has brought me up to date on your situation. Can I look at this painting of Angel?"

We all walked around our desk to a better viewing angle and George had his first look at the painting. His reaction was similar to Clarence's, except he stood still in surprised shock, before walking to the painting and touching the canvas. When he touched the painting he stiffened for a moment, then collapsed to the floor.

I checked his pulse, which was strong, and he appeared to be breathing normal. I looked at the others and said, "He looks fine, I think he just fainted."

Connie rushed in and hearing what I had said, returned to her desk and retrieved smelling salts, which she waved under his nose, getting immediate results. George looked up at us in confusion and asked, "What happened?"

I answered. "We think you fainted when you touched the painting."

We helped him into a chair and he asked, "Connie, call home and tell Marilyn to come get me. Shut the door behind you as I need to discuss something in private."

After Connie left, George asked for a little help to the conference area where we all sat. "When I touched the painting I had a vision. It was your sister, Barbara, the one in the large painting above your mantel. She told me I had a heart problem that Angel corrected by my touching her painting. I knew of the problem and I'm going to see my doctor soon to see if there's been a change in my condition. I'm sure something's changed because of how I feel, and now I'm a believer. Let me know how I can help when Angel goes public. I need to get to my office now and make some arrangements with my doctor."

After George left our office I asked Clarence, "Should we wait until Angel's healing powers are made public, or go ahead with displaying it in the museum?"

"I have a friend on the museum's board. Let me ask her about getting it put on display. I know I could after Angel's gift becomes public."

We thanked Clarence and I called our leasing agent to ask about the other penthouse on our floor. The agent said that it was coming up for lease next week and was vacant. After making a verbal commitment I asked that the elevator serving our floor be adjusted with a key pad lockout. They asked that we stop by the lease office to sign the lease agreement and talk about the lockout.

We met the school bus at the apartment buildings street entrance and took Angel with us to the lease office. After signing the lease we were told that the elevator already had that option and gave us a key and instructions on how to make it work. I asked, "How many keys are there?"

"Just two. You have one and the office has another in case of fire. The key option hasn't been used before, so no other keys have been made."

"What if your office was broken into and the key stolen? I would like a touch pad installed as well to avoid that possibility."

"We still need the code available for the fire department, so that would still be a problem."

I looked at Jenn for help. "We could install a video camera in the elevator that would require an outside viewer to allow the elevator to proceed to the penthouse. That means we will need security 24/7 to man the station."

"Okay, we'll leave it as it is for now. Later, we may need to make changes."

We activated the lockout when we returned to our apartment floor, and checked out the other penthouse. It was similar in layout to our own, but our view of the Plaza was better. We discussed using it as an office to support Angel at some future time, but at this time we agreed that it would remain vacant.

The next day we had a dozen keys made to give to various family members who visited us and to others as the need arose. We also arranged to have the fire escape penthouse door disabled so that it only opened going down. The fire department had a device to open it if needed. We also arranged to have a security station constructed facing the elevator and fire door. We would wait on installing the video camera and hiring security until needed.

Later that week, Clarence informed us that Angel's painting was on display at The Nelson-Atkins Museum of Art, and would receive a small spread in this Sunday's *Kansas City Star* edition.

That Friday, Jenn and I were putting the finishing touches on our planned defense of a case going to trial the next week, when Connie rushed into our office. "Quick, turn on your TV! There's a news bulletin about a school bus accident from Angel's school."

The live feed from the scene news commentator was a young woman who appeared to be shaken as her face came on the screen. "Information is sketchy, but a large dump truck ran a stop light and hit a school bus carrying over twenty students and adults from the Horace Mann Elementary School. At this time we don't have any information on injuries, but two ambulances have already departed to hospitals."

The TV camera panned to the accident site showing the school bus on its side, with its rear crushed where it was struck by the truck. Jenn and I looked at each other in panic until I caught sight of a street sign on the screen. "I know where that is! Jenn, let's go there and check if Angel's alright."

Ten minutes later the cab dropped us off at a police barricade and we hurried to the scene of the wreck. We saw a group of children sitting on the grass near the accident, so we headed there in hope of finding Angel. Jenn spotted Mary and stooped down and asked, "Mary, are you hurt?"

She looked at Jenn and her eyes cleared as she recognized her. "Ooh Mrs. Pearson! It was so terrible. Angel and I were sitting together, when we were covered in something white and there was this loud crashing noise. We were tossed around for a bit, then I could see a big white bird releasing us. Angel looked at the bird and thanked it, then I realized the bird was an angel. Angel helped me out of the bus and told me to help others to come here."

"Where's Angel?"

"She went back to help the others." Then looking up, said, "There she is now coming out of the bus."

We hurried over and helped Angel get through the torn metal and broken glass. She was covered in blood, but none of it appeared to be hers as we checked for wounds. Angel said, "I'm okay. The blood is from the other kids I went back to help."

With tears in her eyes, she said, "Mommy, I couldn't help everyone I found. Some had already died. I fixed a bunch of kids. One, I even reattached a arm. I hope it works alright, it felt right when I got done."

I picked her up and carried her over to the other group of kids. Angel wouldn't let go of my neck, so I sat down with her in my lap and Jenn sat next to us holding her hand. An EMT came by and seeing all the blood on Angel, asked, "Is she hurt?"

"No, she's fine. It's not her blood."

He looked at us in doubt, but continued on searching for more victims. The TV commentator we had seen earlier, came up to our group and asked if she could interview us. I looked at Jenn, who nodded her head. As the camera crew set up, Mary sat as close as she could to Angel.

The interview started with the announcers introduction, "This Alice Tompkins from the site of the school bus accident with several of the survivors."

The camera centered on Jenn and me holding blood splotched Angel. We were all sober faced as Tompkins asked, "Who are you and how did you get here?"

"We are Jack and Jennifer Pearson and this is our daughter, Angel. We saw your earlier broadcast and hurried here looking for Angel. This is Mary, her best friend, who was sitting next to her when the accident happened."

"Mary, how is it that you don't have any blood on you, while Angel is covered in it?"

"Angel helped me off the bus and then went back to help others."

Tompkins looked at Angel in surprise, then asked, "Were you able to help anyone when you went back inside?"

Angel looked at us and asked, "Should I tell her?"

I nodded my head and said, "Yes, it's okay to tell her."

Angel looked into the camera and smiled. It was the smile from the painting and it mesmerized the TV audience. "I don't remember the exact number I helped, but I concentrated on those who were gushing blood that I stopped, and healed the wounds. I reattached Bobby's arm and I think it's okay, but I'm not sure. I couldn't save everyone I found because some were already dead."

Tompkins took a big breath before saying, "Are you a healer?"

Angel gave her the smile again and replied, "Yes, I've healed before."

Mary spoke up. "She healed a gash on my head about two years ago and you can't even tell I was cut." She then pulled her hair away from her forehead. "See, nothing is there."

Jasper, one of the children sitting nearby, said, "I saw her work on three kids before I left the bus."

Two more children spoke up and verified that she did heal other children in their presence. Tompkins gave her call sign and ended the interview. She then looked at us considering. "I want another in-depth interview with you at the station. If I can arrange it, will you be open to such an interview?"

"We are both attorneys, so we will have to work around prior commitments. If we can agree upon a time we will be happy to meet with you. If I were you, I'd interview all the people here and the hospital to see what they can remember of the accident."

Jenn and I went to a policeman, gave him our name, Angel's, and Mary's, telling him we were taking the girls home. He asked for our IDs and then released us. On the way to our apartment Jenn called our office and told Connie to tell Alice Ortega that we had her daughter at our apartment and she was unhurt. Once home, Jenn took Angel to the bathroom and gave her a shower and then a good soak in the tub. I stuffed Angel's blood soaked clothes in a plastic bag, saving them for a future need.

I stayed with Mary and kept her occupied watching TV until Angel could join her. Alice Ortega knocked on our door soon after and entering the apartment she first checked on Mary's condition before asking me what happened.

After hearing the story, she replied, "Oh my. Please thank Angel, and thank you for taking her away from that awful wreck and bringing her home with you." They soon left to return to their home.

Later that evening we watched the late news to see what the fallout would be from the interview. We watched a replay of our interview with Tompkins and at its end, she said, "This station is in the process of arranging another interview with the Pearson family along with testimony from eyewitnesses. If anyone has information about this amazing occurrence, please notify this station."

Turning off the TV, I said, "I'm glad there's no school tomorrow, but we're going to have to make a decision about sending her to school Monday."

Jenn hugged me, her head on my chest. "Let's not think about it tonight. My mind is overloaded and we have so much to do tomorrow, and I still need to call home and tell my family what happened today."

We were awakened the following morning by our telephone. I looked at the time and groaned. It was five a.m. on Saturday, who would be calling us now? I let voice mail pick it up and headed toward the shower with Jenn following close behind. Later, after coffee was on, I checked to see who had called. The message was from the TV station, so I returned their call.

They wanted us at the station at ten this morning for a follow-up interview, which I agreed to attend. Jenn entered the kitchen as I disconnected my cell and asked who I was talking to?

"The TV station wants us there at ten, so we can have a nice breakfast and time to read the morning paper. When should we get Angel up?"

Jenn looked at the time and said, "Not for another hour. I checked on her and she slept well last night since I didn't hear her screaming from nightmares."

"If it had been me I wouldn't have slept a wink." I said.

Later, after Jenn and I finished breakfast, she went to wake up our daughter. I was watching the morning news and found that our interview at the wreck site had been picked up by the major networks. So far, the news people were only reporting facts and not their personal views.

We arrived at the TV station and were seated in an interview room with George Freeman, the station manager, who wanted our background history. After giving him the information he asked for, he read through it and looked up at us.

"Are you the two attorneys who were stalked by that crazy woman in the U.S. Attorney's Office?"

I replied, "Yes, that was a long time ago. You must have a good memory."

Freeman nodded. "If I remember the story right, two local detectives were killed by her."

"No, but that was close. She put out a bounty for Jenn and me, and for Mary Cullen. Her partner was killed while trying to protect her."

Freeman's face cleared, as he said, "Yes, I remember now. You left the U.S. Attorney's after that and you both now work at Phelps, Phelps and Woodruff. Is that right?"

Jenn and I agreed, and he picked up another piece of paper and did a double take. "You and your wife were in the news about a painting you own that created a stir. What was that about?"

Jenn answered. "We are the financial guardian of Barbara Messing, who is being raised by my parents. Barbara is now an accomplished artist in both water color and oils. The news article you are referring to was the display of her water color paintings by Clarence Woodruff at the annual Art Festival held at the Crown Plaza. We own a self portrait by her and a similar oil self portrait by my deceased sister, Barbara Powers, that we loaned to Clarence. Together, these paintings created quite a stir at the Festival."

"You know Clarence Woodruff?"

"Yes, he is a senior partner at our firm."

"I remember now, the two Barbara self-portraits. One of a little girl and the other a beautiful woman. You say the girl is now an accomplished artist?"

I answered. "Her most recent painting is shown at The Nelson-Atkins Museum of Art and is our family portrait. It's quite good if you care to see it."

Freeman looked at me intently for a moment. He then picked up a phone and said, "Take a crew over to the Nelson Art Museum and cover the exhibit of a new painting by Barbara Messing. Anything else before we start the interview?"

I smiled and shook my head while Freeman left the room calling for Tompkins to get in here and start the interview.

Alice Tompkins started the interview by asking Angel, "Mary Ortega and at least two other children saw you and Mary being protected by a woman with wings who was a brilliant white color. Is that true?"

"Yes. Dad told me she is our Guardian Angel and her name is Olivia."

"Had you ever seen her before?"

"No, but I've seen and talked to Barbara."

"Barbara. Who is Barbara?"

"My Aunt who died. She's in her painting above our mantel."

"You've talked to her? Do you mean you hear her in your head or she stands before you and carries on a conversation?"

"She comes out of the painting and stands in front of me and we talk."

"Can you tell me what you talk about?"

"She's my Aunt and she loves me very much, which she tells me. Sometimes she tells me things that are going to happen or that I can do. She told me once that I could heal people, but that I should only do it if they were in danger of dying. I did it once before with Mary, my best friend. She was bleeding so bad that I fixed her head. My friends on the bus were dying from losing so much blood, so I helped them. Did Bobby's arm work after I reattached it? I never did that before, but it felt right."

"I checked on Bobby Mann and he says his arm works as good as before. He only has a faint line around his arm now and he says it's getting fainter. I pieced together from your classmates that you kept ten children and one adult from bleeding to death. It's no wonder that you were covered in their blood."

Angel looked at Tompkins with a tear sliding down her cheek. "I couldn't save everyone that needed it. Elizabeth was already dead when I reached her, and Billy J. died just as I touched him. There just wasn't any energy left in his body."

Tompkins looked at Jenn and I and asked, "Why did you name your daughter Angel?"

I replied, "When I first held her in my arms, Jenn said she was her little angel. We decided then, that was her name. We thought she might have trouble with that name at school, but with our background we thought she could handle it."

"Angel said that your family had a Guardian Angel...named Olivia. How did that come about?"

"Olivia came to me when I was ten and saved my life in a car wreck which left me a orphan. I was raised by my paternal Grandmother and didn't have any further interactions with Olivia until I started college. She informed me that I had a purposeful life ahead of me and her job was to ensure that I was not harmed. She also taught me Judo to protect myself from non-lethal attacks. Later, she has acted against evil people several times in my defense, and she included Jenn and Angel under her protection."

"Your Guardian Angel killed others to protect you?"

"Yes, not long ago four men who broke into our apartment trying to harm us."

"I take it that a Guardian Angel takes no prisoners?"

"Do you remember your Sunday school lessons about the wrath of God?"

Tompkins face paled as she replied, "You mean like a lightning strike from heaven?"

"Yes, she points her sword at her target and fire is released until only a husk remains. You don't mess with a Guardian Angel."

"Do you have any plans for Angel to be made available to heal people?"

"Not at this time. We've discovered that a family painting of us has healing properties, if touched. I'm thinking of making small copies of that painting with the idea of distributing them to the public if the copies also work. However, that may be wishful thinking on my part. Angel can't reach many people personally and we wouldn't want her to. She's just a little girl and deserves a life of her own."

Tompkins brought the interview to a close and taking her mic and ear piece off, she went over and hugged Angel. "I think you are the most selfless person I've ever met, and I want to thank you for saving all those people in the bus. I wish you and your family all the happiness you can arrange for yourselves in the coming years."

CHAPTER TWENTY-SEVEN

Before heading home, we went to a Chucky Cheese as it was a favorite of Angel's. We had a good time watching Angel interact with the other children as we ate our pizza. When we entered our apartment building, the security firm we had engaged were making a change in the lockout device for our floor and installing a wireless video camera. The workers rode with us on the elevator to our floor, where we found two security officers behind their desk. We showed them our IDs, and they took our pictures for future reference.

Angel and Jenn went to the breakfast bar and started looking over the catalogs of on-line computer courses available. We were considering home schooling for Angel, but wanted to first see what was available. Until we came to a decision she could go to the office with us and study in the conference area. Angel was now too old for the in-house daycare.

Jenn and I started the paperwork for the establishment of a nonprofit organization we named the Angel Foundation. The mailing of the small photos was going to be under its heading.

That evening we all sat down before the TV to watch our interview. Jenn made popcorn to get us into the mood. We watched Angel's reaction to the questions and her responses, deciding that it seemed to have gone well. After the interview, the news program showed a busy scene at The Nelson-Atkins Museum of Art, where

Barbara's painting of Angel and us was being exhibited. There was a long line of people waiting to see it, some on crutches and in wheelchairs. The reporter said that several viewers of the painting had collapsed when they touched it and the museum now required an EMT to be present. Those viewers with medical problems who touched the painting seemed to have been cured, but they all said they were going to check with their doctors to be certain.

"Monday, I'm going to try to get billfold sized pictures made of Barbara's painting of Angel. I'm sure the Museum will have to limit access to the painting and if we hand out the small pictures, maybe that will fill the demand." I said.

Jenn nodded, but then grimaced. "I foresee a black market for those pictures, at least at first. Everyone who has a serious illness will want one and until they are widely distributed, someone is going to try to take advantage of it. Assuming you only charge a dollar to cover costs, they could be resold for hundreds or maybe even thousands of dollars."

"I can think of one way to counter that. We can have Angel say that if anyone paid more than a dollar for the picture, then the healing power would not work."

Jenn looked at me and smiled. "I bet if we talked to Barbara, then she would arrange for that to happen."

"First we need to see if a photo I took of the painting will have healing powers. I'll print out ten on the computer and take them to the Museum tomorrow to hand out to those with obvious disabilities and see what happens. If it works we'll do a mass mailing to people who write in to us, and to those who visit the painting."

Jenn laughed as my mood rubbed off on her. "We will have to hire people to do that, unless we can get some church members to volunteer. That means we need to take Angel around to the various church's in the city to get them behind this effort. Let's start with our church tomorrow and try to get Reverend Black on our side."

"Let's not blind-side him. We better call him today and ask for his help. I'm sure he has seen the news of Angel by now and will be wondering why we haven't contacted him. Do you want me to, or would you rather call and talk to him.?"

Jenn shook her head and then said, "I'll call. The woman always get the job men don't want."

She dug out last Sunday's church program and found his

telephone number. Jenn then took a deep breath centering herself before punching in the numbers. When it was answered, Jenn asked, "Reverend Black?"

When he said yes, she said, "This is Jennifer Pearson, Angel Pearson's mother, the girl on the news. Jack and I would like to ask your help in a project that would benefit the sick and injured of Kansas City. It involves Angel's healing ability and how we can best reach the maximum number of people. We aren't interested in lining our own pockets, but need to charge a small fee to cover costs. To keep costs low we were thinking of asking for volunteers from the church."

Reverend Black thought before he answered. "Mrs. Pearson, I don't believe that you are trying to scam us, but to settle any doubt would you consider having Angel do a demonstration tomorrow during services and if everything works out I'll let you ask my congregation for help. Is that satisfactory?"

"That's great. We will see you at church."

Jenn turned to me and said, "He wants to see Angel perform before letting us ask for help."

"Did he seem to think Angel faked it?"

"I'm not sure. We'll know better after tomorrow."

The next morning at church we were told to sit closer to the front. When the services were about to start I looked around the church, trying to gage if the congregation knew we were present and what their attitude might be. Reverend Black took his place at the pulpit and waited until the music stopped.

Before speaking he looked out over his flock solemnly before saying, "We live in difficult and wondrous times. The local news reports that we have been visited by a Guardian Angel. An angel sent to protect one of our own parishioners, Angel Pearson, the young daughter of Jack and Jennifer Pearson. Even her name brings to mind her divine purpose here on earth. Witnesses have attested to her ability to heal wounds and illness by touch alone. This has got to be at the behest of our God and Savior. No one else could have given her these powers."

Reverend Black left the podium and walked to the center of the stage and bowed his head. "I have a confession to make to you all. I have stage four cancer and have only a short time left here. At first I was lost and doubted my faith until I asked God, why me? Today we

187

will witness God's power and the reason I was inflicted with this deadly disease."

Reverend Black looked down at Jenn and me and asked, "Would you bring Angel up here before us and demonstrate to everyone her healing powers?"

Jenn asked Angel, "Honey, do you think you can heal Reverend Black?"

Without a word, Angel stood and started walking toward Reverend Black, while Jenn and I hurried after her. The church was so silent that you could hear our footsteps on the carpet. Before she reached Reverend Black I stopped Angel and asked her to wait until Jenn and I could support the reverend in case he should faint when she touched him. She nodded her head and waited until we each held one of his arms. Angel then gave Reverend Black her special smile that seemed to brighten the room, and then touched him.

Reverend Black stiffened in our hands and we each felt a slight shock. He wavered a little, but soon regained his balance and said, "I think I'm alright now. Jennifer would you bring that chair over here and I'll sit on it."

After he sat down he raised his hands and said, "It's a miracle! I'm cured of this pestilence that had been in my body. When I was touched by Angel, a angel appeared before me and told me I was cured. If anyone had any doubts about her healing abilities, you can now set them to rest."

The congregation shouted, "Hallelujah! Hallelujah! The Lord has spoken!"

There were several screams of passion from the congregation, followed by fainting women and general confusion. During all this, Jenn and I helped Reverend Black back to his pulpit, where he tried to bring order again to the congregation. When quiet was restored, he said, "I want Jack and Jennifer Pearson to speak to you about their plans for Angel to bring healing to everyone who needs it."

Jenn and I helped Reverend Black to his chair and then we stood before the mike. We took turns telling the story of Angel's abilities and how a painting of her at the local Nelson-Atkins Museum of Art was healing people who touched it. We continued with the idea that a photograph of that painting might also have healing powers and if so, we planned on selling them for a small fee to anyone who wrote in for them. To save on expenses we planned on asking for volunteers from the congregation and other church members in the Kansas City area to respond to these requests.

"If anyone is interested we'll accept anyone from eighteen to eighty, and if you are in ill health you will get a free picture."

Reverend Black took our place at the pulpit and we sat on the stage steps with Angel, facing the congregation. After fifteen minutes the noise of people talking to each other died down and Reverend Black called for their attention.

"If anyone is interested in volunteering, leave your name and telephone number at the front door as you leave, so that you can be contacted."

Before leaving the church I gave Reverend Black my card and told him to mail the names of the volunteers to my office. We then headed for a restaurant we liked before we went to the Art Museum.

After finishing lunch we found the Art Museum parking lot almost full. We went to the Museum's office to see if there was anyone we could talk to. Mary Beth Boyles, the Museum's Curator, was there because of the huge crowd waiting to see Angel's painting. When we walked into her office, she came forward to meet us with a stressful smile on her face. "Mr. and Mrs. Pearson, and Angel. Just the people I wanted to talk to. We aren't equipped to handle such large crowds as we are receiving to view and touch the painting of Angel. I was hoping that we could come up with an alternate method of viewing."

I told her of our plans to sell billfold-sized photographs of the painting and keep the painting out of reach of the viewers. This would hinge on whether the photos actually had healing powers, which I was going to test today. Mary Beth smiled, "You know, I think that will solve my problem. I'll go with you while you test your theory."

When we arrived at the painting, we saw two lines. One for the ill that could touch the picture frame, and one further back for viewing only. I went to where the line split between touching and viewing and started to hand out copies of the photograph of the painting to the ill. The first person I handed a copy to was using crutches and he stiffened as though he was being shocked and grabbed me for support, while dropping his crutches. He looked at me in surprise, then when recognizing me as Angel's father, started sobbing. Then looking down at his legs, he said, "I'm cured! I can feel my legs again.

Glory be, I can feel my legs!"

Museum security helped him move to the side and I gave another copy to a little girl in a wheelchair with the same results. I continued handing out the photos until they were all gone, but Angel continued down the waiting line touching everyone who needed her help until we were out the door.

I turned to Mary Beth and said, "As soon as I get a supply of photos to hand out I'll get them here. What were you charging people who wanted to touch the painting?"

"Five dollars plus the normal entry fee."

"When you get the copies, sell them for one dollar extra where they pay the entry fee. You can still use the painting as a draw to the museum, but Angel's Foundation will get the dollar to offset expenses. Move the painting to a wall out of reach of viewers when you start selling the copies. I'll make sure that the Museum gets publicity that they are the sole distributor outside of direct mail."

We returned home to make plans for the next day. I called George and told him we were taking tomorrow off to work on a project for Angel, but would be ready for our Wednesday court case. Jenn was going to take Angel to school Monday and make arrangements for her to be home-schooled, while I took care of making copies of the painting. I also needed a supervisor to handle the direct mailing, and arrange for church volunteers.

The next morning while Jenn was getting Angel ready for school, I was checking the yellow pages for a place to make the photo copies of Angel's painting. I made a list and called each business for a comparison on prices, settling on one whose location wasn't very far from the apartment.

Later that day Jenn returned from the school with Angel and the study requirements for the remainder of the school year. I was on number six on my calls to local churches and so far no one was turning my request down cold, and said they would mention my request at the next service. I was calling all Christian churches and Jewish temples. They all believed in God and his miracles.

I called George and asked him if he knew of anyone who would be interested in supervising a bunch of volunteer church members collecting money and sending out photos of Angel's painting. He replied, "How about Marilyn? She does volunteer work and I can ask her."

"This is going to be a lot of work and may involve supervising ten to twenty people. We need to keep track of who we send the photos to and be able to program the addresses for printing on the return envelopes, so some computer skills will be necessary. I was thinking of using the other penthouse as our work office, what do you think?"

"How are you going to get the volunteers past your security."

"I'll have them come by the office and I'll give them a special badge to use when they arrive at the penthouse. I hope the mailing will start slow so we can learn as we go."

Later, while taking a break from my calls to local churches, Marilyn called me. "Jack, George told me what you plan on doing and I'd be happy to work with you. I've done mailings before and I'm sure I can be of help. How much are you asking for the photographs?"

"One dollar. Do you think that's going to enough?"

"How much is the unit cost of the picture?"

"Twelve cents. I could have gotten them a little cheaper, but I wanted them laminated."

"The cost of mailing has gone up even using the bulk mail rate, and with the cost of envelopes would eat up over 50 cents. We also need a mailing machine, computer, and a printer to address the envelopes. In addition, we also need work tables, furniture, break room refreshments, and other incidentals that will bring the unit cost to over a dollar. Two dollars should be enough of a cushion to cover unexpected costs."

"Okay, I can keep the charge of a dollar at the Museum, since the extra costs only apply to those we mail. Would you and George stop by and look at the penthouse I plan on using for a workplace?"

"I'll talk to George and get back with you on when we can come over. Talk to you later."

CHAPTER TWENTY-EIGHT

I told Jenn that Marilyn agreed to supervise the mailing operation and why I had to up the price to two dollars for the photos we were going to mail. "Marilyn said she'd call back and tell us when she and George would come over to inspect the other penthouse."

Jenn came over and gave me a hug. "It's starting to come together. It's good Marilyn has had prior experience. That takes a load off my mind now that I won't have to worry about that part of the operation. I've looked at Angel's school requirements for the next two years and I feel confident that she can jump at least one grade. The principal said to bring her in this fall and see how she tests out."

"How is she absorbing all this attention her powers of healing has brought her?" I asked.

"She appears to well grounded and the news reports about her have pretty much ended, at least for now. She's handling it like a little trooper, nothing seems to faze her. If it was me, I don't think I could have done it."

"What is she doing now?"

"She's looking over what she is expected to learn before testing next fall."

"Does she appear overwhelmed, or just curious?"

"When I left her she asked me if she could study what she was interested in when she finished these requirements. So, no she's not overwhelmed. If anything, I think we have a very intelligent little girl who's going to breeze through the requirements so she can do what she wants to do. Let's monitor what she is striving toward, so that we can guide her if it becomes necessary."

The next week was busy for the two of us. We had a trial to win for our client; its outcome was as we expected. What was unexpected was the media attention we received because of Angel and our publicity from our interviews on TV. The two days of court were packed with the media and other viewers. The judge limited the media's number to no more than five after the lunch break the first day of the trial, allowing more of the public to attend.

Angel's presence at the office was too distracting for us, the other attorneys, and for her. Jenn started interviewing for a nanny to stay with her in the apartment. Angel was helpful as we watched how she reacted to each prospective nanny we interviewed. The third applicant, Alicia Bishop, was young for a nanny. She was in her late twenties and attending night classes, trying to finish up for a degree in teaching. She met our criteria, so we had her sit with Angel and watched them interact.

Alicia sat down across from Angel in the conference area and asked. "What are you studying?"

Angel gave Alicia her special smile, which brought a smile to her face. "I'm doing a reading assignment. It's Tom Sawyer, by Mark Twain. The book assigned me was too easy, so Mom thought I would like this."

"Do you have a problem with the language Tom uses when he speaks to his friends?"

"It was strange at first, but that was how they talked to each other in that time and place."

"What did you think of Becky's character? Could you identify with her in any way?

"You mean because she's a girl or because she's of a higher class of people in Hannibal?"

"Either, or maybe you picture yourself as Tom or Huck. Living to have fun on the river?"

"I think it's interesting to see how the various characters interact with each other. How they care for one another and try to help when they can. The bad characters are there to show what not to be, and how good overcomes evil."

Jenn and I sat with them and Jenn asked, "Angel, do you think Alicia would be a good person to have as your nanny?"

Angel stood and then sat next to Alicia, and took her left hand in both of hers. She looked into her eyes and gave her a small smile. "Yes, Alicia is a good person and she can help me with my studies."

I asked, "Will you be available week days from eight to six and do you have any questions relating to your work requirements?"

"How much is the job going to pay?"

"Until we see how you and Angel interact, you'll start at Ten dollars an hour for the first eight hours, then twelve for anything over that. Sometimes we run late and some days we might have you come in early. Is this going to be a problem?"

"No. However, I have a question. I've seen Angel and you on TV. What happens if you two and Angel have an interview during the hours I'm supposed to be with her? Will I need to go home or stay here?"

"You can stay here until we return, work on your studies and continue to be paid. You will have full access to the food and drink here. Leave a list of what you like and we will try to be accommodating. The same goes for any future needs. If there's nothing else, we expect you at eight Monday morning. I need to take your picture, so that you can get through security when you arrive for the first time."

Alicia looked at us in surprise. "Security? Oh, because of Angel. Okay, that's understandable."

* * *

Monday morning, Alicia arrived early at 7:45 and I let her into the apartment after I checked the video monitor. Once inside, I showed her the security monitor, in case someone should ring for entry. "Don't open for anyone without first checking with me, unless it's security, police, or firemen. You can talk to people outside by holding down on this button."

I led her into the living room where Alicia stopped as her eyes were caught by the two Barbara paintings. "Ooh my. I remember reading about these paintings. The larger one is Mrs. Pearson's sister?"

"Yes, and the other is by Barbara Messing in the same style. Their works are now both highly sought after."

"The older Barbara is very beautiful and the girl resembles her."

I took Alicia through the house and showed her Angel's room and the spare bedroom we had turned into a study area for her. Jenn and Angel joined us and Alicia took Angel's hand and asked her to show her around, while we left for work.

Later that morning, I called Alice Tomkins at the TV station and explained what I wanted to do about mailing out pictures of Angel to people in need of healing. I asked if she would include a notification on the news. She took the information down and said she would get back with me today. I then faxed the same notification to the *Kansas City Star.*

An hour later, I received a call from the *Star* asking for an interview and a picture of the three of us for a full page spread. I got Jenn's attention and told her what they wanted and she agreed. I arranged to meet them in the lobby of our apartment building at noon. I then called Alicia and told her what was going to happen and suggested she fix lunch before or after we left.

Alice Tomkins said that the station would air my notification at the evening broadcast. I thanked her and told her the *Kansas City Star* was also going to run a piece soon. I then started calling the churches and temples again asking if anyone had volunteered to help in the mailings. I received a total of sixty-four volunteers, which I had Connie transcribe to a single page in alphabetical order, showing which church or temple they were coming from. I gave a copy to George so that he could give it to Marilyn later, and to tell her to watch the news tonight and the *Kansas City Star* for our announcement.

We arrived at our apartment building a little early, but the *Star* reporter and photographer were waiting on us. When we got on the elevator and pushed the button for the penthouse, I gave the prearranged signal to the camera monitored by my security. When we stepped off the elevator, security took their pictures before we continued on to our apartment. I pushed the numbers for the entry code, and if you were listening closely you could have heard the four bolts sliding back into the frame as the lock disengaged.

I opened the door and Jenn led the two into our apartment, while I followed. Jenn introduced the two reporters to Angel and Alicia, before asking where they wanted the picture taken. They both stopped in front of the two Barbara's and after looking at each other, one said, "We want the paintings as background, so stand there."

We wound up having the same pose as Barbara Messing's painting, except this one had the paintings as background. They took another picture with only Angel before starting the interview. Before we finished, I said, "I had a fear of profiteering from the sale of the photos and wanted everyone to know that if a person paid more than two dollars for their copy of the painting, then it wouldn't have healing powers. They should then tell the police where they had purchased the copy."

The reporter asked, "How does that work?"

Jenn spoke up. "God knows how much you paid for it and he is the one who is channeling the healing power. The price is low to cover our costs and so everyone can afford to pay for a copy. If there is profiteering or fraud involved, then the healing will not work. We have asked the local churches and temples for volunteers and we will start calling them in by alphabetical order when we need them. This is how we can keep the price low. Any extra monies we receive will be given to the churches and temples we receive volunteers from."

"Is healing going to continue at The Nelson-Atkins Museum of Art?"

"Yes. However, that is going to change somewhat. The painting will continue to be available for viewing, but not for touching. A copy of the painting can be purchased for one dollar at the ticket counter. The price is less because our costs are less for this venue."

After the reporters left the apartment, Jenn and I checked with Alicia on how her first day with Angel was going. "I did a quick testing of the topics she was going to need to study and found her only weak area was writing. I thought I would concentrate on that this afternoon."

Jenn asked Angel, "Are you and Alicia having fun together?"

"No, but I like her and she is helping me with my studies, and she knows a lot about different things. Did you know she went to Paris and knows a little French?"

We left the apartment and picked up the first batch of 40,000 laminated photos on our way back to the office. We planned on leaving 10,000 photos at the Museum on our way home that evening. Marilyn had already arranged to have portable worktables and other equipment delivered to our penthouse office. The U.S. Postal Service had furnished mail trays and would start pickup when we were ready.

CHAPTER TWENTY-NINE

The TV and *Star* news coverage looked good about the availability of the painting copies that would have the same healing powers as the original. Now we would wait and see what the response would be. Wednesday we got our first indication of the demand, when the museum called and said they had sold over half the photos and needed more. I called our supplier and ordered another 100,000 copies ASAP, and where to deliver them.

The next morning the postal service delivered three bags of mail to the penthouse office. I called Marilyn to tell her the mail had arrived and she needed to start work with her volunteers. That evening when we returned to our apartment, Marilyn had just released her crew from work for the day and they were waiting for the elevator when we stepped off.

Marilyn was still in the office making determinations on what remained to be done and who to call tomorrow. She looked up when we entered the apartment. "Wow! That was something. I had to call the supplier to deliver what photos he finished because I thought we were going to run out. We had 1,000 left of our original supply when we finished that first batch, and the supplier delivered 50,000 more this afternoon. You better call him and tell him to deliver that much every day until you tell him different."

I smiled at Jenn. "I guess our little enterprise is going to be successful. Marilyn, how did your volunteers work out for you?"

"I called in ten, some I had worked with before, which helped. By the end of the day we had a system established and those ten trays of mail will be picked up in the morning when they deliver more for us. We need to ask for more trays, at least three times what we have now. I'll bring in more volunteers tomorrow, whether we need them or not, so that they can be trained for replacements."

I said, "Keep track of the numbers from each church who volunteer, so we can donate any excess funds to their church or temple according to how many volunteers they send. How are the refreshments holding out for them?"

"They expressed a desire for tea and hot chocolate, in addition to the coffee you had. Something sweet was also mentioned, and we need to furnish lunch for them. We can have it delivered, so that shouldn't be a problem."

"How about you? How are you holding up on this first day?"

"I need to train a permanent second in command, so I can get away from this sometimes. I'm enjoying being in charge of this operation. By the way, here's the first day's receipts." Marilyn said as she handed me a large bank bag.

I lifted the bag and smiled, then said, "I better run this across the street to the bank branch before it gets any later. I'll see you tomorrow."

I soon returned to the apartment and found Angel recounting her day to her mother, but when I entered the room she ran to me and jumped into my arms. "Daddy, I learned some French today and tomorrow Alicia said she would teach me some Spanish. I finished the whole book of writing assignments and will start on geography next."

I complimented her on how well she was doing and said to Jenn, "It looks like we should increase Alicia's pay. She's doing far more than nanny duties."

Jenn considered. "You're right. When she gets here tomorrow let's tell her we're going to double her salary. I thought we were paying her too little anyway."

"Daddy, what are you going to fix us for dinner?"

"How about chicken and pasta?"

"Can I make the salad?" Angel replied.

"Why don't you and your mother do that and if you do a good

job, that'll be your job from now on when we have a salad."

"Oh goody. Mommy, hurry up and get changed so we can get started."

Angel Foundation's healing project had been in operation one month and seemed to have settled down to an average of 32,000 daily requests for mail delivery and 5,000 in sales at the museum, or almost $70,000 a day. The Foundation had been approved as a non-profit organization and its profits were not taxed. We hired a local CPA firm to maintain its financial records. Marilyn had trained all the volunteers from the various churches and temples and had set up a schedule where they each worked two consecutive days a week.

Marilyn now had two supervisors trained, which meant she only came in to the office on a spot basis or when one of the other supervisors couldn't work. The news organizations continued to monitor the success of the project, which now had started to reach other countries. The medical profession gave us mixed reviews as it was starting to affect their bottom line. The majority of their new business was now from injuries.

Reverend Black came to the firm wanting to talk to us about the Angel Foundation. Connie showed him into the office, where we offered him a seat in our conference area. Jenn asked him about his health.

"My cancer is gone, just like the angel told me. Our church is planning a trip to southwest Africa on a medical missionary project to an area where disease is rampant. I was hoping that you would donate 10,000 of your healing photos for use in this project."

I looked at Jenn and we excused ourselves, after telling the Reverend we needed to discuss this. After discussing it for a few minutes we returned and sat down. "Reverend Black, we are concerned about the safety of your missionary team. As we understand the situation there, even the military is rogue and can't be trusted. We will give you all the photos you need, but only if the missionaries distribute them from a place of safety. They will get to the people you want to help because the photos can be used more than once." I said.

Reverend Black's understood what I was saying. He then said, "I don't suppose you could lend them your Guardian Angel."

I smiled at his request. "You know it doesn't work that way. I'm sure God will be watching over the missionaries, but we should take appropriate precautions when dealing with evil. Let me know when you need the photos and I'll have them delivered to you."

Reverend Black smiled at us gratefully, shook our hands, then departed. Jenn shook her head in frustration. "I wish we could do more!"

"Other than drop the pictures from the air, I don't know what else we can do."

Jenn started to speak, then realized the futility of that option. "Oh well, I hope the missionaries get the job done without any harm to themselves."

Another month passed without any problems from the mailing project. The number of sales at the museum had declined, which was not unexpected as local people with health problems were being cured. Mail orders continued to climb as word of the healing powers of Angel became more believable.

Jenn received a phone call from a major TV network wanting to discuss a possible segment on their weekly news magazine show. She asked them to send a representative and they would discuss the matter. They agreed and would arrive Saturday afternoon for discussions.

That evening at home we told Angel about the pending meeting with someone from the XYZ Network about a news magazine segment. "Oh, is George Pepper going to do the interview? He is so impressive on the shows I've watched. Alicia said she likes him too. I hope he doesn't think I'm a fake."

Jenn hugged her and said, "That's what the meeting is for. We want to find out what kind of show this is going to be about. An expose', or a report on how much you have helped cure people with a disease or injury. Whoever they send will want to talk to you. Is that going to be alright?"

Angel looked at her mother and smiled. "Oh Mom, you know I'm not shy. Besides, I may be able to tell if he is not being truthful with us. We can always sic Aunt Barbara on him if he gives us trouble."

Jenn looked at me in a panic, causing me to say, "Let's not sic her on anyone before we discuss it first, besides that would be Olivia's job."

"Ooh Daddy. I was just joking. I know Aunt Barbara is only a messenger."

"Did she tell you that?"

"No, but so far that's all she's done. Olivia is our Guardian Angel and is God's warrior."

"Have you talked to any other angels?"

"No, but there has to more to be able to take care of the whole world."

We slept in on Saturday morning, not getting up until Angel came into our bedroom, jumping on the bed with us and hollered. "Hey sleepy heads! Get up, I'm hungry."

We groaned and chased her out, telling her to go get dressed and we would start breakfast. After a shower together that took longer than it needed to because of our antics, we met Angel in the kitchen. When we arrived, she asked with a frown, "What took you so long?"

Jenn blushed and answered, "Your daddy needed his back scrubbed, so it took longer than normal. What do you want to eat?"

She arched her eyebrow at her mother, but didn't pursue it further. "I haven't had French toast in a long time, is that okay?"

Mary Ortega was scheduled to come over this morning for a play date with Angel. Since the person from the network was not due until this afternoon they didn't cancel it. Angel and Mary continued to meet on their weekly play dates, even after Angel began home schooling. Alice and Mary Ortega were due to arrive at nine a.m., so they needed to hurry and clean up the breakfast mess.

Jenn and Angel were in Angel's room, where Jenn was supervising it's cleanup when the door bell sounded. I checked to make sure it was the Ortega's, before letting them inside. I told Mary that Angel was in her room cleaning up her mess and asked if she and her mother wanted something to drink while we waited.

Five minutes later, Jenn came out closely followed by Angel, who motioned for Mary to come to her room. The adults sat in the living room and started catching up on each other's activities since they had last gotten together. Alice wanted to know how Angel was doing in her home schooling.

Jenn was happy to report that Angel completed all her courses to finish the third grade and now was working on courses for the fourth grade. "She is also beginning computer courses that interest her. She's taking high school biology and science courses, and according to Alicia, is doing well."

Alice grimaced. "I knew Angel was smart, but I had no idea she had that much ability. She must have been very bored with the classes she was taking with Mary. Mary misses her at school, but these weekly play dates seems to help them both."

"Has Mary made any new friends at school?"

"Yes, but none as close as Angel."

Jenn thought a moment. "Angel hasn't had any opportunity to make new friends her age. She's close with her nanny, but except for Mary all she knows are adults. Jack, let's start her in youth judo classes or some other kid's group."

"We can ask Alicia to check out what's available and see if Angel is interested. Judo might be too soon, but dance seems right. I bet we can find something that we can work into her free time."

CHAPTER THIRTY

At three p.m. I got a phone call from the XYZ Network representative. She was downstairs in the lobby and waiting for my arrival per my instructions. On the way to the elevator I told security that I was bringing someone up to our apartment and would check her in with them when I returned.

When I arrived in the lobby I approached the only person there and asked, "Ms. Parsons?"

At her nod, I responded with my name and shook her hand. She was in her mid-thirties and dressed to the nines in a conservative business suit, that must of cost twice what I paid for my best suit. She was slim with a good figure that the suit failed to hide, and had an attractive face framed by red hair cut short in a style not yet seen this far west.

"Let's go upstairs to the penthouse level, where I'll help you go through security." She nodded and started pulling her luggage, following me into the elevator. After having her picture taken and checking her ID at the security station, we walked down the hallway and I pointed out the door where our work office was located, before we reached my apartment. I punched in my code on the entry pad, waited until the locks disengaged, then entered the apartment.

I introduced Elizabeth Parsons to my family and invited her into the living room, where we all took seats. I noted that she had kept her luggage with her, leaving it next to her chair. Before we started I asked if she needed to freshen up or could I get her anything? She declined, but asked if she could look at the paintings on the mantel and hear their story.

Jenn led her where she could comfortably observe the paintings. She told Ms. Parsons about the two pictures history and asked if she had any questions. Elizabeth was looking at the larger painting as she said, "I've heard about this painting from a friend. His description doesn't do it justice. How old was she when she did this, eighteen or nineteen, not much over that. She's absolutely captivating... I'm sorry, I lost my train of thought."

Angel said, "Aunt Barbara is pretty, but can you feel the love coming from her. Just stand there and look at her face."

Elizabeth stood transfixed, staring at the painting for a good ten minutes, until I cleared my throat. She blinked her eyes and then looked at us with a little fear in her eyes. "I don't know what came over me. I got lost looking into her eyes and it seemed she was talking to me."

Angel asked, "What did she say? She talks to me all the time."

"You're not putting me on are you?"

Jenn answered. "No, we all have had conversations with her. We believe she is one of God's messengers."

Elizabeth's face turned white and staggering, she put a hand out looking for support, which I grabbed and helped her to a chair.

"Oh my! Mother told me I would see the light one day and regret my wasted youth. Ooh my! Barbara told me I was to show Angel as proof that there is a God who is healing people through her touch. How am I going to do that? The Network won't let us say that."

I said, "Just show what she is doing in healing people. Let her voice provide the words you can't say. We can start with the healing Angel did after the school bus wreck, then the painting Barbara Messing did of Angel, which started the healing from touching the picture. We now send small pictures of the painting world-wide where healing is done by touching them. Then ask Angel where she thinks she gets this power from."

Elizabeth grabbed my hand. "I can do that. We'll just ease into it showing how Angel does it and at the end we'll get her take on it. I think that will work...no problem, yes that will work!"

Elizabeth shuddered. Then she looked at me and said, "I want to see the work office and an idea on how it works."

"If you want the full detail I'll need to get the supervisor here to go over it with you."

"Do it! Let's go over your other outlet at the local museum and where you get your supply of pictures."

Marilyn arrived after we returned from the museum, and after giving her own background, she told Elizabeth how the volunteers got the mail out. Elizabeth didn't finish until midnight and then realized she had missed her flight back to New York. We offered to put her up for the night, which she accepted after making another reservation for eight a.m.

The next morning Elizabeth left the apartment at five-thirty, but not before she stood before the portrait of Barbara one last time. One week later we received a letter from XYZ Network that they would be in Kansas City in two weeks to film the segment, but an advance crew would arrive three days before to prepare for the shooting.

On Thursday afternoon, the week before the network people were to arrive, Elizabeth Parsons arrived at our firm. She had three others with her when she arrived at Connie's desk and was told to wait until our client meeting was finished. Twenty minutes later Connie showed them into our office and we sat in the conference area.

Elizabeth introduced her crew, James McGraw, Peter Withers, and Sally Dillard. She asked if one of us could accompany them to the various points where they intended to shoot scenes. I conferred with Jenn and checked our schedule for the day before reaching the decision that it would be me going with them.

I asked, "Have you rented a car?"

Elizabeth said "Yes."

"Good, because my Prius is not big enough to haul five people."

When we got to the garage she pointed at a large Suburban and asked me to drive. After we were all inside I asked, "Where to?"

"Let's go to the museum first and make arrangements for filming."

I guided the group to the Curator of the Museum, Mary Beth Boyles, and left it to Elizabeth to explain why they were here. Ms. Boyles was happy to help them when she found out The Nelson-

Atkins Museum of Art was going to receive national recognition. She led the group to the Gallery where Barbara Messing's painting of Angel was displayed.

The long lines were gone since the pictures of the painting were now sold at the entrance, but still fifteen people were waiting to view the painting. Mary Beth explained why the lines were now absent, but many people still wanted to view the actual painting. On the way back outside I suggested that they could get footage of the original crowds from the local TV station as well as the interviews with Angel at the bus wreck and later at the station.

Elizabeth said, "That's already been arranged. Peter, I want inside shots of the painting and a view of the outside of this building. Jack, take us by the building of your supplier of pictures. I think we only need a view of that building's exterior, and we need a shot of the workroom where the volunteers are working. In fact, I want George Pepper to do an interview with Marilyn while we get a shot of them working."

After we were back in the car heading for my photo supplier, Elizabeth said, "The bulk of Pepper's interview will be at your apartment with the Barbara paintings in the background. I'd like you to tell their story again, but I'm not sure we have the time. If we run out of time, we can always cut it. I told my crew about Barbara talking to me and they think I was delusional, so I'm not telling that story on the air."

I looked at her crew in my rear view mirror and saw Sally roll her eyes and the other two slump down in their seats. I said, "We know better, don't we."

She grabbed my arm and gave it a squeeze, before turning around and sticking her tongue out at them, causing everyone to laugh. I smiled at her and said, "You seem different now than when I first met you. Not so uptight."

Sally snickered and then said, "You mean she doesn't have a stick up her ass anymore."

I looked at Elizabeth, who was blushing. "I'm a different person now. If these three had my experience with Barbara, they would understand."

I parked outside the building where the painting photos were reproduced. "If you want an inside shot I'm sure it can be arranged, they do 50,000 copies every week day."

"No, we don't need it. Let's go to the workroom. I want these people to see the security you have in place."

When we were in the apartment lobby I called security and told them to expect me and four people from the XYZ Network, one of which had already been cleared. Security cleared the three newcomers and I took them to the workroom, where the volunteers were still at work. Marilyn was not working today, so I introduced her replacement, Janet Willis. Janet told them their routine from start to finish. There were twenty people in the room and it was obvious that they were putting the finishing touches on today's work. The majority of the volunteers were female and ranged in age from eighteen to seventy.

Elizabeth went over to a girl dressed like a typical teenager in jeans and sweatshirt, and asked her what her name was and what she did. "Hi. My name is Dotty and I do the data input into the computer, then later I print out the addresses on the return envelopes."

"How often do you work?"

"It varies, but usually two days a week. The job is easy and the perks are nice. They furnish snacks, drinks, and lunch. We also get a fifteen minute snack break in the morning and afternoon."

Janet said, "We do our own clean up each day, which doesn't take long. That way the next crew has a clean work environment waiting for them."

I took them to my apartment and after I punched in the code, Elizabeth said, "Wait for it!"

Then they heard the soft clunk as the bars disengaged from the door frame. Opening the door, I entered the apartment calling out for Alicia. She hurried into view, closely followed by Angel. I introduced Elizabeth and her XYZ crew to them and explained Alicia's duties as a teacher/nanny.

Elizabeth took Alicia aside and got her background, as well as learning how Angel was progressing in her studies. While she was doing this, I noticed that her crew found the Barbara paintings and were standing before them as though transfixed. Angel asked, "Should we do something?"

"Not yet. Let's give them some more time and see what happens."

It wasn't long before Elizabeth and Alicia joined us as we

watched the enthralled crew. Alicia said, "I lost thirty minutes once doing that. I wonder what Barbara is telling them?"

I looked at her in surprise. "I didn't know you and Barbara were acquainted. When did that happen?"

"Angel told me about her painting and how sometimes she talked to her. I was curious to see if Angel was making up a story or if it was true. Barbara appeared before me and told me what I should do in teaching Angel. I don't know if she left the painting or if it was all in my head."

A few minutes later, the crew members each gave a shudder and looked at each other in wonder. Sally gasped. "Where's the bathroom, I think I wet myself."

* * *

Alicia took her arm and they hurried to the hall bathroom. Sally was sobbing as she took off her pants and panties, then took a wash cloth from Alicia to clean herself. Alicia confided, "I almost wet myself too when she first appeared to me, but I made it here in time."

Sally looked at her in surprise. "You've talked to her too?"

"Of course. I take care of Angel. You don't think her Aunt wouldn't hesitate to give me instructions on how to take care of her. What did she say to you?"

"She just wanted us to know she was real, and that we should reevaluate our lives with the knowledge that God was watching how we live our lives. She scared the piss out of me, is what she did."

Alicia smiled. "Yeah, I know the feeling."

I fetched a clean pair of undies and gave them to Elizabeth, who knocked on the door, handing them to Alicia. "Sally, when you are ready, come out here and we can talk about it."

* * *

While we were waiting on them, Jenn came home and I explained what had happened. Just as I finished, Alicia and Sally came out of the bathroom and joined us. James McGraw spoke first. "Elizabeth, I want to apologize for the hassle we gave you when you told us about Barbara talking to you. What can I do to make up for it?"

Both Sally and Peter echoed his apology before Elizabeth

answered. "We knew we were covering something unusual when we got this assignment and should have approached it with an open mind. Now we know, without any doubt, that God has a hand in this. So give me all the help you can to get this right."

CHAPTER THIRTY-ONE

Two weeks later the program aired while we were in Coffeyville visiting family. Grandmother was holding Angel in her lap while we all watched the program. They had so much material that the whole hour was devoted to Angel's healing. George Pepper, the networks star announcer, carried the audience from Angel's first public display of her healing powers at the school bus accident, the painting of Angel by Barbara Messing that had healing powers when touched, and the mailings of pictures of the painting that spread her healing powers world-wide. Testimonies touting the salvation they received from being cured, were shown, some with before and after pictures. To the family, what we were most proud of was how they depicted Angel, the little girl with the big heart, with a talent to cure other peoples' hurts.

A week after the broadcast, Angel started getting hate mail from a person or organization, postmarked from Denver. After the third letter, I called Detective Mary Cullen and reported the threat. She and her partner, Peter Jackson soon came by the firm where I gave them the letters.

Detective Cullen looked at the letters and frowned. "These are disgusting, but they may only be a nut looking for attention. I'll contact the Denver PD and ask them to look into it for us. Have you had any other problems?"

"No. I'm surprised that this is the first of this kind of

correspondence. We get the good kind. What do we do with them if we get more?"

"Save them and we'll pick them up every week, unless the tone becomes more threatening. If that happens, let us know right away."

Jenn and I put the threats down to a nutcase, someone living in the Denver area, and as long as he stayed there, what was the problem. Two weeks later our family was in the apartment garage preparing to drive to one of our favorite restaurants, when we were accosted by three scruffy looking men. They started out calling us vile names, but as they approached they pulled knives and began chanting Kill, Kill, Kill!

In a flash of light Olivia appeared before us facing the men, their faces blanched in fear as they faced the Guardian Angel. Olivia's wings were spread in attack mode, but she did not attack. Instead, she stepped toward the men, who turned and ran away screaming in fear. Olivia turned and smiled at us, saying, "These evil men will spread fear among others like them; however, if they return I will take stronger measures." She then disappeared.

Angel exclaimed, "Wow! Olivia is powerful, yet beautiful to behold. Not just pretty like Barbara, but scary when she spreads her wings like that. When you told me about her I didn't visualize that."

I smiled. "I guess you had to see her to get the full benefit. I'm hungry, how about the rest of you?"

* * *

Six years later, Angel had just celebrated her fifteenth birthday. She was still being home schooled and was studying high school senior level courses as well as college classes on-line. Alicia Bishop had finished her work for a degree in Education and was teaching in a local middle school, but she still supervised Angel's education on a part time basis.

Angel was taking judo classes and was assisting the instructor with new students. She and Josh Richards had reconnected when he started taking classes three years ago, after Angel began. Jenn and I were at the Judo studio to watch the awards ceremony where Angel and two others received their first level black belts. Angel had just finished her last big growth spurt and stood at 5'10", the same as her mother, but without many of her curves.

The three stood together facing the instructor, who stripped off the old brown belts and fastened new black belts around their waists. After the ceremony, Angel and Josh rushed over to us with big smiles on their faces. Josh was a Junior in high school, having skipped a grade himself, and stood almost six feet tall. His mother died last year and his father stood with us congratulating him.

We stepped forward taking turns hugging our daughter, causing tears to flow down the faces of mother and daughter. I shook hands with Josh after he received his hug from his father. Josh had gotten his growth early and appeared to not be done yet. His father was 6'3" and played football in high school, so the potential was there.

We waited while our kids changed into street clothes before we headed out to celebrate at a restaurant of their choice, which turned out to be pizza. Mary Ortega and her mother were already there waiting for us. The three teenagers sat together having fun, while the parents talked, catching up on what was new in their children's lives.

Brad Richards smiled at Jenn as he said, "Josh told me he never would have gotten his black belt without Angel's help. She drilled with him until he got it. Your daughter is strong both mentally and physically and she was determined that Josh would get the belt. At first, he was afraid he might hurt her since he outweighed her by eighty pounds, but when he found himself on his back every time he tried to grab her, he got over that fear."

Jenn looked at the three friends interacting and thought to herself, *I hope Mary doesn't get left behind as Angel and Josh jump ahead through school.* Mary and Angel were the same age, and where Angel's growth was upwards, Mary's body at 5'6", had filled out in curves which may have caused her mother some anxiety.

Later that evening after we returned to our apartment, Angel took our hands and had us sit down in the living room, saying she had something to tell us. Jenn and I sat down wondering what problem our teenager was going to drop on us.

Angel stood before us, working up the courage to speak. She took a deep breath and said, "Mom, Dad, I don't have my healing powers anymore. I've twice tried to heal muscle injuries of my fellow students at the Judo Studio with no results. However, I knew where the muscle injury was and through massage I was able to lessen the pain. Yesterday I asked Aunt Barbara about my powers and she confirmed that I could no longer heal by touch, but was given another power. She said I could sense where a problem was inside a body and that I should train myself to correct it. I've already taken premedical college courses, but I need your help in planning on how to gain entry into the best medical school I can get into."

I asked, "Do the pictures of your painting still provide healing?"

"Barbara says they still work, but at some point that too will stop. She will let you know when to stop selling the pictures."

Jenn and I stood and took Angel into our arms and held her tightly. Jenn said, "I'm so sorry. Does it feel like there's something missing inside you?"

"I've felt strange for about a month, but the new gift filled any void left when I lost my healing powers. I'm glad I lost that power. Maybe now I can have a normal life."

"We can contact Alicia and ask her if she can recommend someone to help us plan your education. You're still young to enter college, but it's been done before and we'll get it done."

Alicia got us an appointment to meet with Doctor Paula Richards, the head of admissions at MU, Columbia, Missouri. When we arrived, Dr. Richards had us take a seat while she looked at the courses Angel already completed. When she finished, she looked at Angel for a few moments considering before speaking. "Impressive, but you will need to test out for some of these courses and for your high school degree. Why do you want a medical degree when you have healing powers?"

Angel answered. "I've lost those powers, but instead have acquired diagnostic abilities that I need medical knowledge to fulfill. I need to finish the courses required to enter medical school."

Dr. Richards looked at her and smiled. "Well, it's obvious that you can handle college courses. I'll set you up to take the tests that will get you into the next term this fall. You are required to stay in a dorm for the first year since you live in Kansas City, even though you already have enough credits to start as a second year student. Be here tomorrow morning at eight to start your tests. My assistant, Becky Norcroft, will take care of you."

* * *

Jack rented a car and returned to KC, while Angel and I stayed in Columbia. We took a tour of the campus and asked to see a dorm room before checking into a motel for the night. The next night we returned to KC after Angel completed the tests. When we entered the apartment, Angel appeared happy, but tired. I fixed dinner, which she ate and then went to her room for the night.

* * *

I asked Jenn how it went? "I couldn't stay with her, but she took tests for seven hours with a break for lunch. On the drive home she said that she thought she did well, but was exhausted and slept most of the way. I hope in the future she doesn't overdo her studies in her attempts to complete them."

The following week Dr. Richards sent Angel the results of the tests she had completed. She was now a high school graduate, getting a perfect score on the GED. She had also received a perfect score on her SAT, and had passed all the tests relating to the college level correspondence courses she had taken. Her IQ was rated at 156, well into the upper level range. Dr. Richards had also included a list of courses she needed to complete to qualify for medical school.

I hugged Angel and said, "Well done, especially on the SAT. A perfect score is hard to do. Your IQ level is not a surprise since we always knew you were smart. You even beat out your mother, whose IQ is 148 and me at 139. I've always considered your mother as the smart one in our family, but now we have you to carry the banner."

Jenn hugged her daughter too and kissed her cheek. "Let's look at these courses and see how we can plan getting them finished in the least amount of time."

We made the trip to Coffeyville that weekend and picked up Grandmother at the farm on the way. It had been over a month since Grandmother had seen Angel and when she hugged and kissed her she asked, "What's happened to you?"

Angel gave her a lopsided smile, then replied. "I've lost my healing powers Grandmother."

Grandmothers face reflected her great granddaughter's loss, which caused Angel to break down in tears and hug the matriarch. Grandmother looked at me for guidance, but I had no idea Angel felt the loss so deeply. Jenn and Grandmother steered Angel towards a seat where we told her what happened and Angel's plans to enter MU the next fall.

"My, my, my darling Angel. Gods gifts sometime happen this way, but he did give you another gift to take its place. It's possible this gift will be even more important for you in the years to come, long after I'm gone. When you go off to college your life will enter a new chapter where you will leave the old healer persona behind and start another grounded in the medical profession."

Angel blew her nose, kissed her great grandmother, and smiled at us. "Okay, I'm cried out and ready for the rest of the family."

When we arrived in Coffeyville, the first to reach the car was Barbara Messing. She grabbed Angel as she left the car, holding her tightly to her chest as they both cried in each other's arms. Barbara was now twenty-four and lived nearby in her own home. Somehow she knew Angel was coming today and was here to meet her.

Jenn's parents, her brother Ben, and his wife were all standing nearby watching Barbara and Angel's emotional exchange. Jenn went over and explained about Angel's loss of healing powers, which caused distress for everyone. Barbara and Angel composed themselves and wiping their eyes, joined the others.

Barbara now looked like a older version of Jenn's sister, so much so that it was hard to remember that they were not the same person. Barbara had taken control of her trust when she reached twenty-one and purchased a home less than a mile from the family who raised her. One of the first things she did was construct a art studio with a south facing wall of windows. She was joined by a young man that appeared to be her age, but was new to us.

Barbara introduced him as Jesse Stone, a fellow artist, who was one of her new students. She had started teaching last year, but this one appeared to be more than a student. She said she had a dream last night where the other Barbara said Angel was coming here with news of her loss of healing powers. She had to meet her when she arrived to show her support.

Ben and Judy Ellsworth married two years now, were expecting their first child in six months. Ben was working at one of the oil companies in Bartlesville, OK, as a computer analyst. The family went inside and after everyone was settled, Angel told them of her future plans and that she was starting classes at MU in the fall.

Ben looked at his sister and shook his head. "I always thought of you as the brain, now your daughter is going to MU, and she's only fifteen."

Jenn stuck her tongue out at her brother. "Not only that, but she's already got a year's worth of credits accumulated. I don't want to give her a big head, but she has a higher IQ than either Jack or me."

CHAPTER THIRTY-TWO

Two months later Jenn and I were helping Angel move into her dorm room, which was on a segregated women only floor. Her roommate, Lilly Williamson, had already moved in and was helping Angel settle in. She was a eighteen year old light skinned black woman from Hannibal, Missouri. She was quite beautiful, with her long hair pulled into a pony tail. This was her first time away from home and her Baptist minister father, who had raised her on fire and brimstone and a fearsome God. She was able to afford college because of a basketball scholarship.

We each gave Angel a hug and told her to call us every day so we can keep in touch, before we left her with Lilly. Angel made some adjustments of her things before sitting on her bed trying to keep from crying.

* * *

Lilly said, "Angel. Why did they give you a name like that? Are they some kind of religious nuts?"

Angel looked at her in surprise for a moment. "What, do you live in a vacuum. Don't you know who I am?"

"No, should I? Are you somebody famous?"

Angel gave her a crooked smile. "No, I suppose not, not anymore."

Lilly gave her a surprised look, then shook her head. "No, you're not her. God wouldn't do that to me, would he? Tell me you're not that girl that heals people!"

"Surprise! I'm not little anymore and I've lost my healing powers."

Lilly's face got paler as she looked at Angel. "If my father was here he would be laughing at me and praising the Lord. When I left home, I told him I was getting away from him and his religion. Now here you are as my roommate. It's got to be God's joke on me."

"I promise not to preach at you if you keep quiet about my history."

"Deal! How smart are you, because I need all the help I can get with my studies. I'm barely a B average student and I need to maintain at least a C to keep my scholarship."

"I'll help you if you watch after me. I'm only fifteen, and my social graces are nonexistent as I've been home schooled."

"Oh you poor kid. I thought I had a depressing childhood until now. Okay, let's get out of here and go to the student union and meet some boys."

My first few months of college passed in a blur as I experienced so many different things and made new friends. Lilly and I became like sisters and she taught me how to survive as a girl turning into a young woman. After three months, Lilly's parents made their first appearance. I was in my room, when there was a knock and Lilly stuck her head in and asked, "Are you decent, my parents want to meet you."

"Come on in, I'm just studying."

Reverend Williamson and his wife June, followed Lilly into our small room. We had them take our chairs, while we sat on our beds. After a quick glance at the room, her father turned his attention to me. "Are you a God fearing woman?"

I looked over at Lilly and smiled, which caused her to roll her eyes. "What do you mean?"

"I mean do you fear God's wrath if you don't follow his ways."

"More than you know."

Reverend Williamson looked at me in surprise and then at his daughter in suspicion. "Daughter, are you trying to make me look ridiculous."

"No Reverend. It's obvious that Lilly hasn't told you who I am.

I'm Angel Pearson, of the healing angel persona. I've had intimate contact with God and know of His power."

He looked at me in surprise for a moment. "What are you doing here?"

Lilly answered. "Angel no longer has healing powers and is preparing herself for medical school. She says God has given her another power to replace the one He took back. He wants her to prepare herself to properly use it."

"But, your pictures still heal, don't they?"

"Yes, but that will stop too, but I hope not until I'm ready to use my new power."

"Can you tell me what this power is?"

"I can tell by touch what causes a person's illness. I need medical knowledge to make use of this diagnostic power."

"Not as dramatic as your healing power, but still a useful gift. Now that I've discarded my own bias, I can see God's glow around you. I hope He keeps you safe from the evil of this world."

"My Guardian Angel is still with me. Olivia has taken good care of me in the past."

"Daughter, we'll take our leave from you and I'm happy that Angel is your roommate."

After Lilly's parents left, she jumped up and sat next to me on the bed. "You have a Guardian Angel! Didn't you think that might be of interest to me?"

"She only manifests when I'm in mortal danger. I didn't think you would ever have cause to see her."

"Still, it's nice to know she's there. What if it's only a mugger that comes after you, what then?"

"I have a black belt in Judo for that case."

Lilly looked at me with new respect. "Girl, I'm going to stick even closer to you now."

We had several general requirement courses together, and biology gave Lilly problems. I told her that all she needed to do was memorize the terms and how they fit together. She responded, "That's easy for you to say since you have an eidetic memory and can recall everything you read."

I grimaced and said, "Alright, then you need to repeat the terms over and over again until it sticks in your head and doesn't leak out. Keep at it and I'll test you later to see if anything stuck."

She stuck her tongue out at me after I returned to my desk that I caught sight of in the mirror. "I saw that! Don't make me call Olivia on you."

I got a pillow to the back of my head as her response.

One day I went down to the basketball court to watch Lilly practice, but I didn't understand the game since I'd only seen tiny parts of a game as I switched channels while watching TV at home. Lilly was fast and pushed the ball down the court with grace and agility. After the others left, she stayed to shoot baskets. I called to her as I walked onto the floor and complimented her on how well she played.

Lilly grinned at me. "Yeah, how many games have you watched?"

I blushed, then motioned for her to pass me the ball. I imitated how she threw the ball, which fell far short of the basket. "Wow, you must have muscles I don't have."

I moved closer and tried again, this time hitting the backboard and bouncing away. I looked at her and smiled. "I guess it takes a lot of repetitions to get muscle memory trained to make those baskets."

"Okay, smarty pants I get your analogy. Let's get back to the books after I shower and we get something to eat."

When we arrived at the dining hall and picked out our food, we sat down with some of the other members of Lilly's team. Most were older, juniors and seniors, but seemed to accept me because of my friendship with Lilly. The gap in my age was somewhat mediated by my size, as I was almost as tall as their tallest player.

Patty Gifford, the senior star player, asked me, "You keeping Lilly straight on her studies? We can't afford to lose her on the games coming up."

"Lilly's doing fine. She just needs a little more work tonight." I said.

During spring break, Lilly took me home in KC where we spent a few days before she planned to spend the remainder of the break at her home. Lilly had a six year old VW bug that looked a little rough, but ran great. When we arrived at the penthouse level and went though security, Lilly now realized how I lived. We entered the apartment and announced our arrival, then I realized my parents were still at work. I showed Lilly the apartment and the spare bedroom and bath, which we both used. I then took her into the living room and showed her the Barbara's on the mantel.

I introduced her to my Aunt Barbara and told her of the paintings history. Lilly looked at the painting in awe. "She's so beautiful and she died so very young, about my age."

"Yes, my mother doesn't know I know this, but my father and Barbara were engaged before her death in a auto wreck. Mother and he never saw each other again until she went to work as an attorney with the Kansas City U. S. District Attorney office where father worked. I don't know the details, but they were married soon after. I guess it was love at first sight."

"Wow, that's a strange story. Your mother married her sisters first love and she has her picture on the wall."

"Barbara doesn't hold any bad feelings over their marriage, in fact I think she helped arrange it."

"You know, I believe you look a little like Barbara, except for your hair. The white hair makes you fit your name. The little painting somehow goes with the larger. What's its story?"

"That's Barbara Messing, and she now looks just like the older Barbara. She's an orphan, who was in my parents' office when her Aunt died. Mom said she looked just like her sister did when she was ten, and Mom and Dad got her named as their ward. My grandparents raised her and she has the same artist talents as their first daughter. She also has some connection with my Aunt."

"This is some strange family you have. I can't image growing up with a gift from God and talking with angels."

"Do you want to ask Barbara anything? I'm not sure she will talk to you, but there's no harm in trying."

Lilly stared at the painting for a moment, considering, when Barbara stepped out of the painting and stood before them. Lilly stepped back a step in surprise and said, "Wow, you startled me. My father is the head of our Baptist church in Hannibal and he raised me to be fearful of God, lest He toss me into the fires of hell. Angel has shown me a different side of God, a loving God. Which is He?"

Barbara smiled at Lilly. "What do you believe after getting to know Angel?"

Lilly considered a moment. "Perhaps both. Father was trying to scare his flock into walking the straight and narrow following His commandments, while Angel is showing His loving side. I prefer the loving side. Angel's influence may have saved me a lot of heartache when I was ready to rebel against my father."

"God's message is salvation if you believe His gospel message. He gives everyone the freedom to choose their path in life. You have been granted greater insight than most people, so I'm sure you will choose wisely."

Barbara stepped back into the painting and Lilly stood for a moment, tears in her eyes. I touched her arm and she turned to me, hugging me for a few moments, until with a sigh she let me go.

"I don't know if my father would believe me if I ever told him of this experience, but I may some day."

I hugged her again, placing my forehead against hers. "I have a feeling we are going to be friends for life, so if ever you feel a need for a shoulder to cry on, you know I will be there for you."

Mom and Dad soon arrived and were delighted to find us there, wanting to know what our plans were and where we wanted to go to eat.

THE BEGINNING

ABOUT THE AUTHOR

Hugh A. Flowers retired after almost thirty years with the Federal Deposit Insurance Corporation as a bank examiner. He now spends his time reading and writing novels and short stories.

Salvation is his fourth published novel. It's the first of a spiritual trilogy. You won't want to miss the sequels.

www.ingramcontent.com/pod-product-compliance
Lightning Source LLC
Chambersburg PA
CBHW051435170626
46809CB00006B/2472